hrjc

CARTOON NETWORK

STEVEN UNIVERSE

WELCOME TO BEACH CITY

kaboom!

WWW.BOOM-STUDIOS.COM

STEVEN UNIVERSE: WELCOME TO BEACH CITY, November 2019.
Published by KaBOOM!, a division of Boom Entertainment, Inc.
STEVEN UNIVERSE, CARTOON NETWORK, the logos, and all related
characters and elements are trademarks of and © Cartoon Network.
A WarnerMedia Company. All rights reserved. (S19)   Originally
published in single magazine form as STEVEN UNIVERSE: GREG
UNIVERSE SPECIAL No. 1, STEVEN UNIVERSE 2016 SPECIAL No. 1 ©
Cartoon Network. A WarnerMedia Company. All rights reserved. (S15,
S16) KaBOOM!™ and the KaBOOM! logo are trademarks of Boom
Entertainment, Inc., registered in various countries and categories.
All characters, events, and institutions depicted herein are fictional.
Any similarity between any of the names, characters, persons, events,
and/or institutions in this publication to actual names, characters,
and persons, whether living or dead, events, and/or institutions is
unintended and purely coincidental. KaBOOM! does not read or
accept unsolicited submissions of ideas, stories, or artwork.

For information regarding the CPSIA on this printed material, call:
(203) 595-363 and provide reference #RICH - 865880.

BOOM! Studios, 5670 Wilshire Boulevard, Suite 400,
Los Angeles, CA 90036-5679. Printed in USA. First Printing.

ISBN: 978-1-68415-466-1, eISBN: 978-1-64144-583-2

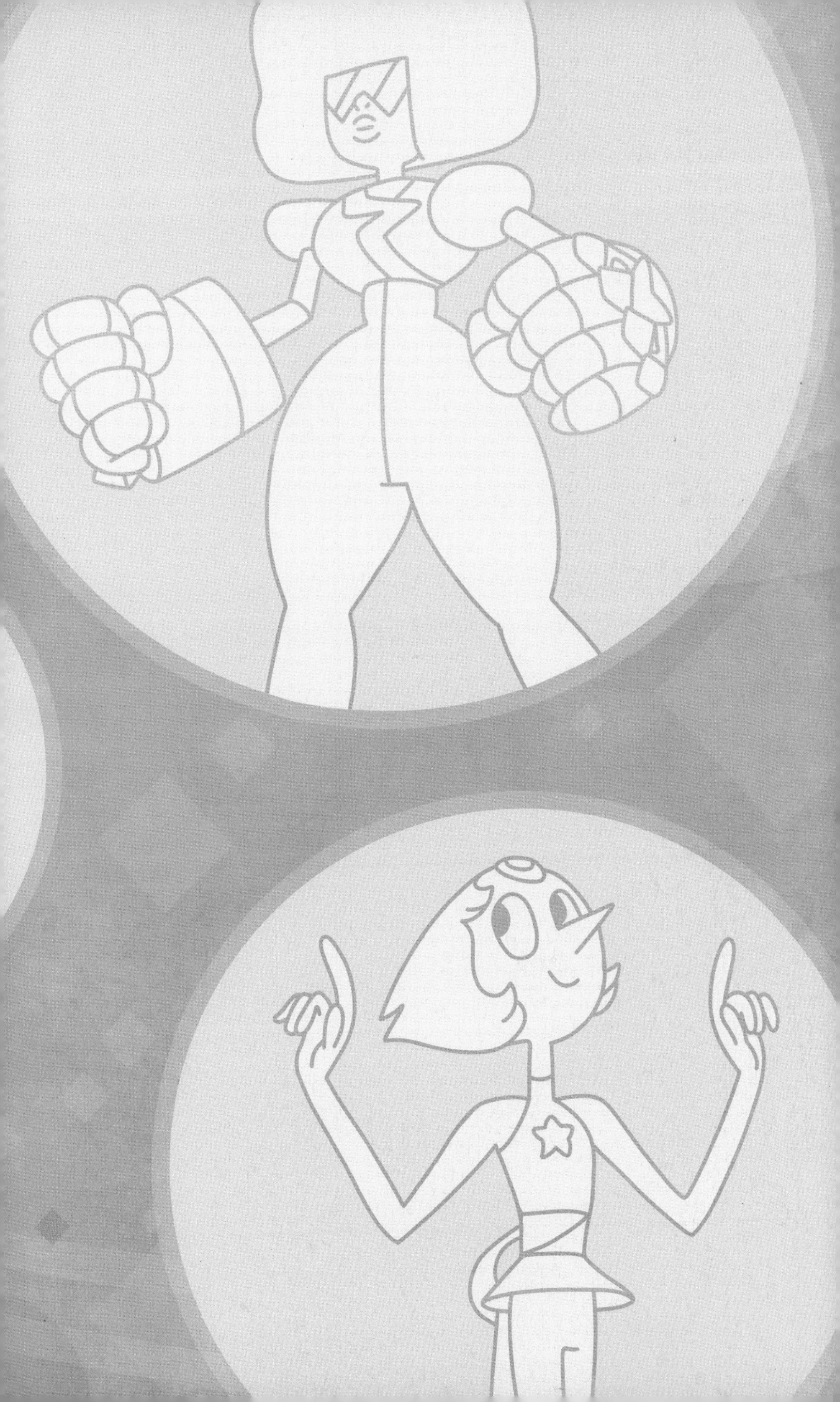

Cover by
Ayme Sotuyo

Series Designers
Michelle Ankley, Jillian Crab,
and **Grace Park**

Series Associate Editors
Whitney Leopard and **Chris Rosa**

Series Editor
Shannon Watters

Collection Designer
Marie Krupina

Collection Assistant Editor
Michael Moccio

Collection Editor
Matthew Levine

With Special Thanks to
Marisa Marionakis, Janet No, Austin Page, Conrad Montgomery, Jackie Buscarino and the wonderful folks at **Cartoon Network**.

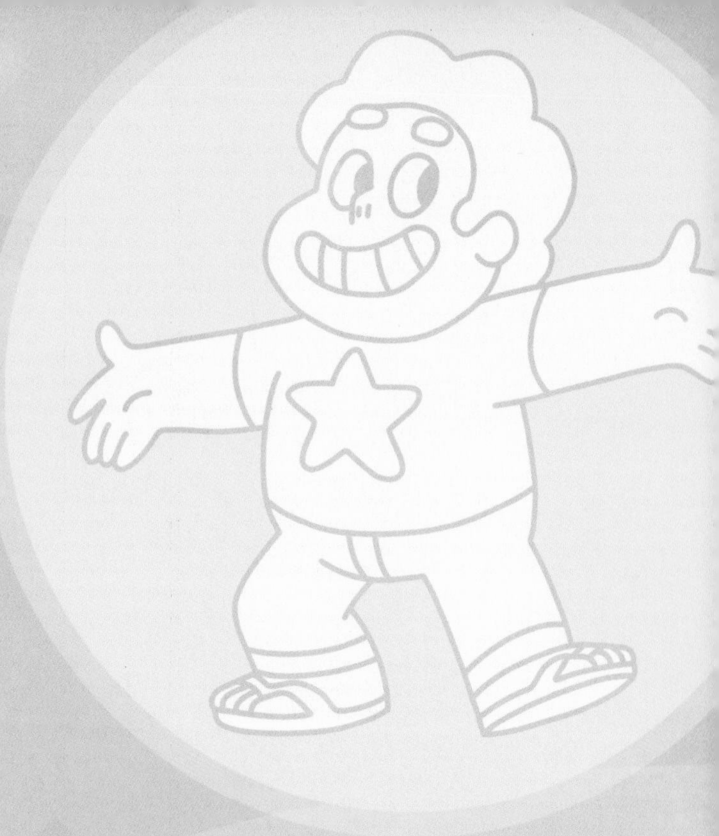

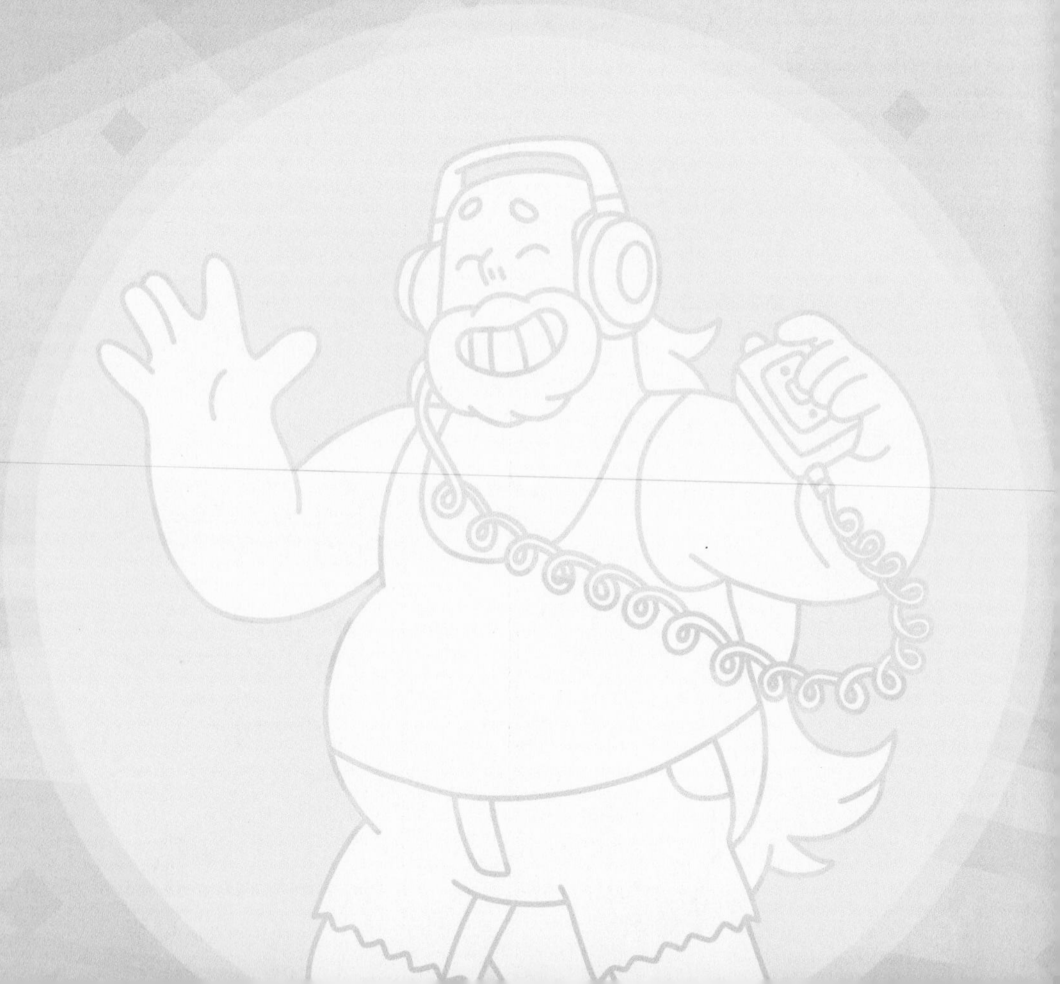

CARTOON NETWORK

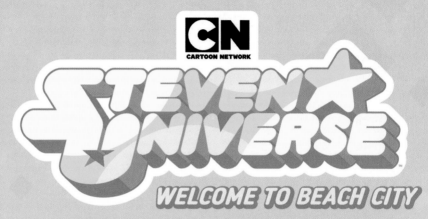

STEVEN UNIVERSE

WELCOME TO BEACH CITY

Created by **REBECCA SUGAR**

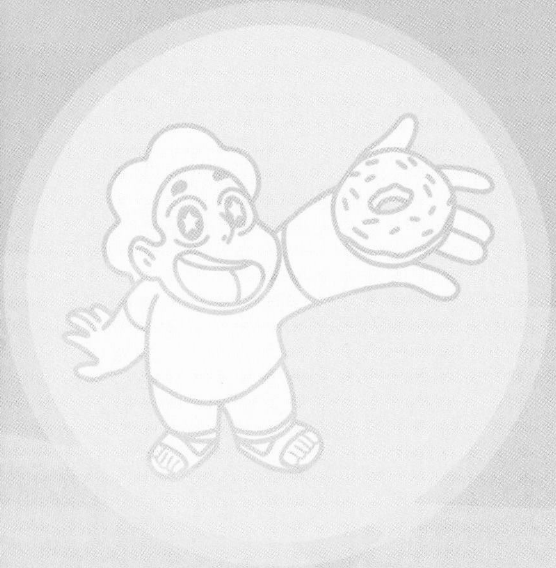

"UNIVERSE AND THE MOON"
Written & Illustrated by .... **Jeremy Sorese**

"PINK ELEPHANT IN THE ROOM"
Written by .... **Liz Prince**
Illustrated by .... **Rachel Dukes**

"NOW IN 3D"
Written & Illustrated by ... **Chrystin Garland**

"BY HEART"
Written & Illustrated by .... **Grace Kraft**

"GREGARIOUS GAMERS"
Written & Illustrated by .... **Coleman Engle**

"SNAP SHOTS"
Written by .... **Grace Kraft**
Illustrated by .... **Kelly Turnbull**

"SLAM BUDDIES"
Written by .... **Kevin Panetta**
Illustrated by .... **Jared Morgan**

"CLASH OF THE GLUTTONS"
Written & Illustrated by .... **Sara Talmadge**
Lettered by .... **Jim Campbell**

"THE BIG DONUT CONTEST"
Written & Illustrated by .... **Queenie Chan**

"THE DONUT THIEF"
Written & Illustrated by .... **Katie Jones**
Colored by .... **Laura Langston**
Lettered by .... **Jim Campbell**

"HEALTH INSPECTION"
Written & Illustrated by .... **Rii Abrego**

"HOW TO DONUTS"
Written & Illustrated by .... **Ayme Sotuyo**

"FOOD FIGHT"
Written & Illustrated by .... **T. Zysk**

"DONUT DERBY"
Written by .... **Nicole Andelfinger**
Illustrated by .... **Cara McGee**
Colored by .... **Laura Langston**
Lettered by .... **Warren Montgomery**

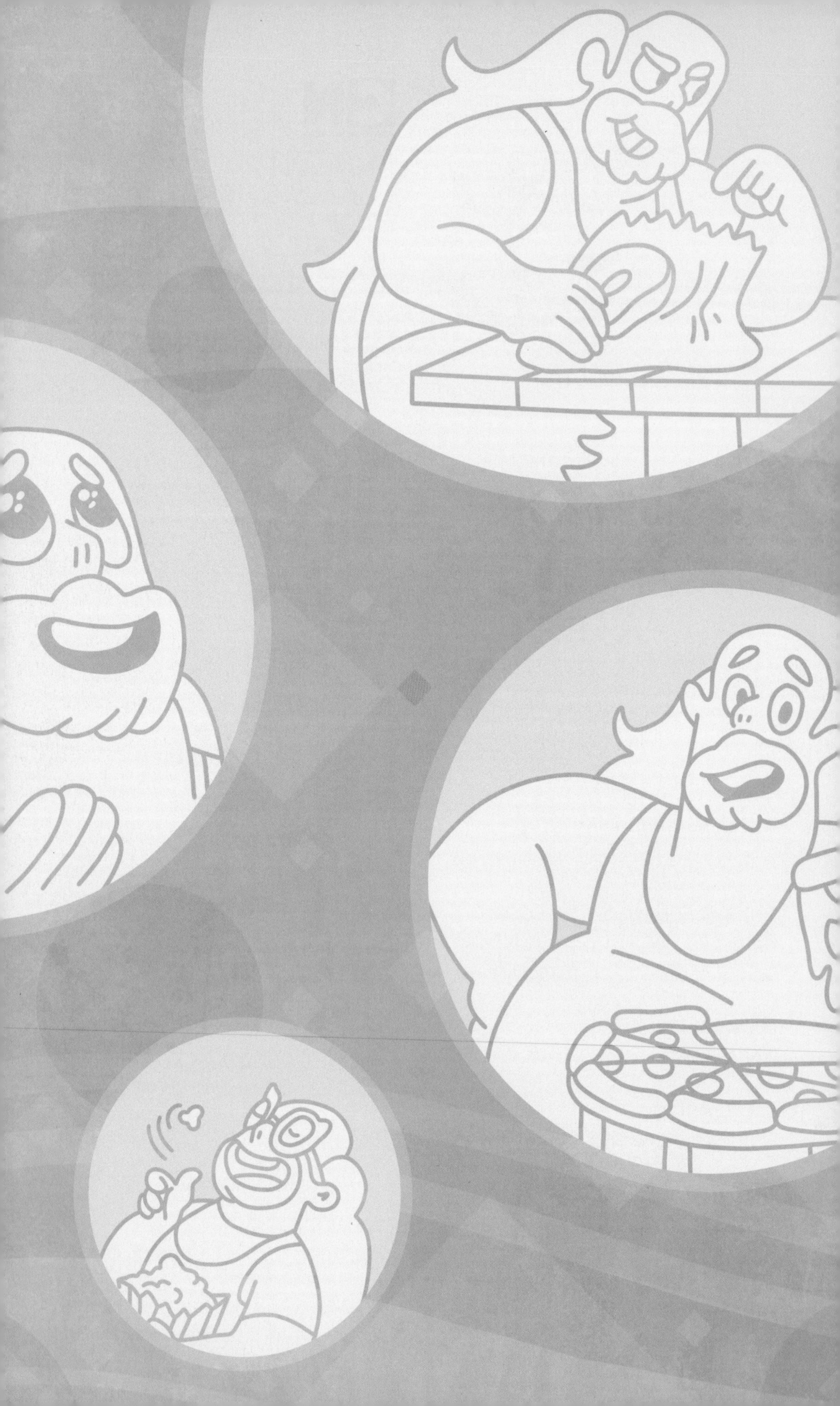

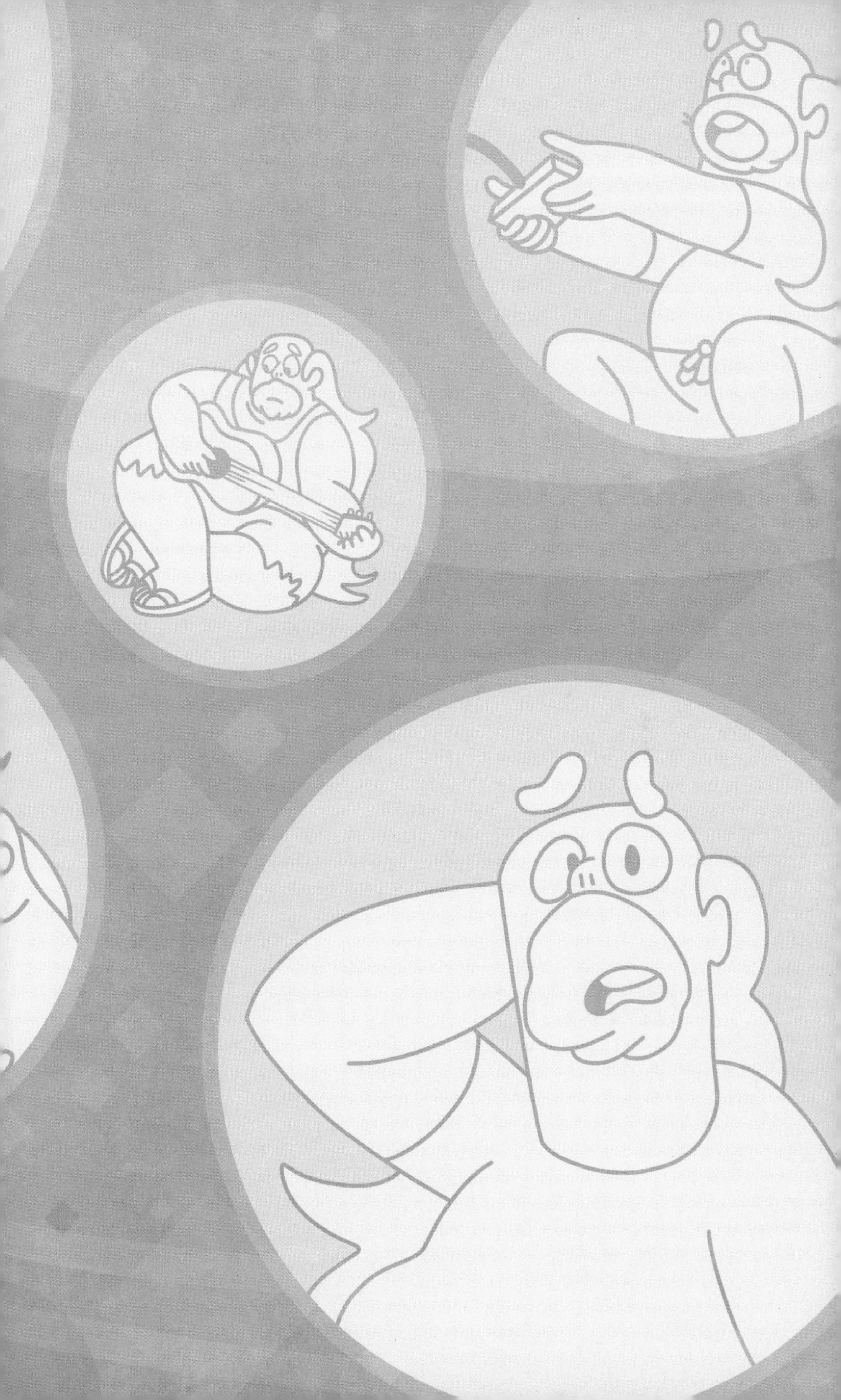

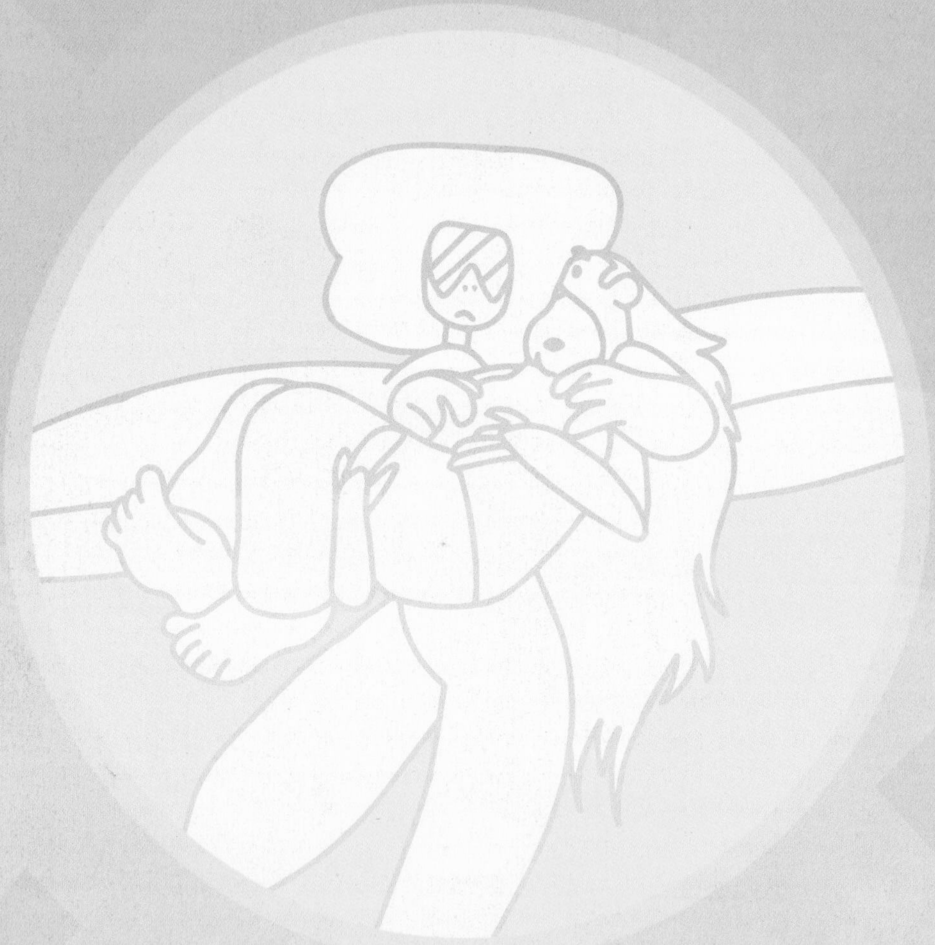

UNIVERSE AND THE MOON

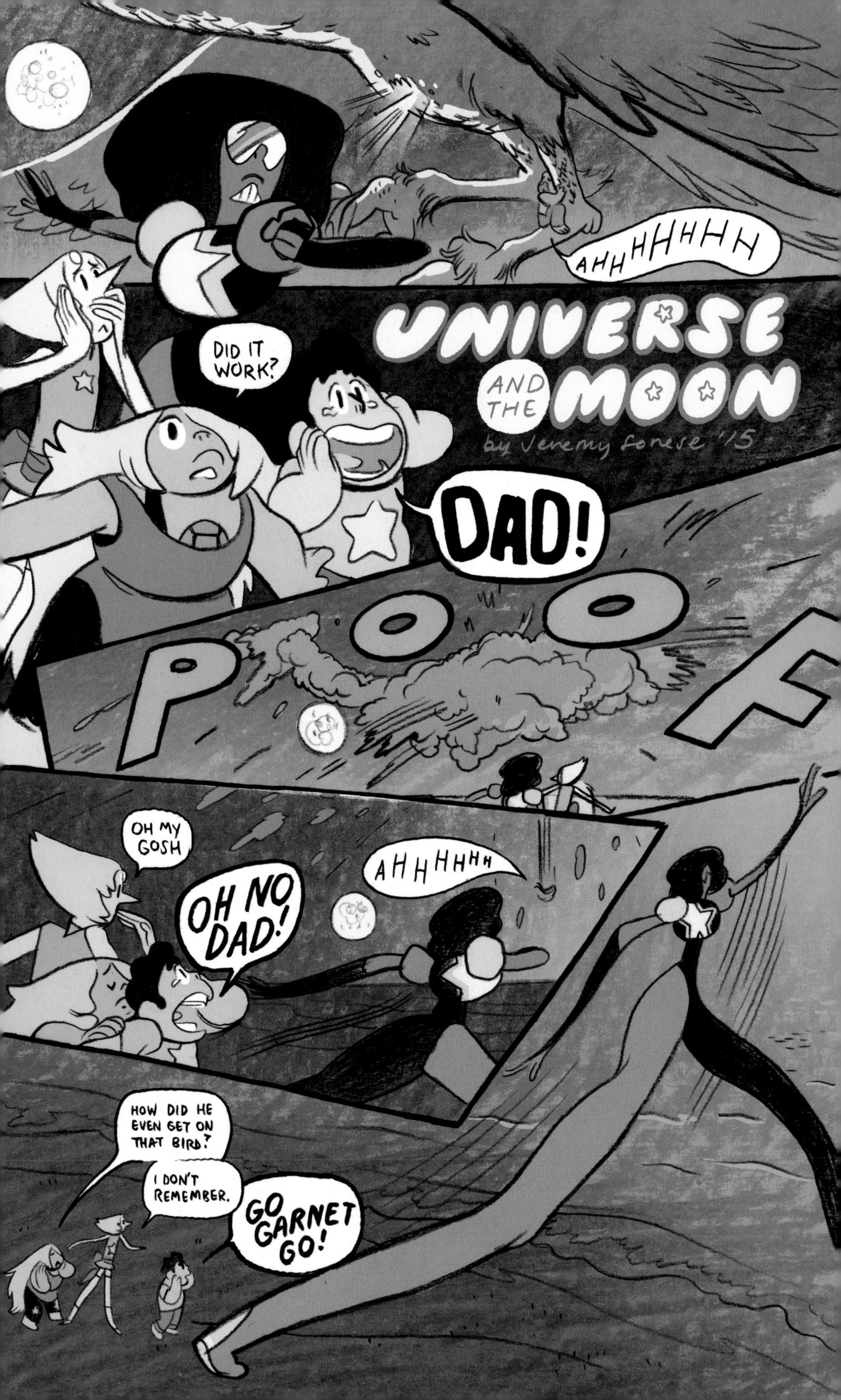
AHHHHHHH
UNIVERSE AND THE MOON
by Jeremy Sorese '15
DID IT WORK?
DAD!
POOF
OH MY GOSH
OH NO DAD!
AHHHHHH
HOW DID HE EVEN GET ON THAT BIRD?
I DON'T REMEMBER.
GO GARNET GO!

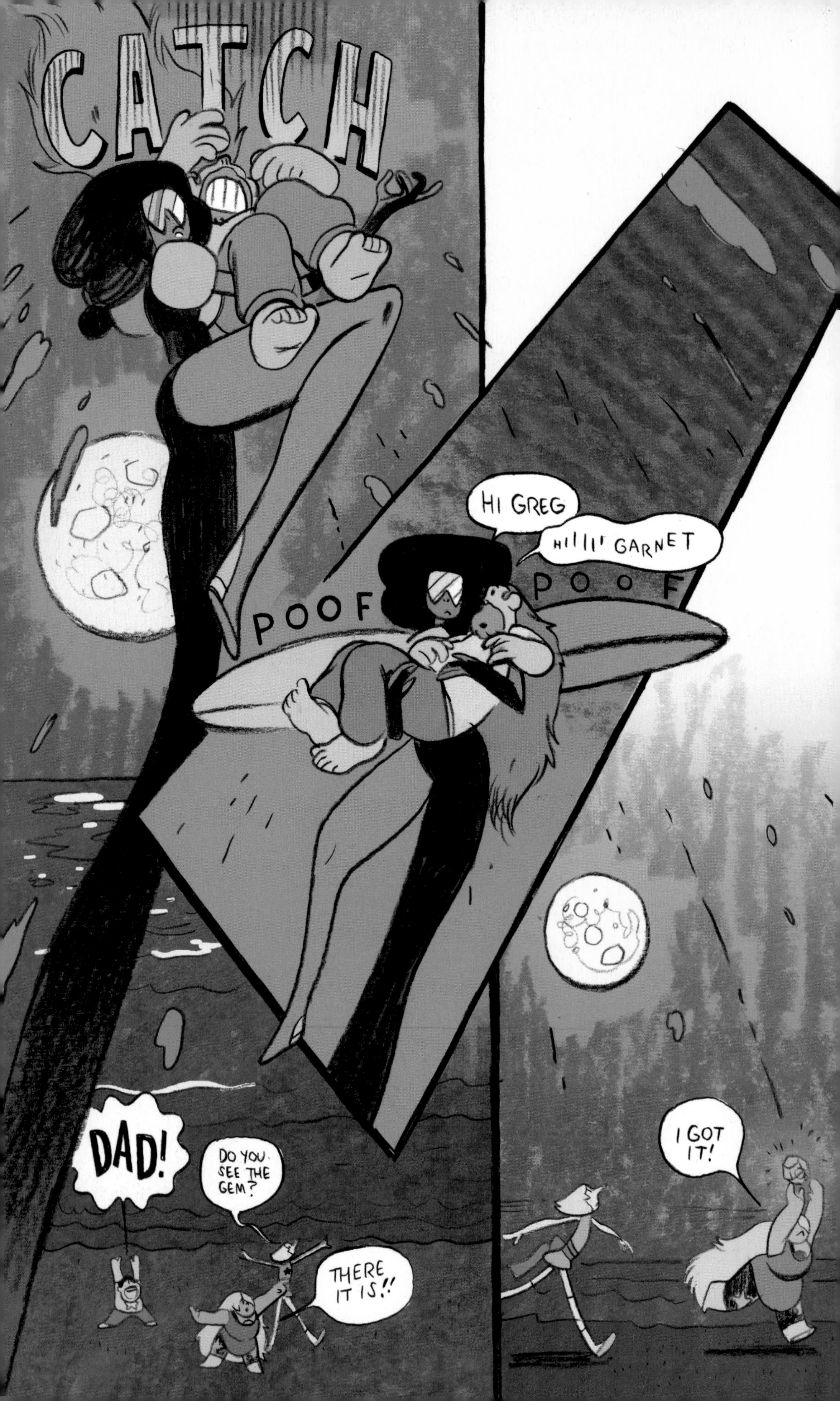
CATCH
HI GREG
HIIII GARNET
POOF
POOF
DAD!
DO YOU SEE THE GEM?
THERE IT IS!!
I GOT IT!

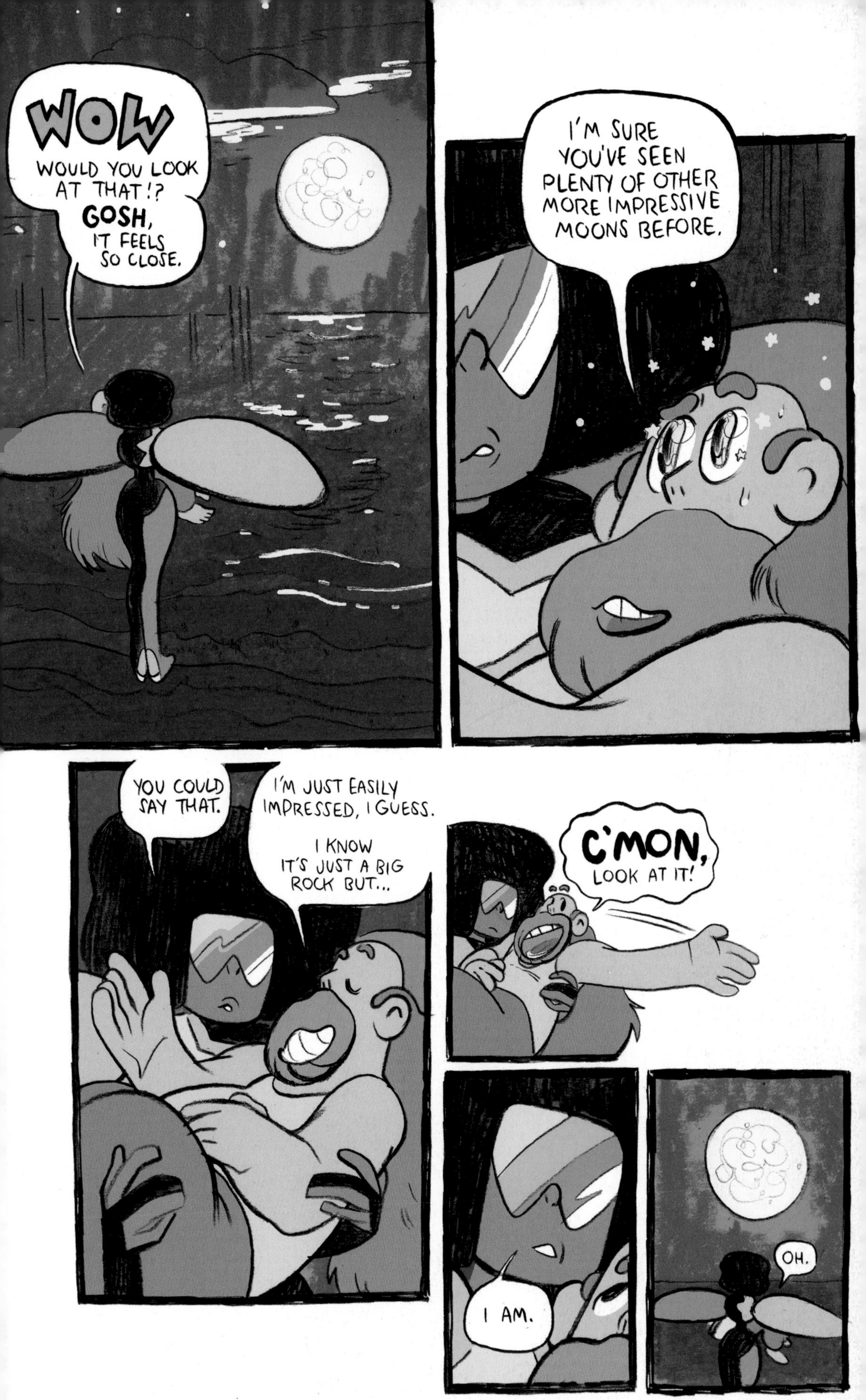
WOW
WOULD YOU LOOK AT THAT!? GOSH, IT FEELS SO CLOSE.
I'M SURE YOU'VE SEEN PLENTY OF OTHER MORE IMPRESSIVE MOONS BEFORE.
YOU COULD SAY THAT.
I'M JUST EASILY IMPRESSED, I GUESS.
I KNOW IT'S JUST A BIG ROCK BUT...
C'MON, LOOK AT IT!
I AM.
OH.

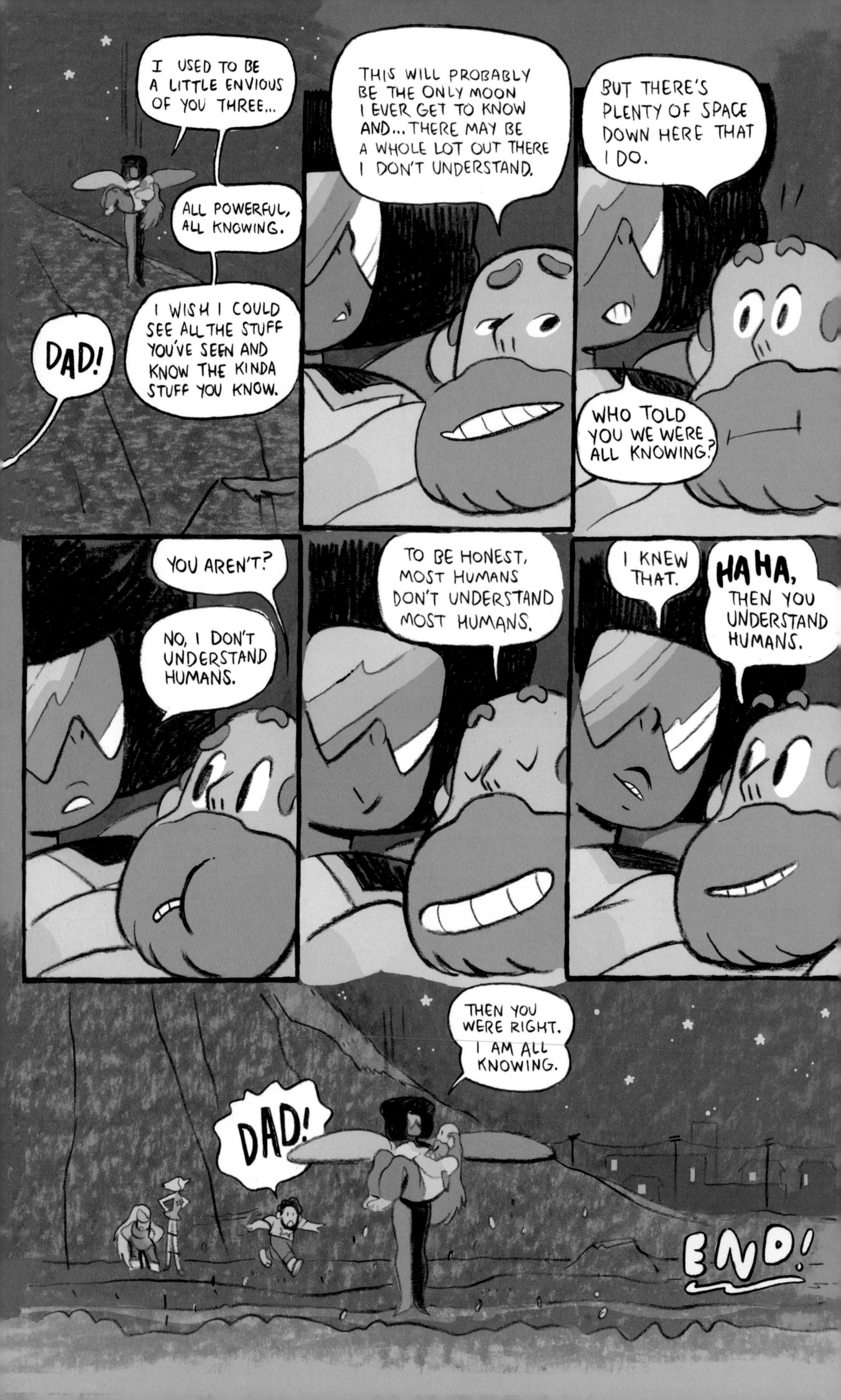

I USED TO BE A LITTLE ENVIOUS OF YOU THREE...
ALL POWERFUL, ALL KNOWING.
I WISH I COULD SEE ALL THE STUFF YOU'VE SEEN AND KNOW THE KINDA STUFF YOU KNOW.
DAD!
THIS WILL PROBABLY BE THE ONLY MOON I EVER GET TO KNOW AND... THERE MAY BE A WHOLE LOT OUT THERE I DON'T UNDERSTAND.
BUT THERE'S PLENTY OF SPACE DOWN HERE THAT I DO.
WHO TOLD YOU WE WERE ALL KNOWING?
YOU AREN'T?
NO, I DON'T UNDERSTAND HUMANS.
TO BE HONEST, MOST HUMANS DON'T UNDERSTAND MOST HUMANS.
I KNEW THAT.
HA HA, THEN YOU UNDERSTAND HUMANS.
THEN YOU WERE RIGHT. I AM ALL KNOWING.
DAD!
END!

PINK ELEPHANT IN THE ROOM

PINK ELEPHANT IN THE ROOM

by Liz Prince

=DRAWN BY RACHEL DUKES=

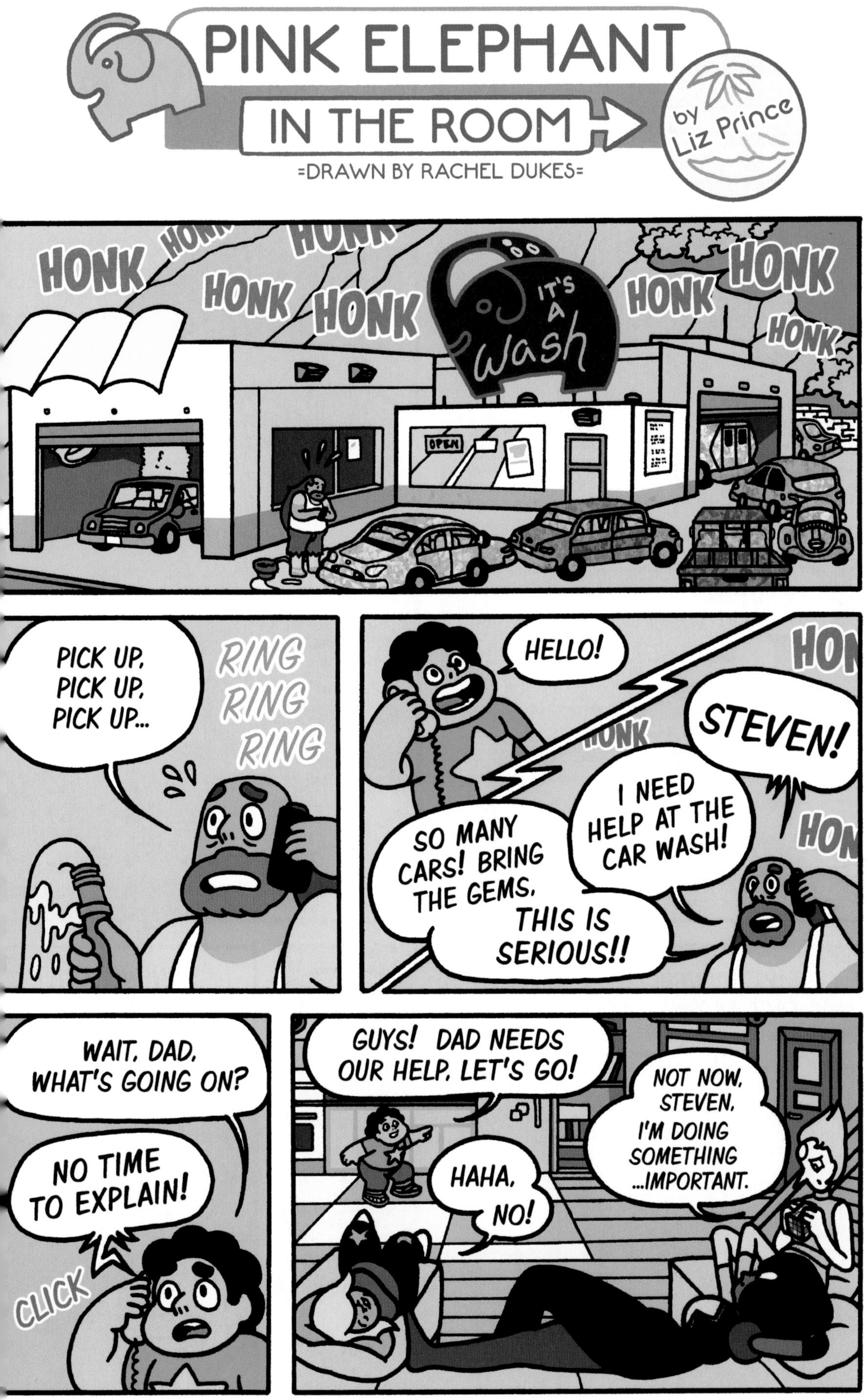
HONK
HONK
HONK
HONK
HONK
HONK
HONK
IT'S A wash
OPEN
PICK UP, PICK UP, PICK UP...
RING RING RING
HELLO!
STEVEN!
I NEED HELP AT THE CAR WASH!
SO MANY CARS! BRING THE GEMS,
THIS IS SERIOUS!!
WAIT, DAD, WHAT'S GOING ON?
NO TIME TO EXPLAIN!
CLICK
GUYS! DAD NEEDS OUR HELP, LET'S GO!
HAHA, NO!
NOT NOW, STEVEN, I'M DOING SOMETHING ...IMPORTANT.

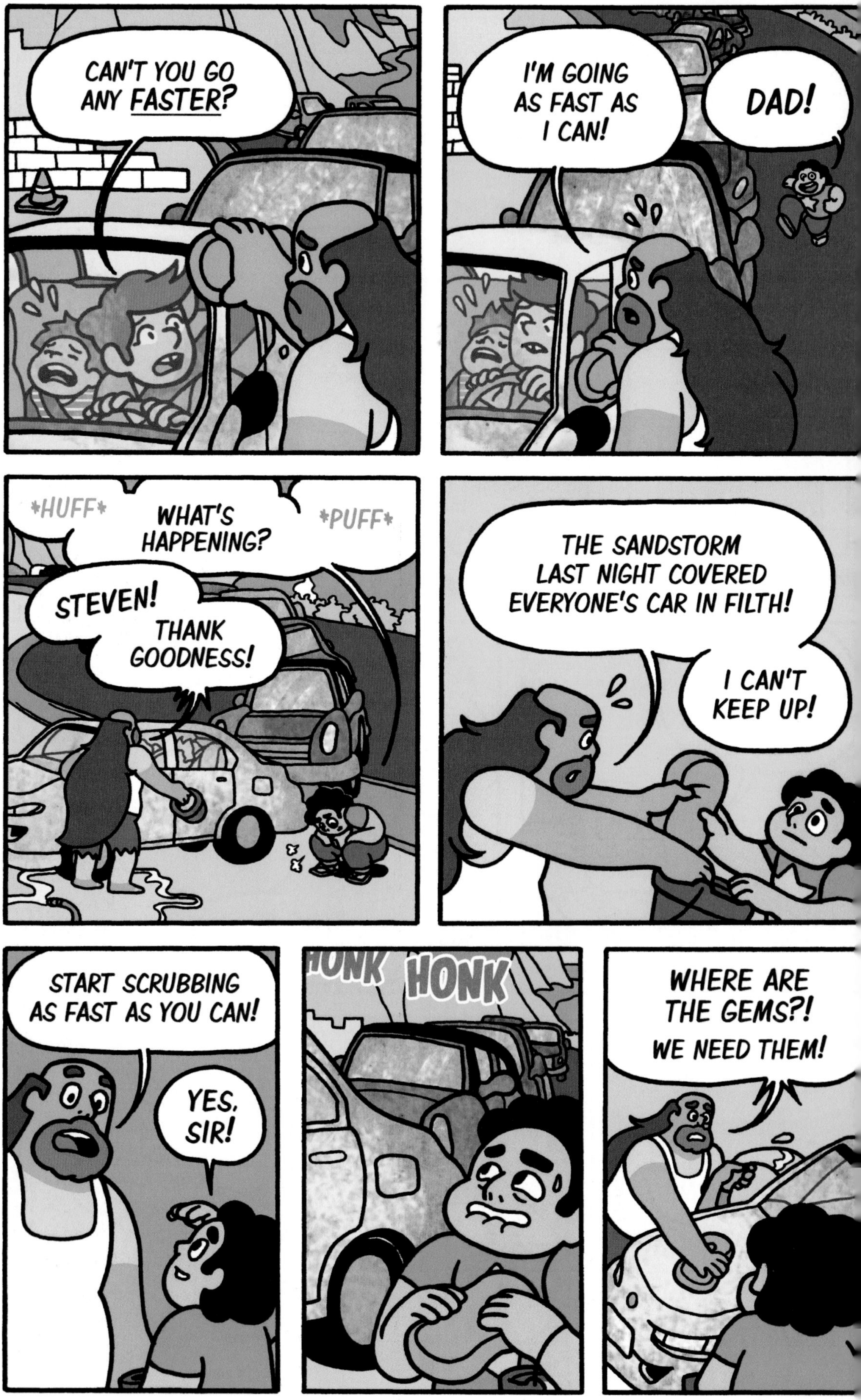
CAN'T YOU GO ANY FASTER?
I'M GOING AS FAST AS I CAN!
DAD!
HUFF
WHAT'S HAPPENING?
PUFF
STEVEN!
THANK GOODNESS!
THE SANDSTORM LAST NIGHT COVERED EVERYONE'S CAR IN FILTH!
I CAN'T KEEP UP!
START SCRUBBING AS FAST AS YOU CAN!
YES, SIR!
HONK
HONK
WHERE ARE THE GEMS?!
WE NEED THEM!

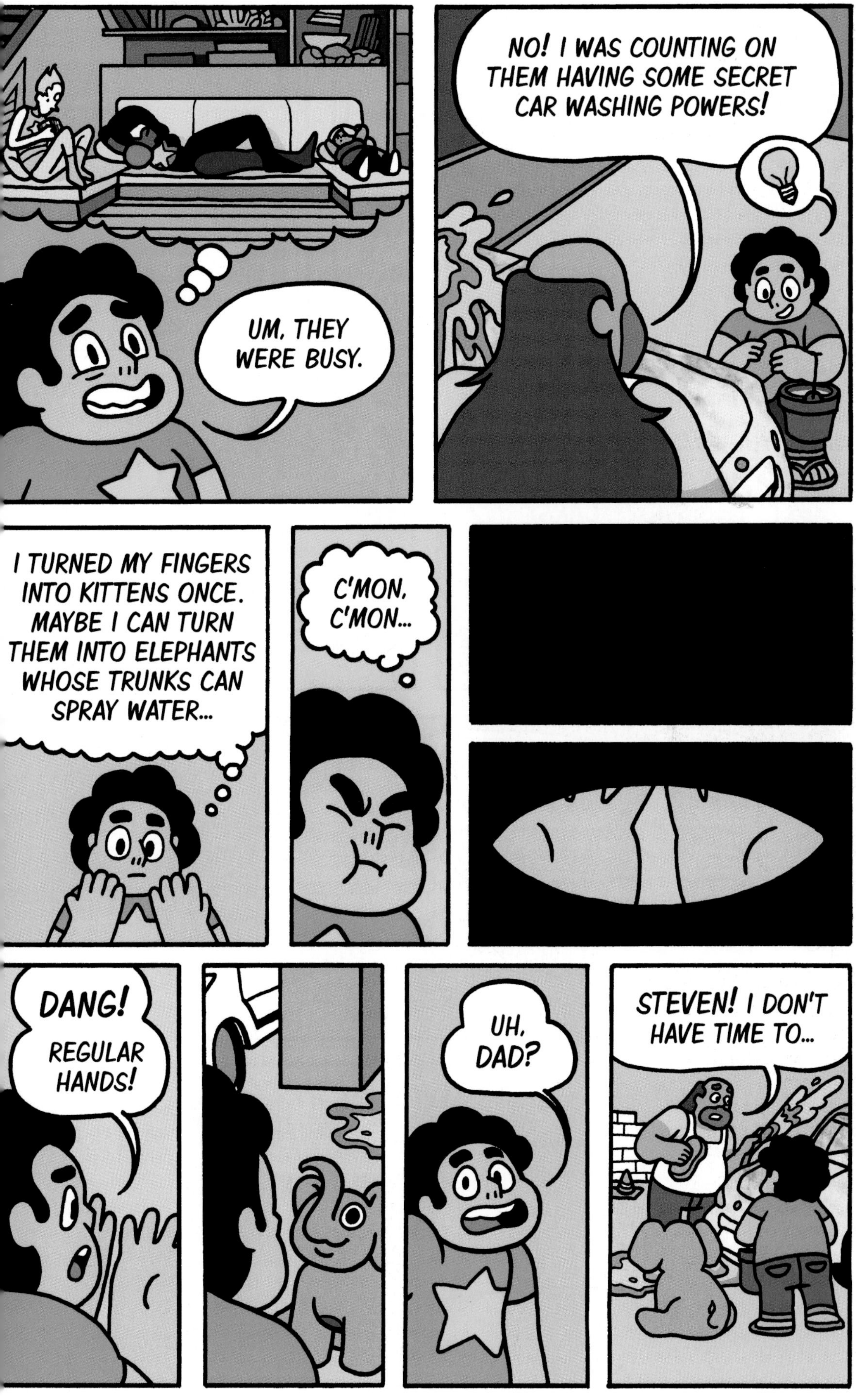
UM, THEY WERE BUSY.
NO! I WAS COUNTING ON THEM HAVING SOME SECRET CAR WASHING POWERS!
I TURNED MY FINGERS INTO KITTENS ONCE. MAYBE I CAN TURN THEM INTO ELEPHANTS WHOSE TRUNKS CAN SPRAY WATER...
C'MON, C'MON...
DANG!
REGULAR HANDS!
UH, DAD?
STEVEN! I DON'T HAVE TIME TO...

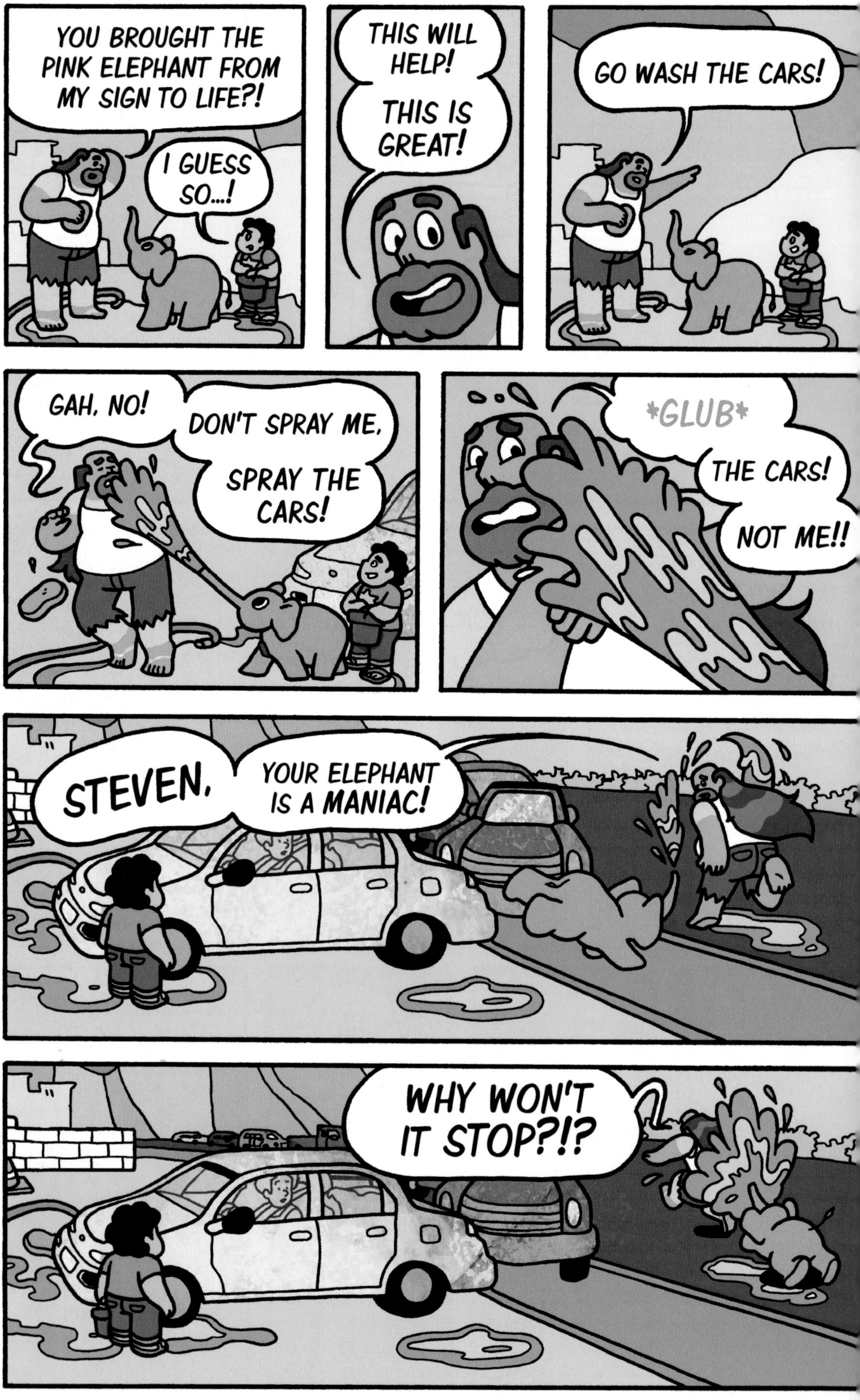

YOU BROUGHT THE PINK ELEPHANT FROM MY SIGN TO LIFE?!
I GUESS SO...!
THIS WILL HELP!
THIS IS GREAT!
GO WASH THE CARS!
GAH, NO!
DON'T SPRAY ME,
SPRAY THE CARS!
GLUB
THE CARS!
NOT ME!!
STEVEN,
YOUR ELEPHANT IS A MANIAC!
WHY WON'T IT STOP?!?

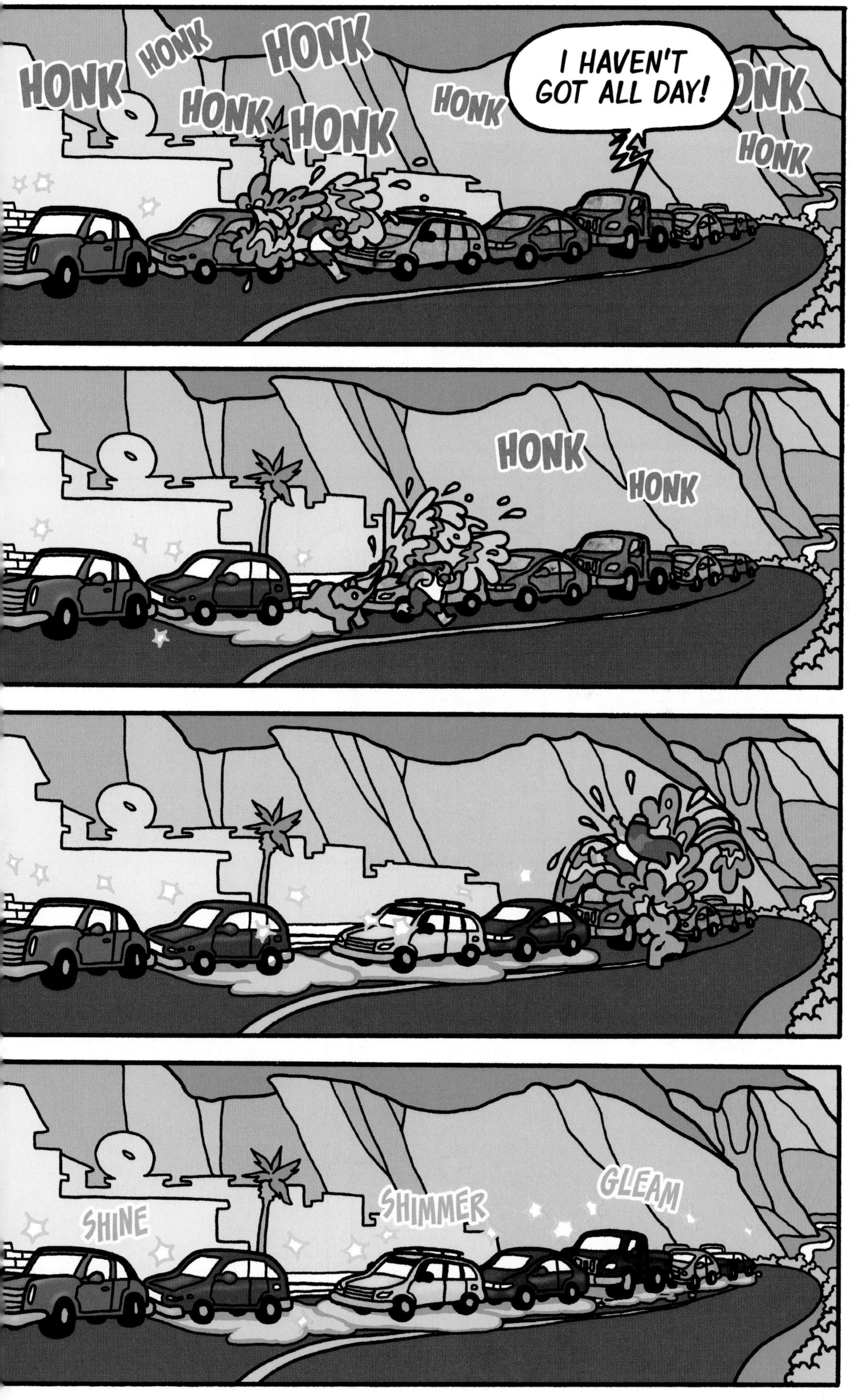

HONK
HONK
HONK
HONK
HONK
HONK
I HAVEN'T GOT ALL DAY!
HONK
HONK
HONK
SHINE
SHIMMER
GLEAM

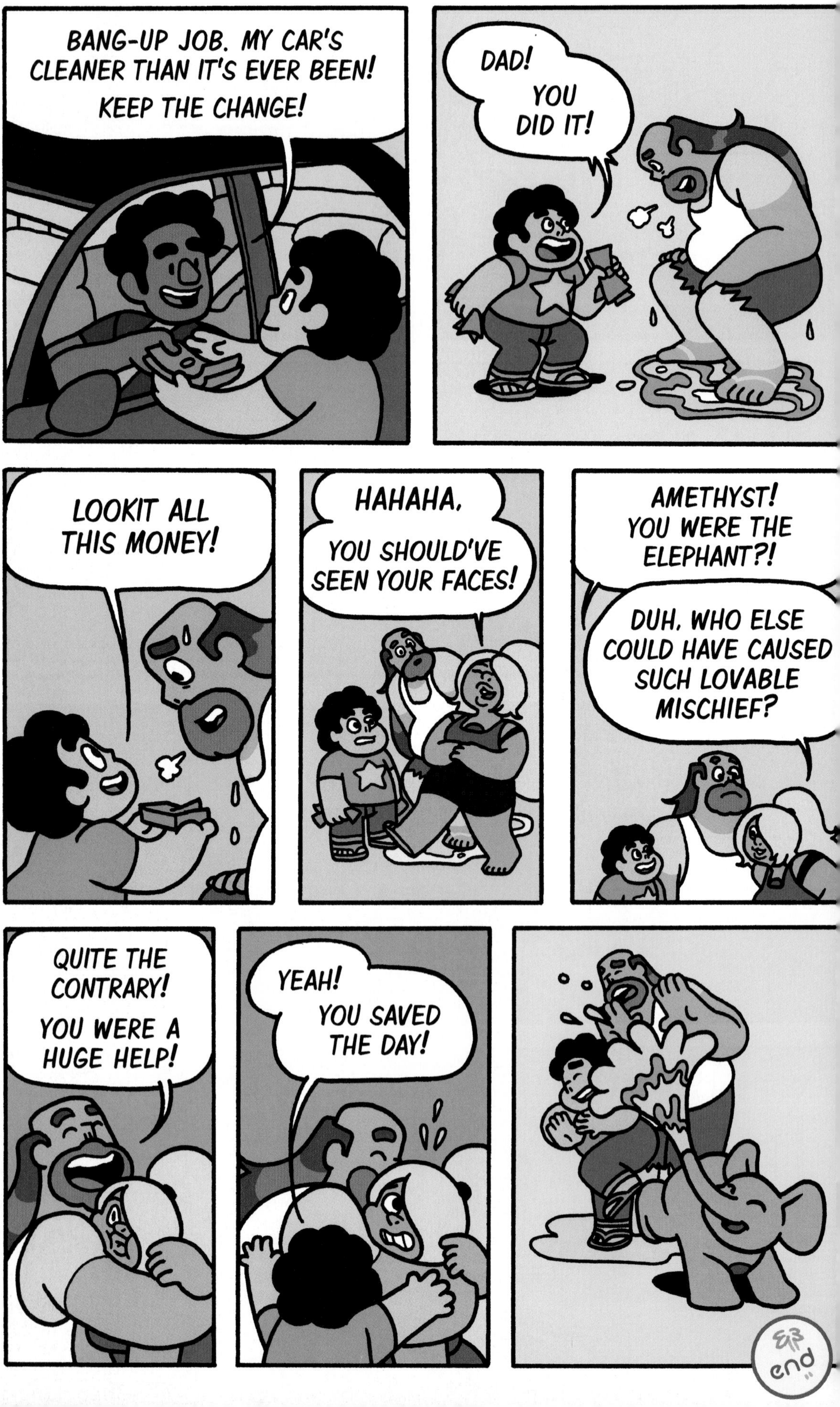
BANG-UP JOB. MY CAR'S CLEANER THAN IT'S EVER BEEN!
KEEP THE CHANGE!
DAD!
YOU DID IT!
LOOKIT ALL THIS MONEY!
HAHAHA,
YOU SHOULD'VE SEEN YOUR FACES!
AMETHYST! YOU WERE THE ELEPHANT?!
DUH, WHO ELSE COULD HAVE CAUSED SUCH LOVABLE MISCHIEF?
QUITE THE CONTRARY!
YOU WERE A HUGE HELP!
YEAH!
YOU SAVED THE DAY!
end

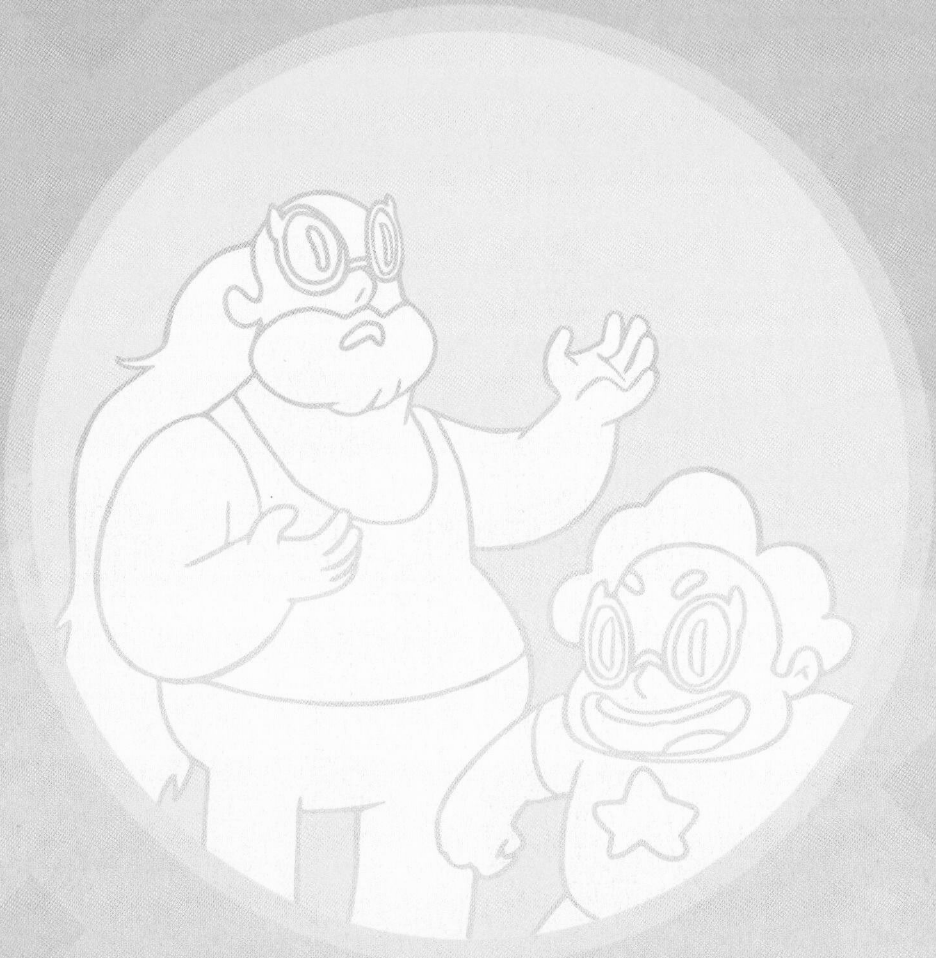

NOW IN 3D

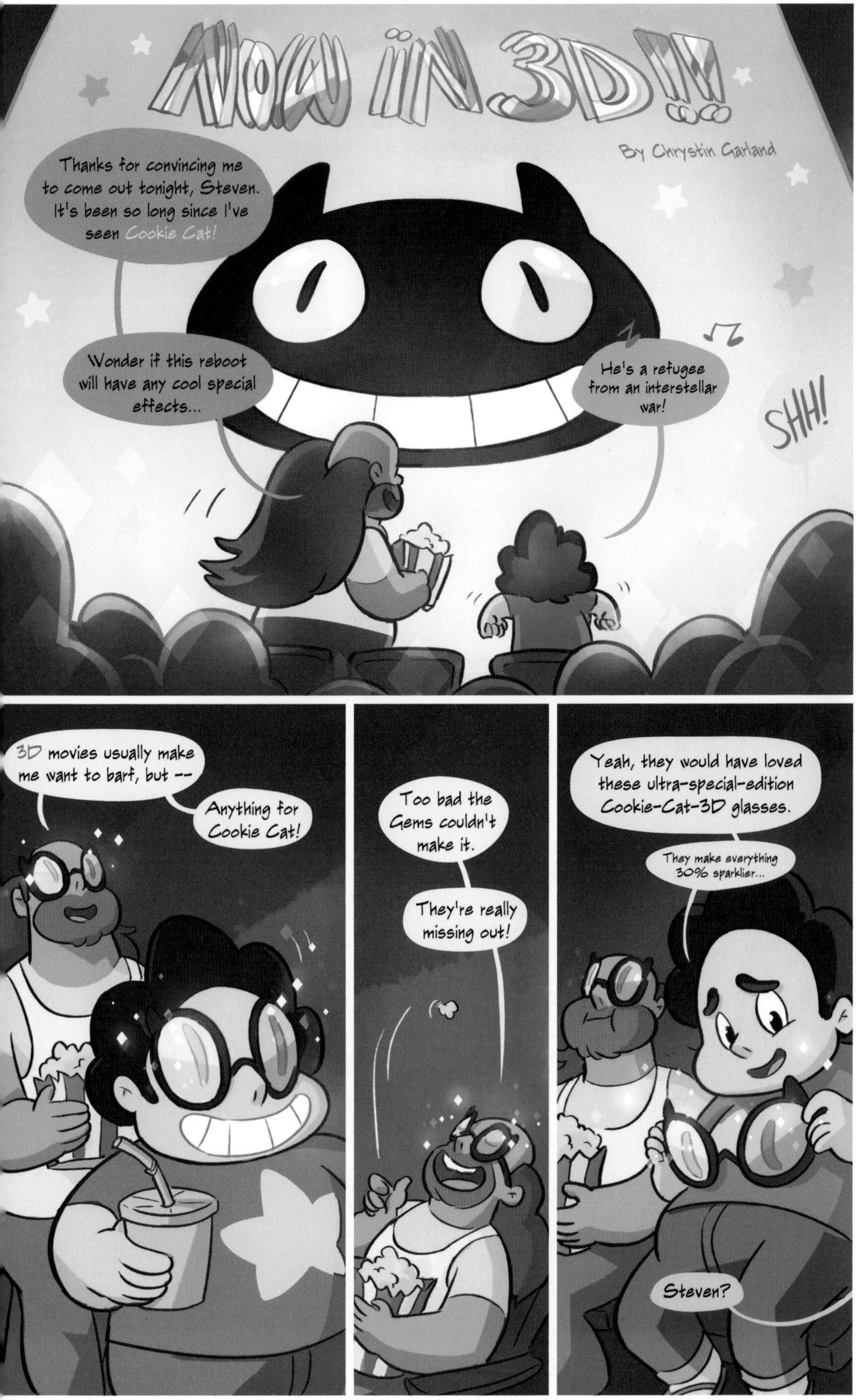
NOW IN 3D!!
By Chrystin Garland
Thanks for convincing me to come out tonight, Steven. It's been so long since I've seen Cookie Cat!
Wonder if this reboot will have any cool special effects...
He's a refugee from an interstellar war!
SHH!
3D movies usually make me want to barf, but --
Anything for Cookie Cat!
Too bad the Gems couldn't make it.
They're really missing out!
Yeah, they would have loved these ultra-special-edition Cookie-Cat-3D glasses.
They make everything 30% sparklier...
Steven?

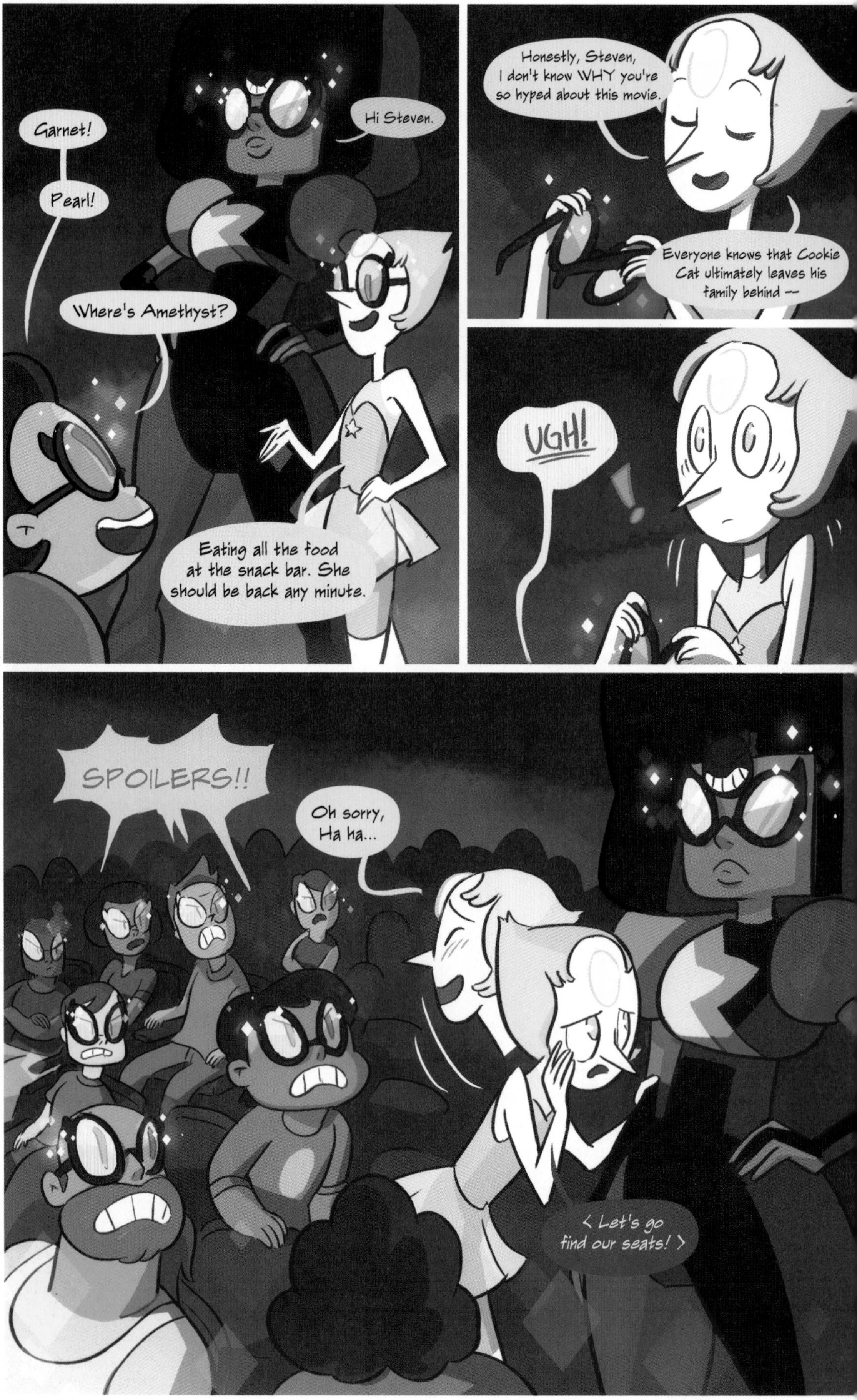
Garnet!
Pearl!
Hi Steven.
Where's Amethyst?
Eating all the food at the snack bar. She should be back any minute.
Honestly, Steven, I don't know WHY you're so hyped about this movie.
Everyone knows that Cookie Cat ultimately leaves his family behind --
UGH!
SPOILERS!!
Oh sorry, Ha ha...
< Let's go find our seats! >

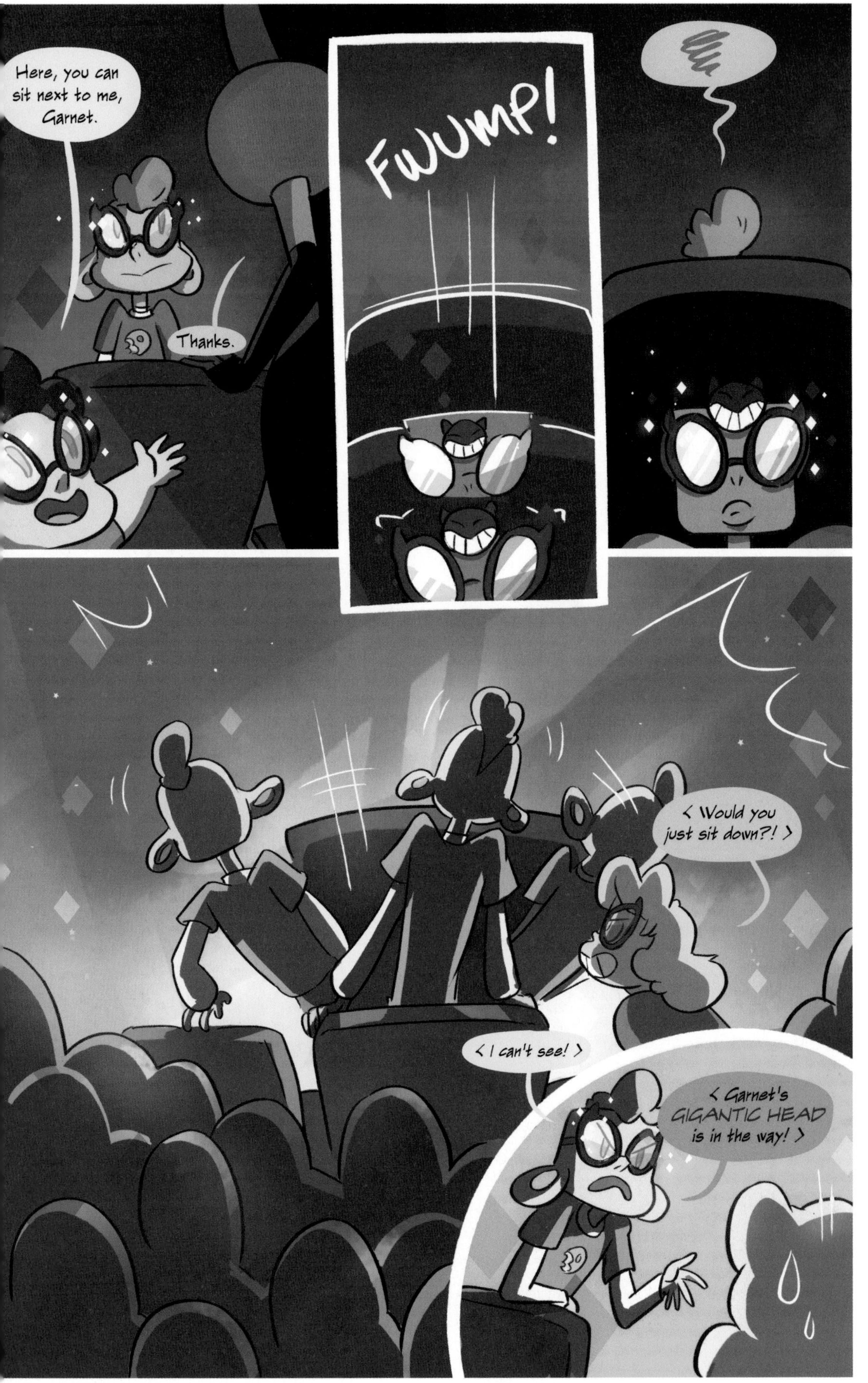
Here, you can sit next to me, Garnet.
Thanks.
FWUMP!
< Would you just sit down?! >
< I can't see! >
< Garnet's GIGANTIC HEAD is in the way! >

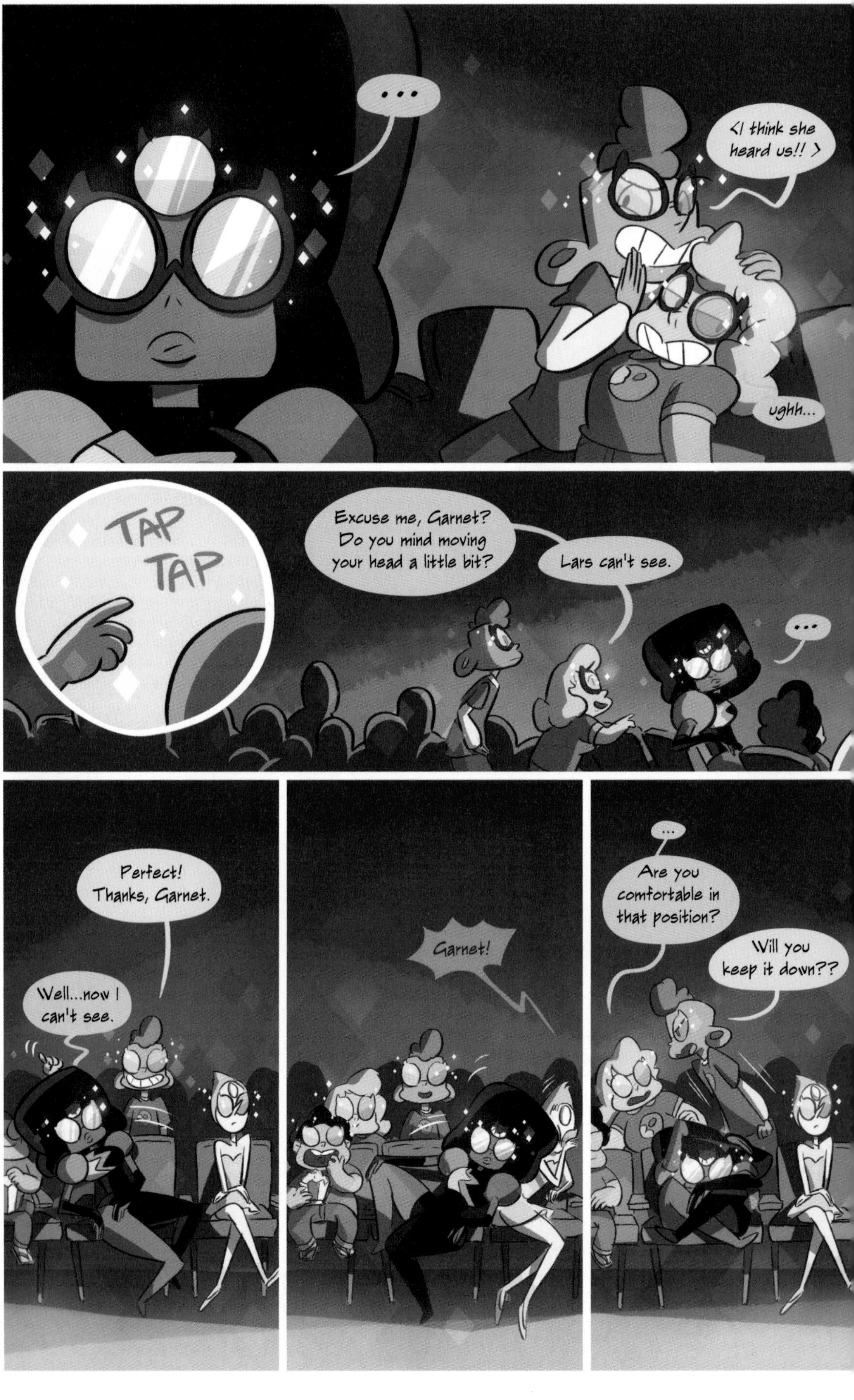
...
<I think she heard us!! >
ughh...
TAP TAP
Excuse me, Garnet? Do you mind moving your head a little bit?
Lars can't see.
...
Perfect! Thanks, Garnet.
Well...now I can't see.
Garnet!
...
Are you comfortable in that position?
Will you keep it down??

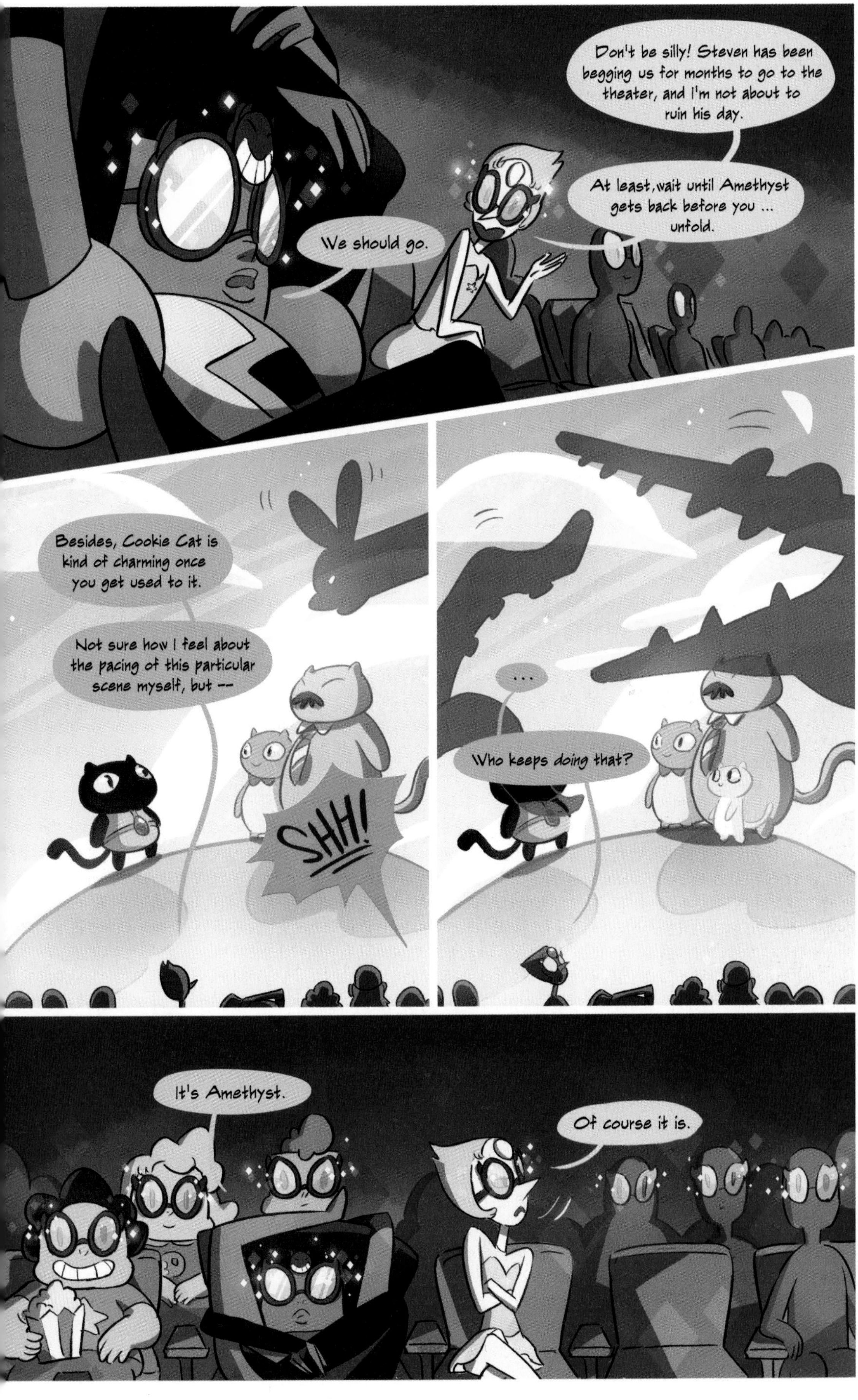
Don't be silly! Steven has been begging us for months to go to the theater, and I'm not about to ruin his day.
We should go.
At least, wait until Amethyst gets back before you ... unfold.
Besides, Cookie Cat is kind of charming once you get used to it.
Not sure how I feel about the pacing of this particular scene myself, but --
SHH!
...
Who keeps doing that?
It's Amethyst.
Of course it is.

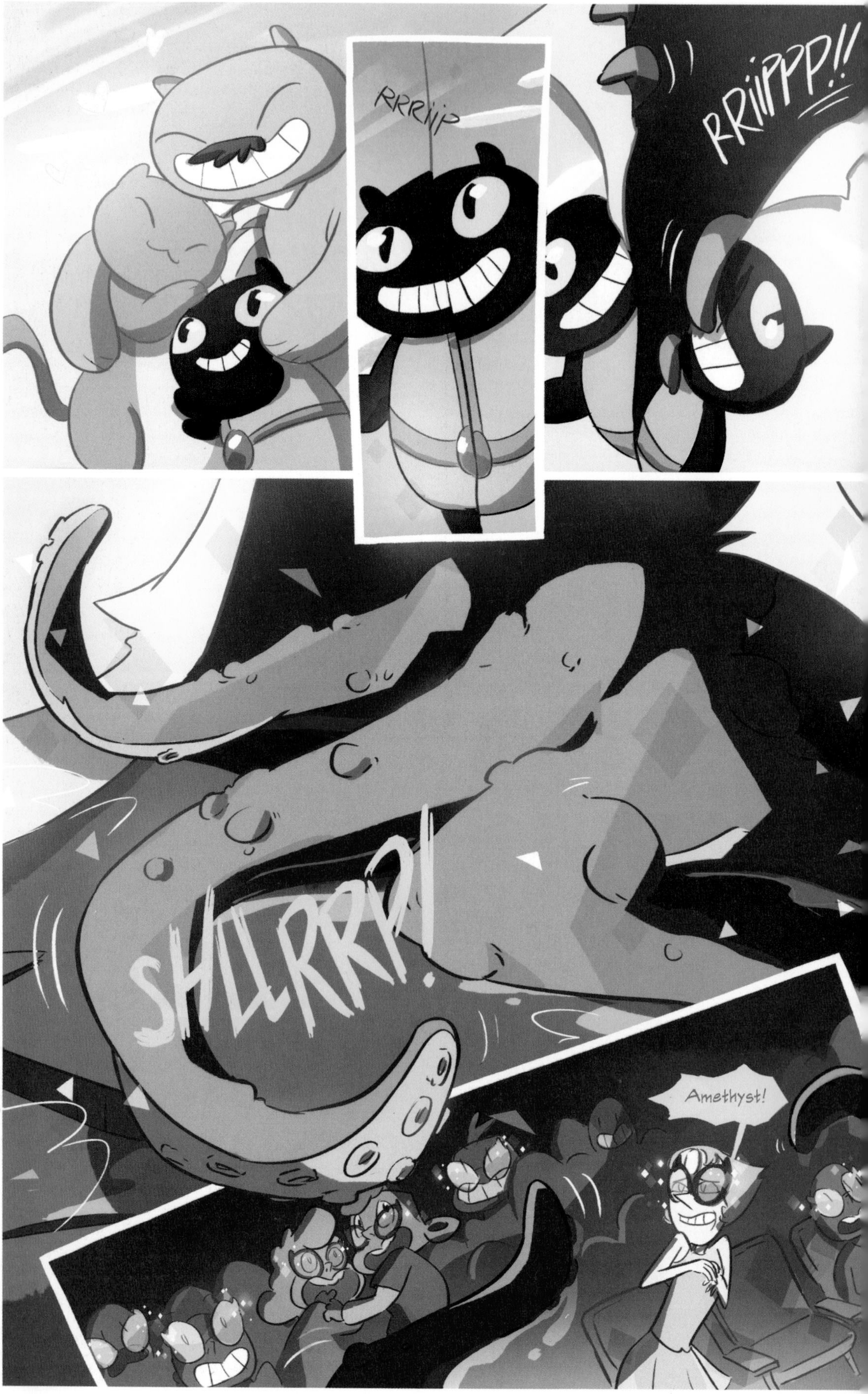

RRRIIP
RRIIPPP!!
SHLRRP!
Amethyst!

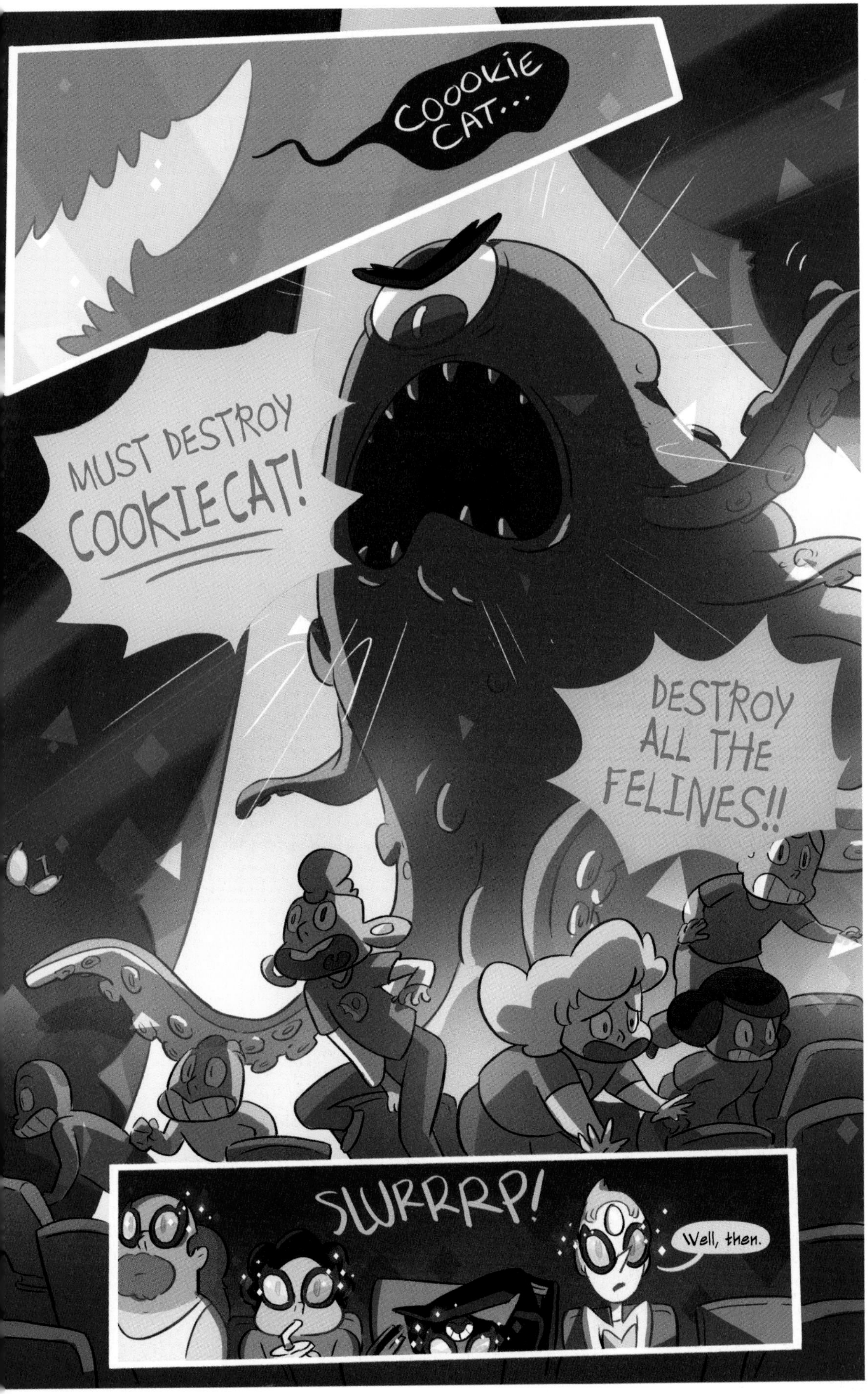
COOOKIE CAT...
MUST DESTROY COOKIE CAT!
DESTROY ALL THE FELINES!!
SLURRRP!
Well, then.

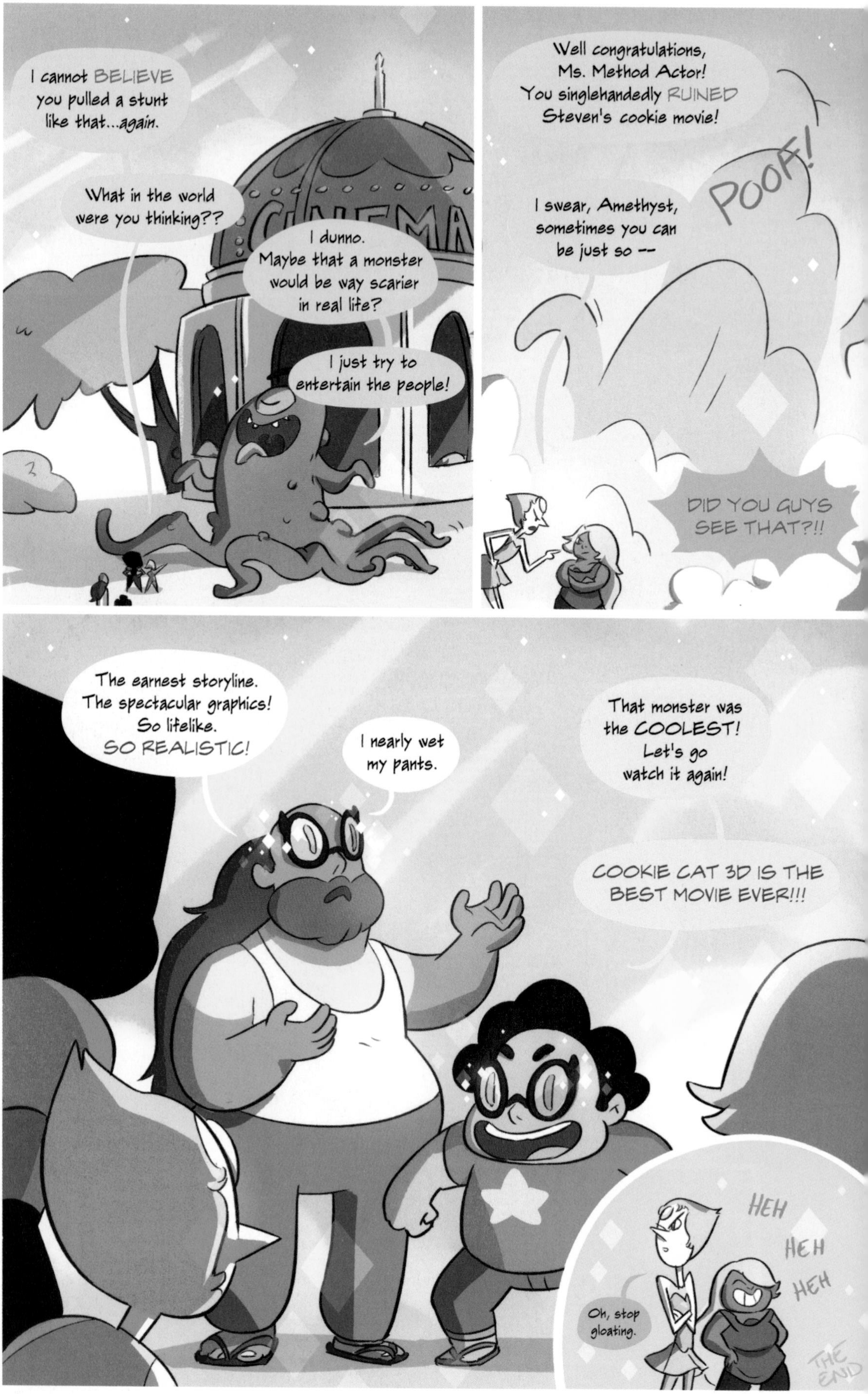
I cannot BELIEVE you pulled a stunt like that...again.
What in the world were you thinking??
CINEMA
I dunno. Maybe that a monster would be way scarier in real life?
I just try to entertain the people!
Well congratulations, Ms. Method Actor! You singlehandedly RUINED Steven's cookie movie!
POOF!
I swear, Amethyst, sometimes you can be just so --
DID YOU GUYS SEE THAT?!!
The earnest storyline. The spectacular graphics! So lifelike. SO REALISTIC!
I nearly wet my pants.
That monster was the COOLEST! Let's go watch it again!
COOKIE CAT 3D IS THE BEST MOVIE EVER!!!
HEH
HEH
HEH
Oh, stop gloating.
THE END

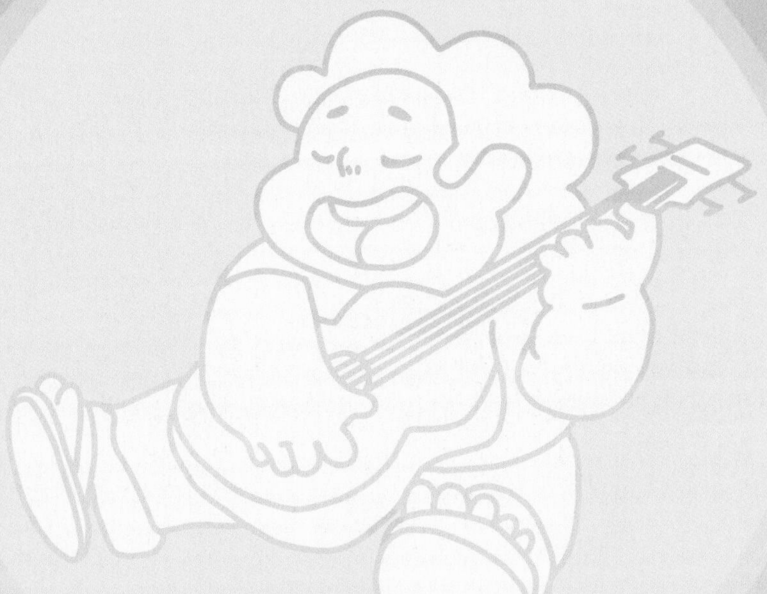

BY HEART

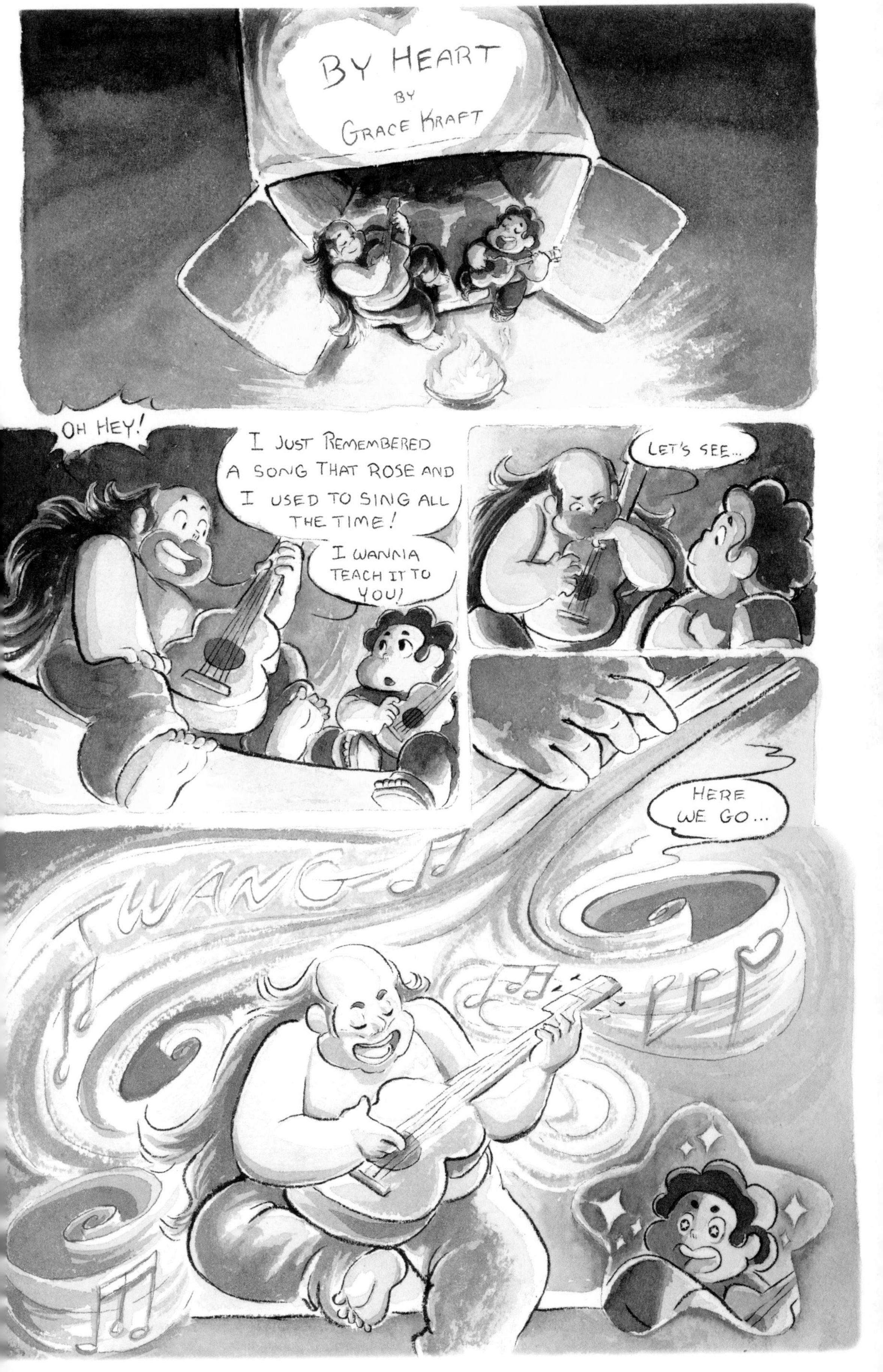

BY HEART
BY
GRACE KRAFT
OH HEY!
I JUST REMEMBERED A SONG THAT ROSE AND I USED TO SING ALL THE TIME!
I WANNA TEACH IT TO YOU!
LET'S SEE...
HERE WE GO...
TWANG

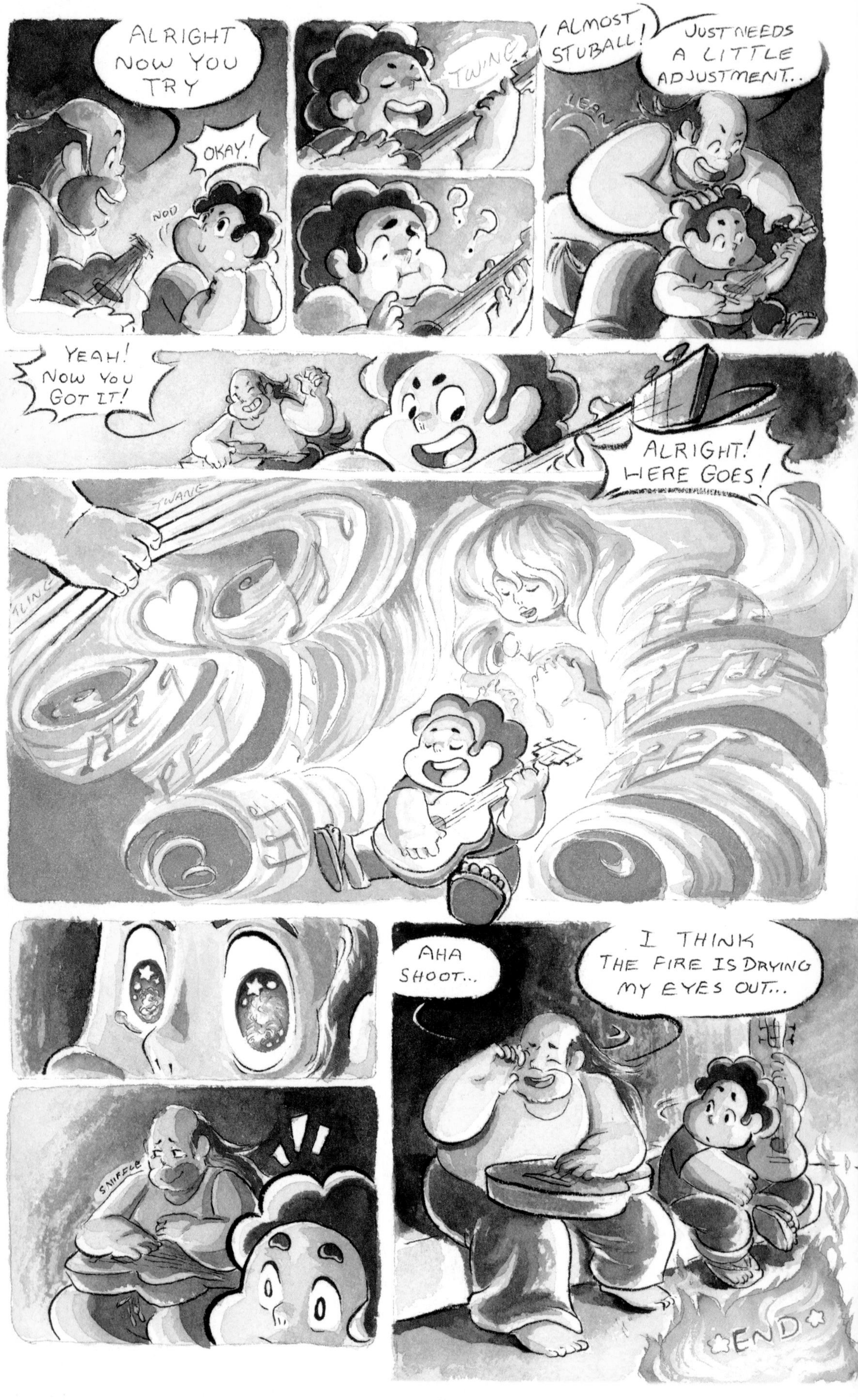
ALRIGHT NOW YOU TRY
OKAY!
NOD
TWING
ALMOST STUBALL!
JUST NEEDS A LITTLE ADJUSTMENT...
LEAN
YEAH! NOW YOU GOT IT!
ALRIGHT! HERE GOES!
TWANG
TWING
AHA SHOOT...
I THINK THE FIRE IS DRYING MY EYES OUT...
SNIFFLE
END

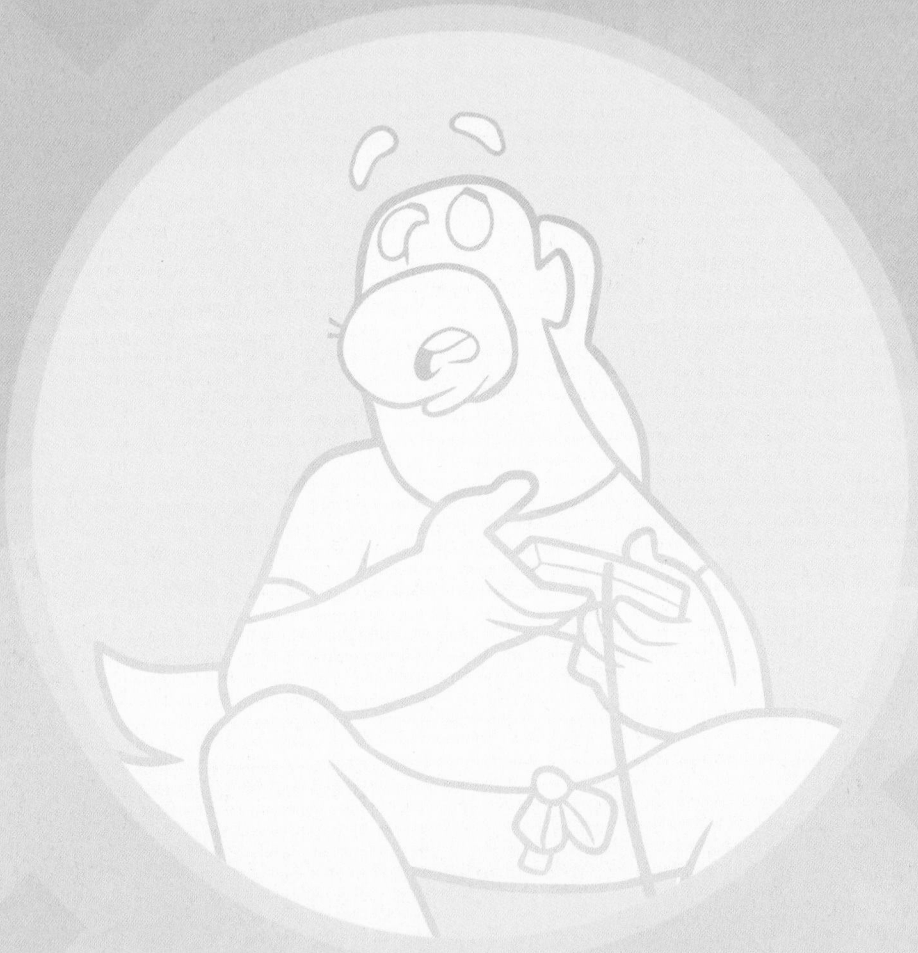

GREGARIOUS GAMERS

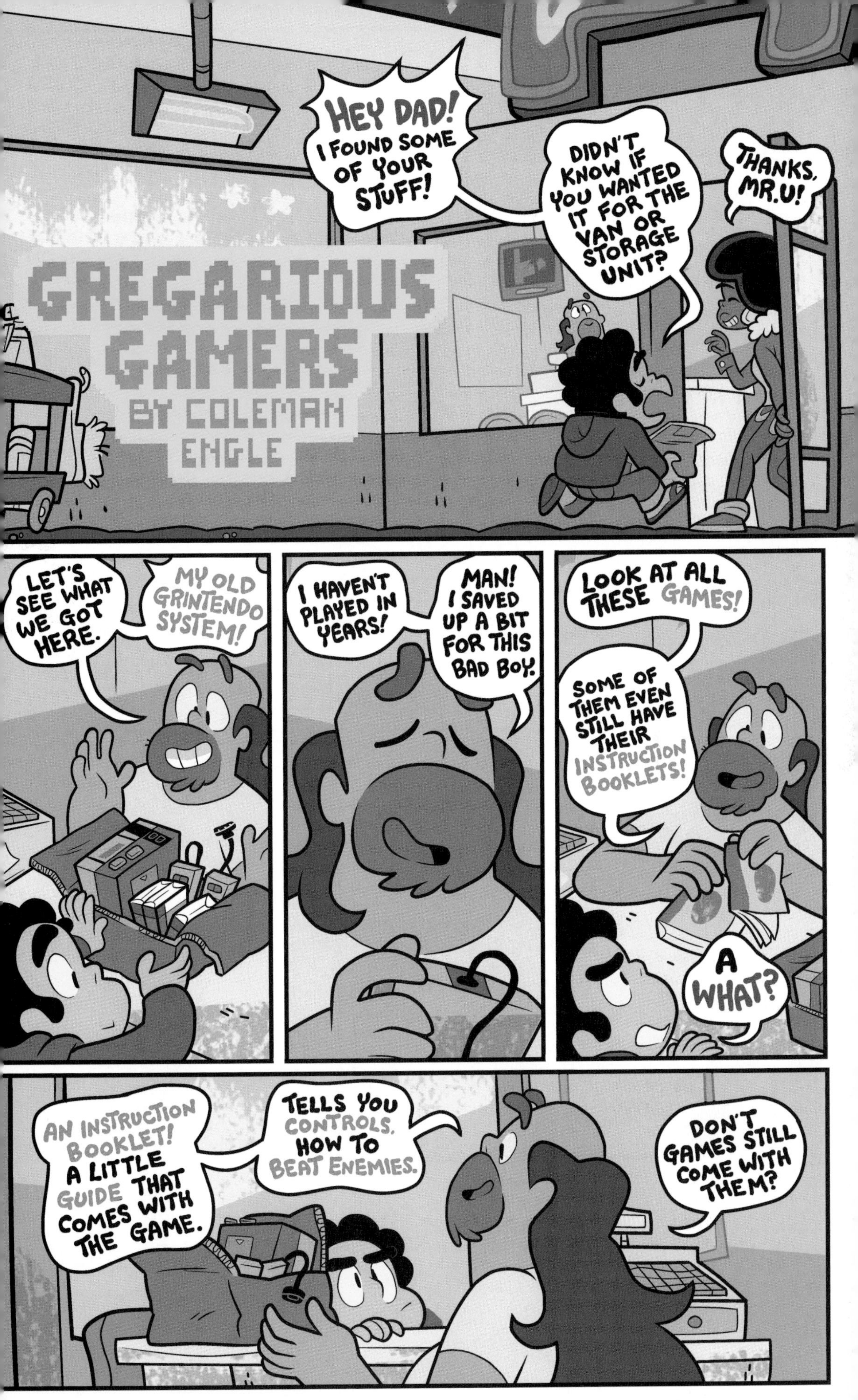
GREGARIOUS GAMERS
BY COLEMAN ENGLE
HEY DAD! I FOUND SOME OF YOUR STUFF!
DIDN'T KNOW IF YOU WANTED IT FOR THE VAN OR STORAGE UNIT?
THANKS, MR.U!
LET'S SEE WHAT WE GOT HERE.
MY OLD GRINTENDO SYSTEM!
I HAVEN'T PLAYED IN YEARS!
MAN! I SAVED UP A BIT FOR THIS BAD BOY.
LOOK AT ALL THESE GAMES!
SOME OF THEM EVEN STILL HAVE THEIR INSTRUCTION BOOKLETS!
A WHAT?
AN INSTRUCTION BOOKLET! A LITTLE GUIDE THAT COMES WITH THE GAME.
TELLS YOU CONTROLS, HOW TO BEAT ENEMIES.
DON'T GAMES STILL COME WITH THEM?

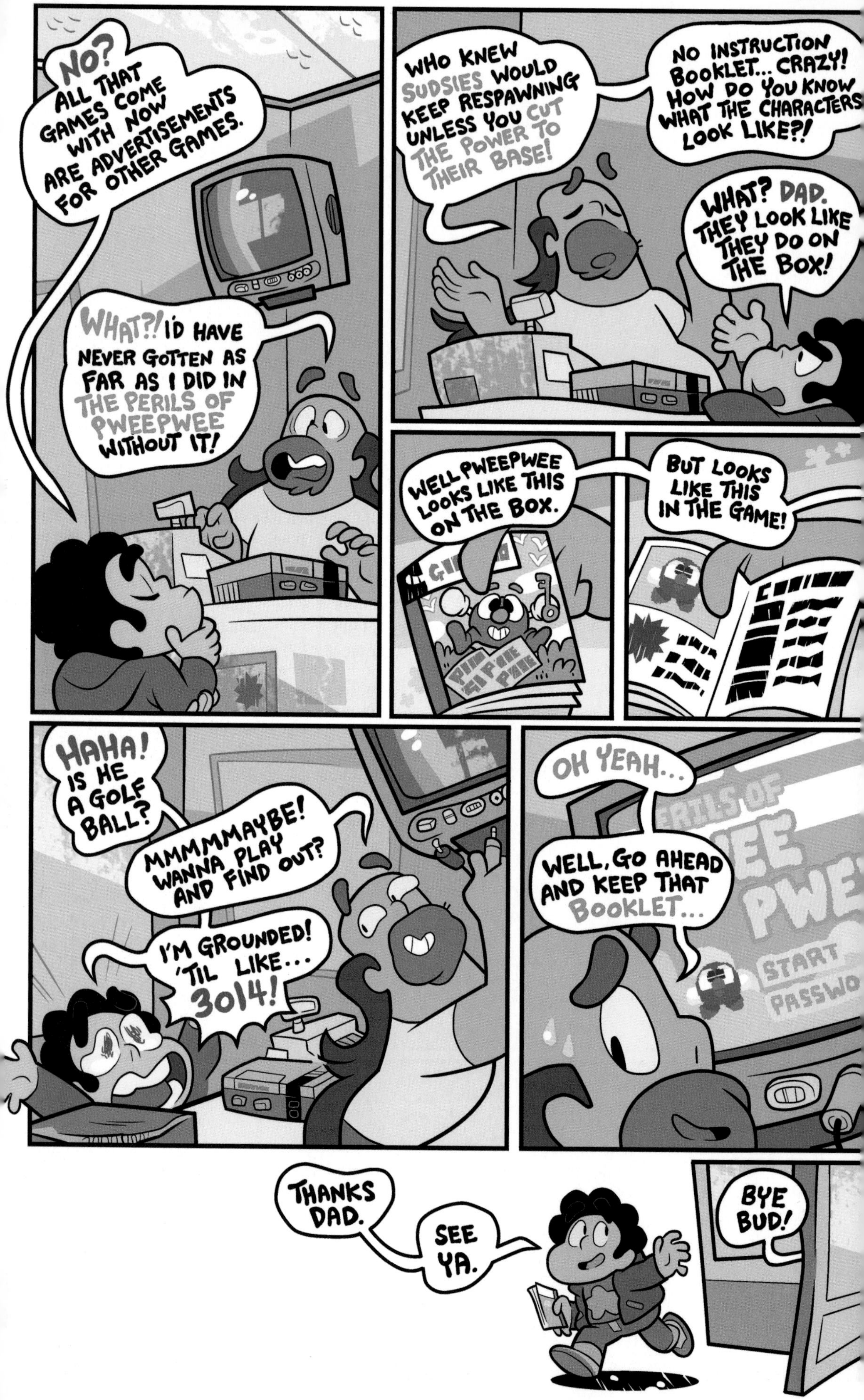

NO? ALL THAT GAMES COME WITH NOW ARE ADVERTISEMENTS FOR OTHER GAMES.
WHAT?! I'D HAVE NEVER GOTTEN AS FAR AS I DID IN THE PERILS OF PWEEPWEE WITHOUT IT!
WHO KNEW SUDSIES WOULD KEEP RESPAWNING UNLESS YOU CUT THE POWER TO THEIR BASE!
NO INSTRUCTION BOOKLET... CRAZY! HOW DO YOU KNOW WHAT THE CHARACTERS LOOK LIKE?!
WHAT? DAD. THEY LOOK LIKE THEY DO ON THE BOX!
WELL PWEEPWEE LOOKS LIKE THIS ON THE BOX.
BUT LOOKS LIKE THIS IN THE GAME!
HAHA! IS HE A GOLF BALL?
MMMMMAYBE! WANNA PLAY AND FIND OUT?
I'M GROUNDED! 'TIL LIKE... 3014!
OH YEAH...
WELL, GO AHEAD AND KEEP THAT BOOKLET...
THANKS DAD.
SEE YA.
BYE BUD!

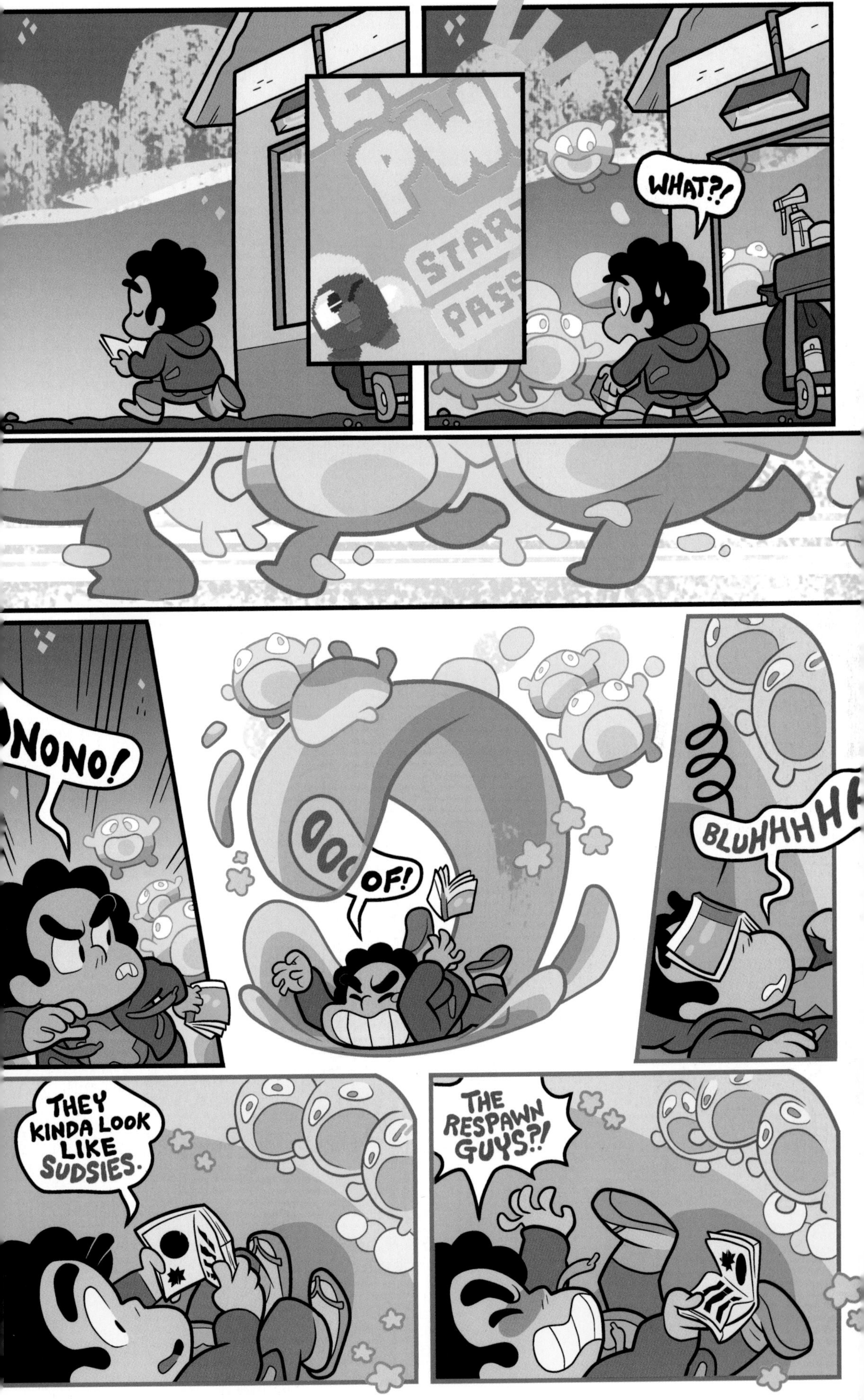
WHAT?!
NONONO!
OOOOF!
BLUHHHHH
THEY KINDA LOOK LIKE SUDSIES.
THE RESPAWN GUYS?!

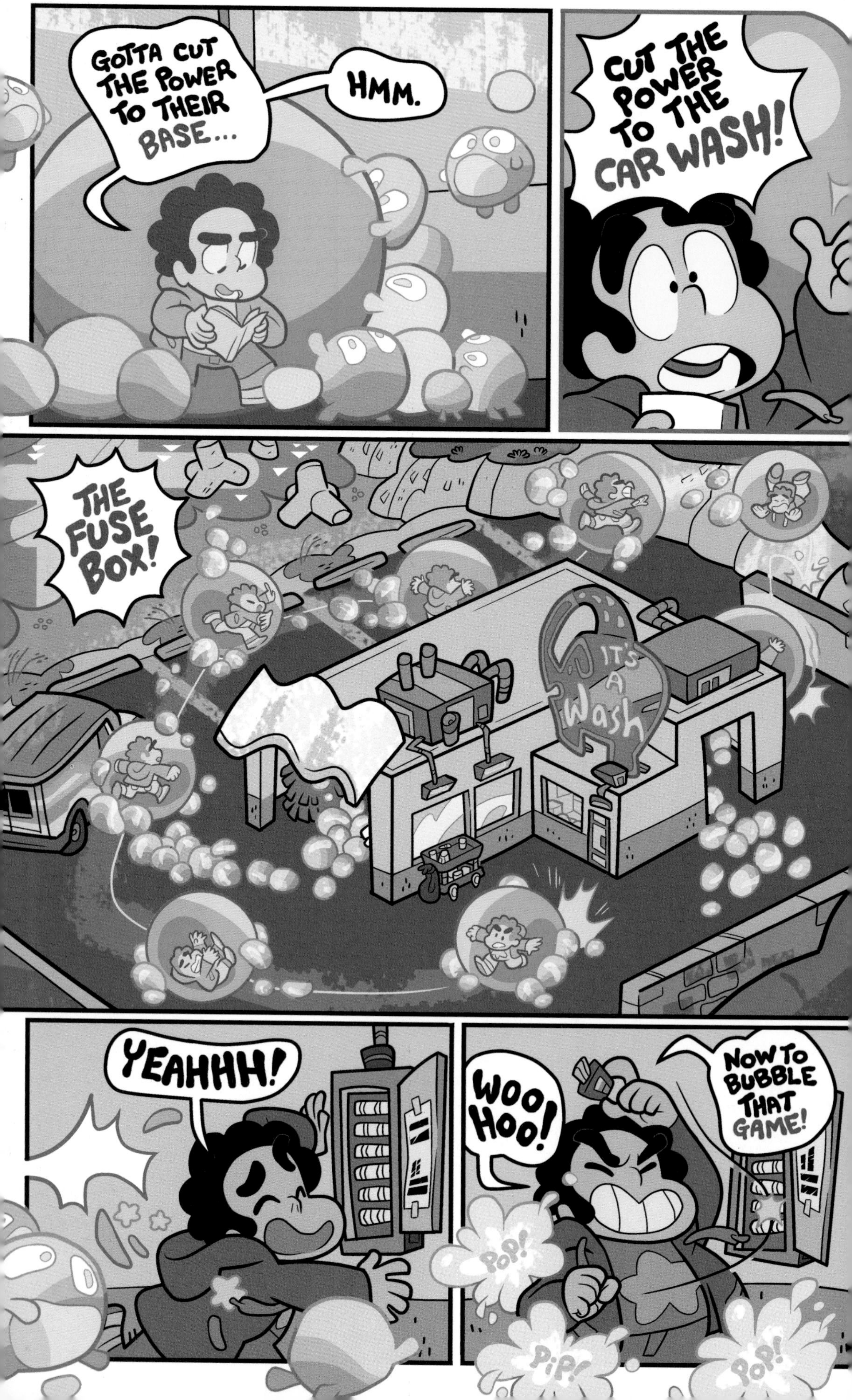
GOTTA CUT THE POWER TO THEIR BASE...
HMM.
CUT THE POWER TO THE CAR WASH!
THE FUSE BOX!
IT'S A Wash
YEAHHH!
WOO HOO!
NOW TO BUBBLE THAT GAME!
POP!
PIP!
POP!

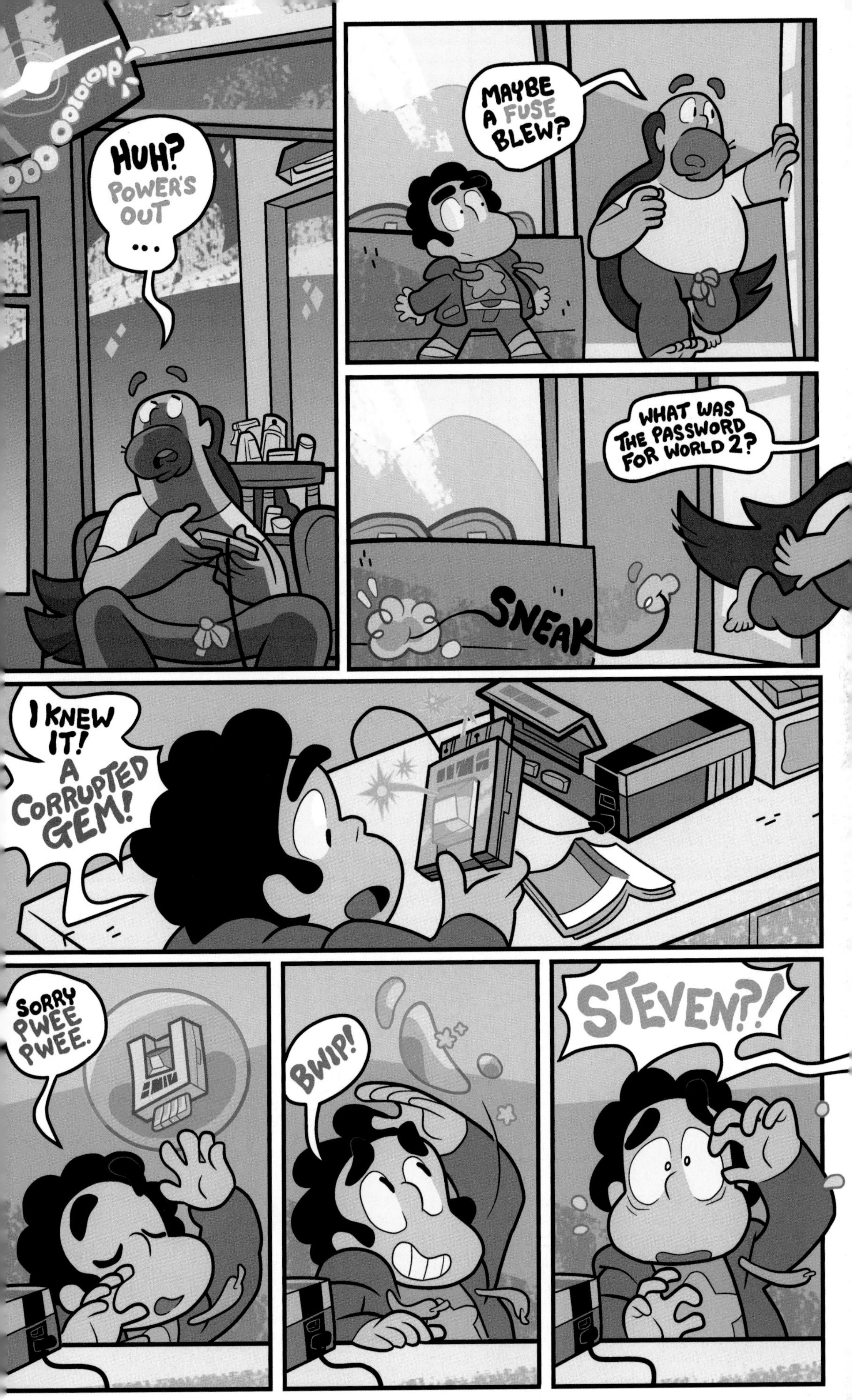
OOOOOOIOIOIOIP!
HUH? POWER'S OUT...
MAYBE A FUSE BLEW?
WHAT WAS THE PASSWORD FOR WORLD 2?
SNEAK
I KNEW IT! A CORRUPTED GEM!
SORRY PWEE PWEE.
BWIP!
STEVEN?!

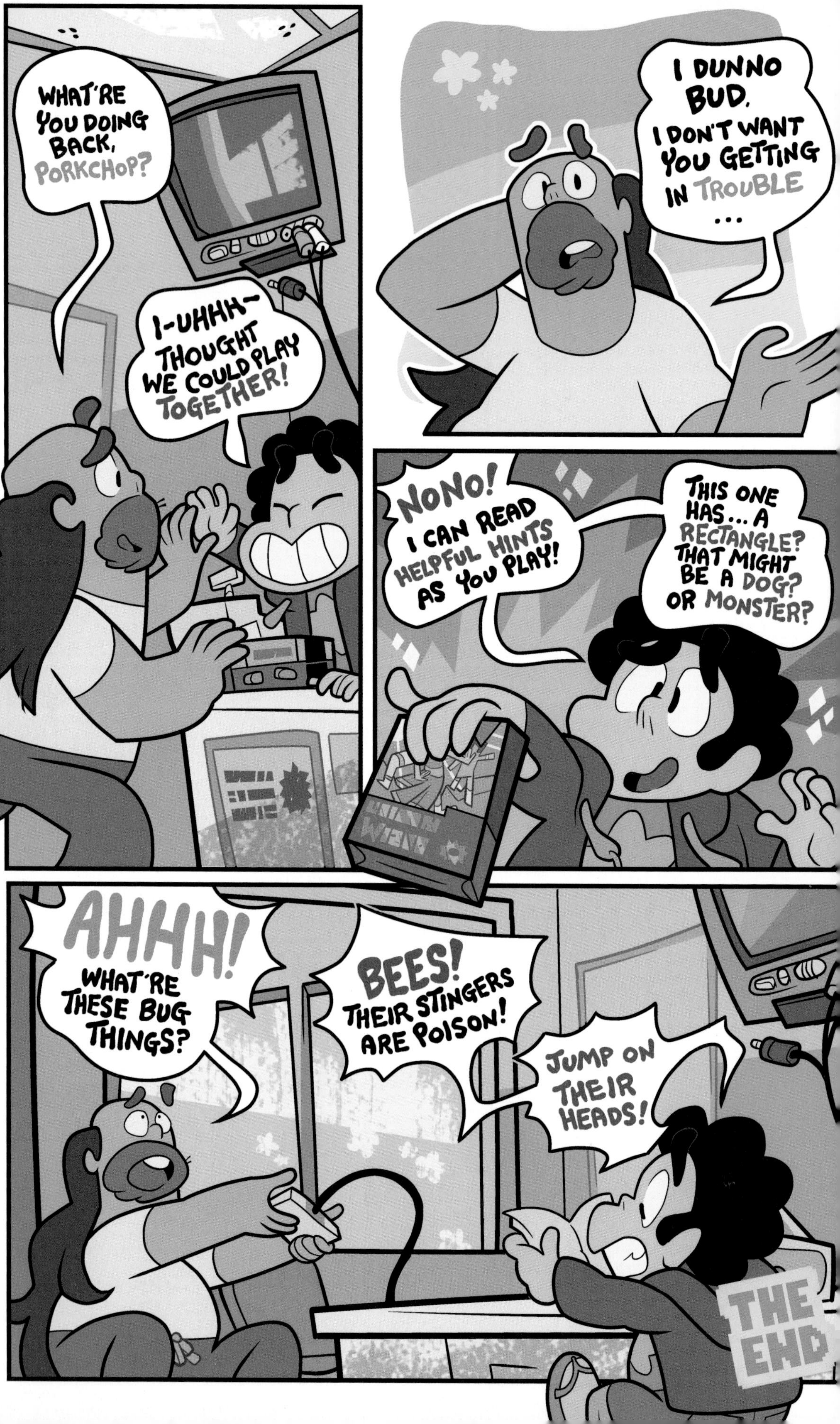
WHAT'RE YOU DOING BACK, PORKCHOP?
I-UHHH-THOUGHT WE COULD PLAY TOGETHER!
I DUNNO BUD. I DON'T WANT YOU GETTING IN TROUBLE ...
NONO! I CAN READ HELPFUL HINTS AS YOU PLAY!
THIS ONE HAS... A RECTANGLE? THAT MIGHT BE A DOG? OR MONSTER?
AHHH! WHAT'RE THESE BUG THINGS?
BEES! THEIR STINGERS ARE POISON!
JUMP ON THEIR HEADS!
THE END

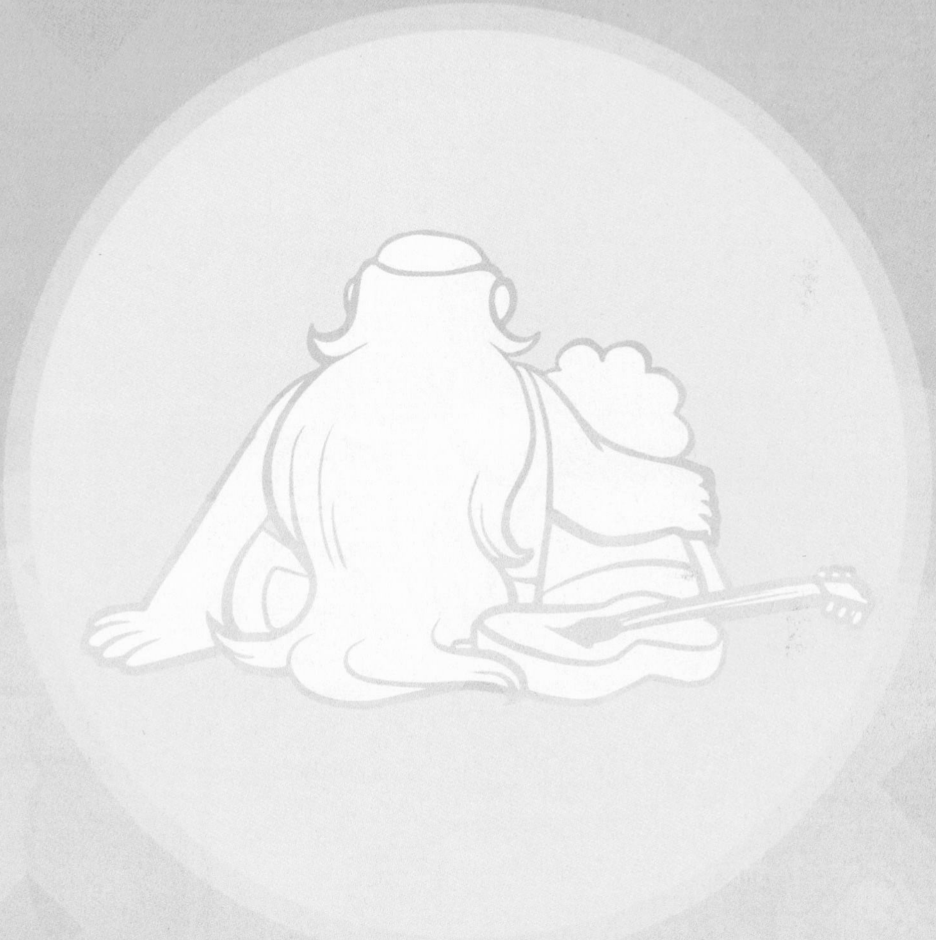

SNAPSHOTS

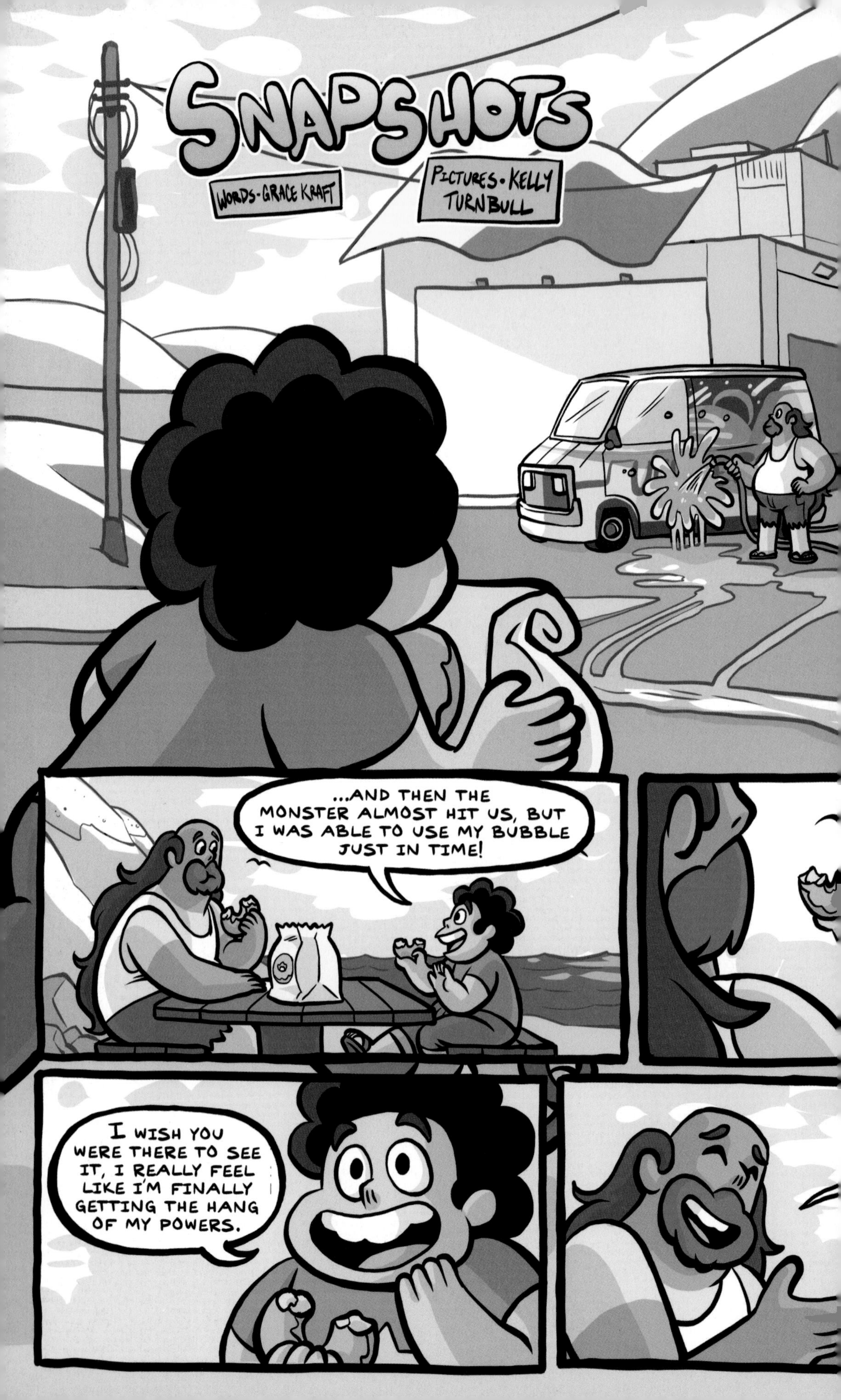
SNAPSHOTS
WORDS-GRACE KRAFT
PICTURES-KELLY TURNBULL
...AND THEN THE MONSTER ALMOST HIT US, BUT I WAS ABLE TO USE MY BUBBLE JUST IN TIME!
I WISH YOU WERE THERE TO SEE IT, I REALLY FEEL LIKE I'M FINALLY GETTING THE HANG OF MY POWERS.

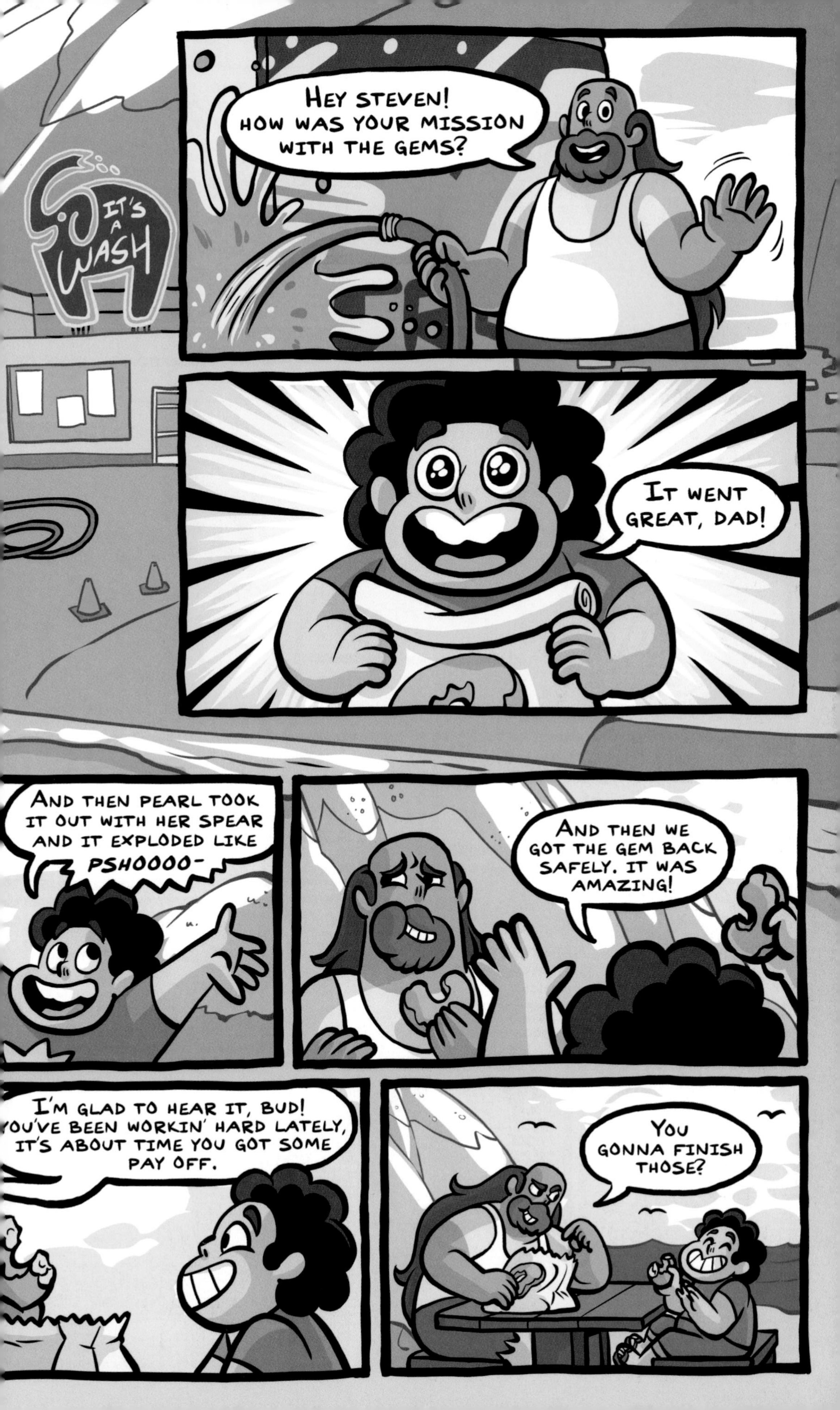
IT'S A WASH
HEY STEVEN! HOW WAS YOUR MISSION WITH THE GEMS?
IT WENT GREAT, DAD!
AND THEN PEARL TOOK IT OUT WITH HER SPEAR AND IT EXPLODED LIKE PSHOOOO-
AND THEN WE GOT THE GEM BACK SAFELY. IT WAS AMAZING!
I'M GLAD TO HEAR IT, BUD! YOU'VE BEEN WORKIN' HARD LATELY, IT'S ABOUT TIME YOU GOT SOME PAY OFF.
YOU GONNA FINISH THOSE?

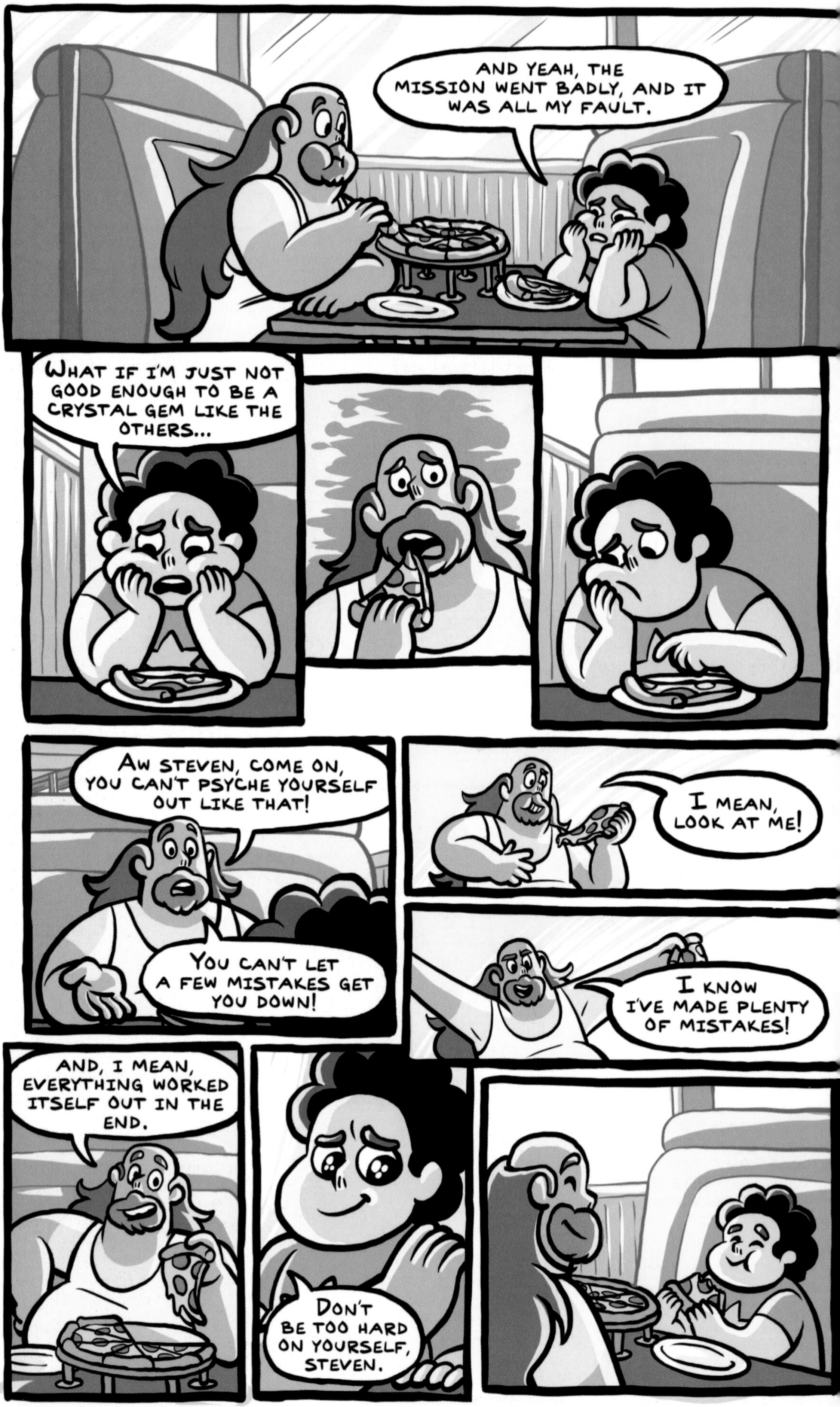
AND YEAH, THE MISSION WENT BADLY, AND IT WAS ALL MY FAULT.
WHAT IF I'M JUST NOT GOOD ENOUGH TO BE A CRYSTAL GEM LIKE THE OTHERS...
AW STEVEN, COME ON, YOU CAN'T PSYCHE YOURSELF OUT LIKE THAT!
YOU CAN'T LET A FEW MISTAKES GET YOU DOWN!
I MEAN, LOOK AT ME!
I KNOW I'VE MADE PLENTY OF MISTAKES!
AND, I MEAN, EVERYTHING WORKED ITSELF OUT IN THE END.
DON'T BE TOO HARD ON YOURSELF, STEVEN.

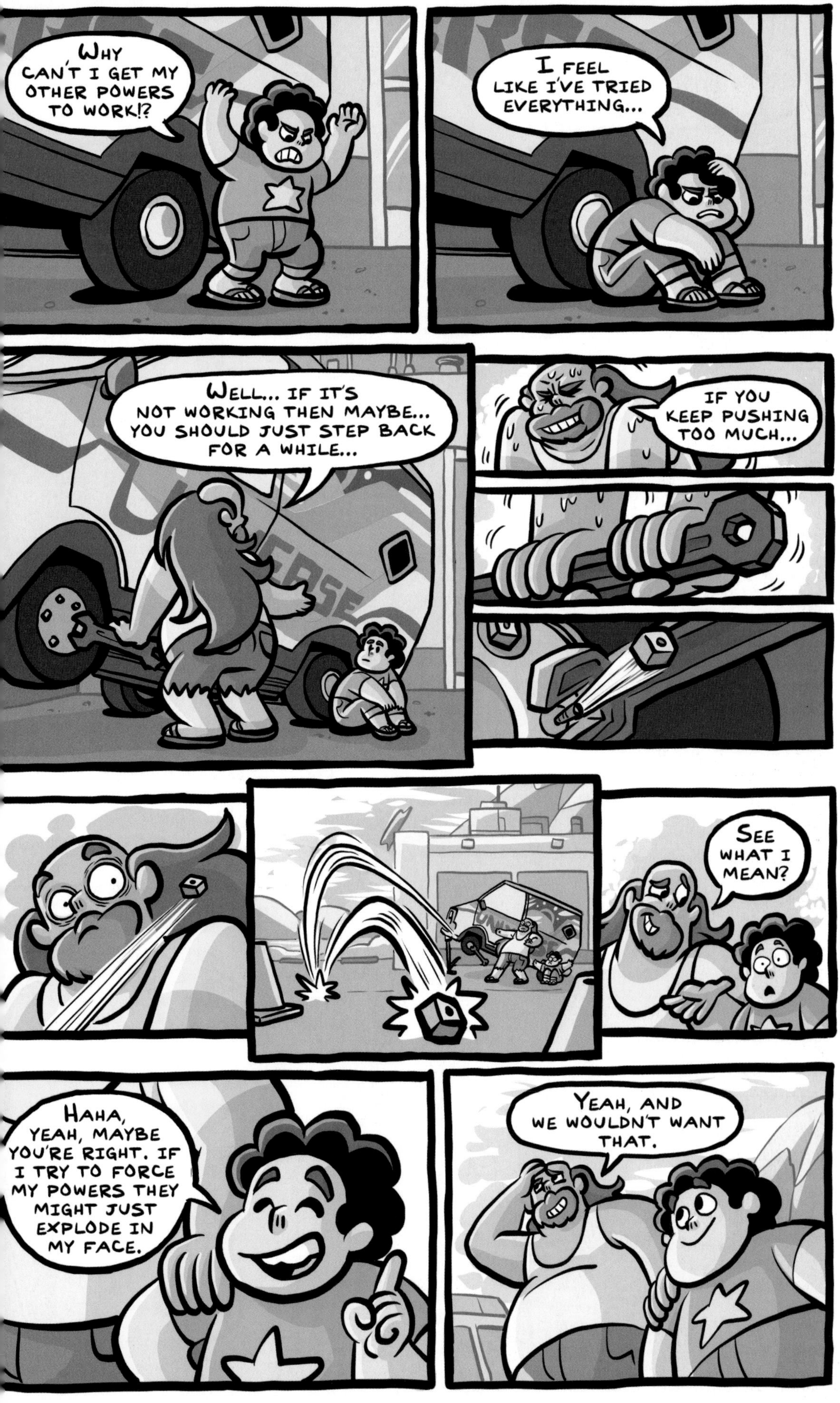
WHY CAN'T I GET MY OTHER POWERS TO WORK!?
I FEEL LIKE I'VE TRIED EVERYTHING...
WELL... IF IT'S NOT WORKING THEN MAYBE... YOU SHOULD JUST STEP BACK FOR A WHILE...
IF YOU KEEP PUSHING TOO MUCH...
SEE WHAT I MEAN?
HAHA, YEAH, MAYBE YOU'RE RIGHT. IF I TRY TO FORCE MY POWERS THEY MIGHT JUST EXPLODE IN MY FACE.
YEAH, AND WE WOULDN'T WANT THAT.

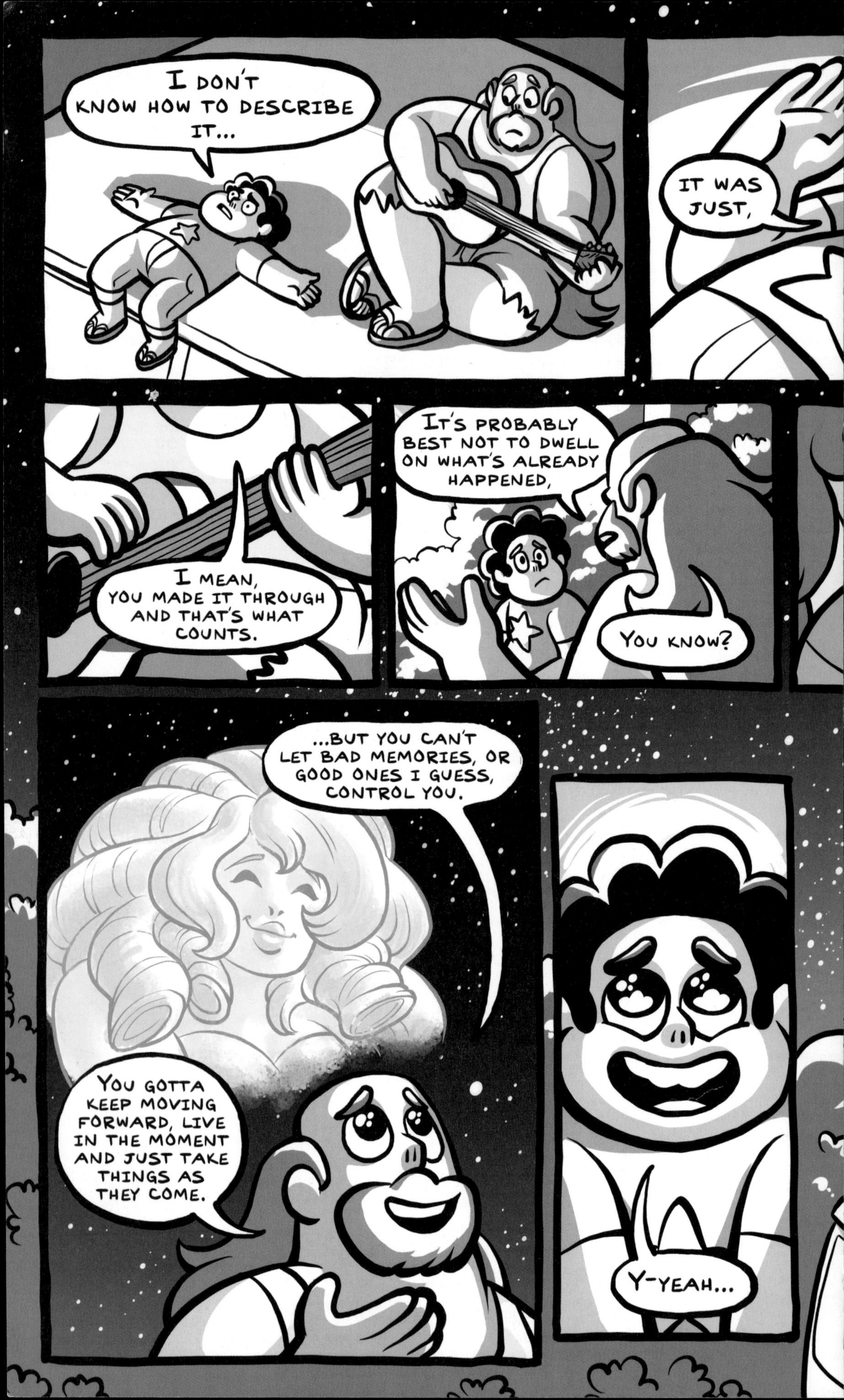
I DON'T KNOW HOW TO DESCRIBE IT...
IT WAS JUST,
I MEAN, YOU MADE IT THROUGH AND THAT'S WHAT COUNTS.
IT'S PROBABLY BEST NOT TO DWELL ON WHAT'S ALREADY HAPPENED,
YOU KNOW?
...BUT YOU CAN'T LET BAD MEMORIES, OR GOOD ONES I GUESS, CONTROL YOU.
YOU GOTTA KEEP MOVING FORWARD, LIVE IN THE MOMENT AND JUST TAKE THINGS AS THEY COME.
Y-YEAH...

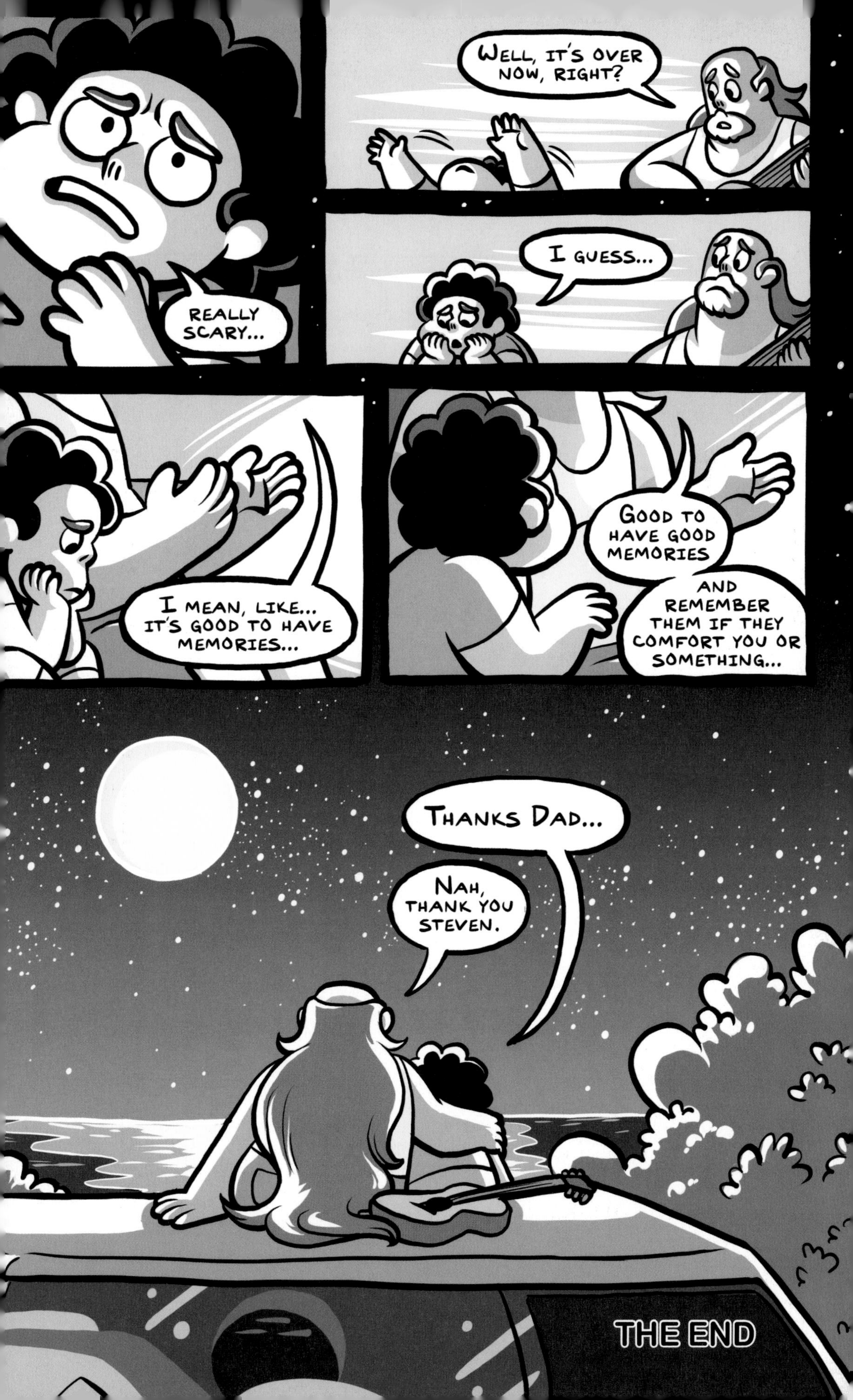
REALLY SCARY...
WELL, IT'S OVER NOW, RIGHT?
I GUESS...
I MEAN, LIKE... IT'S GOOD TO HAVE MEMORIES...
GOOD TO HAVE GOOD MEMORIES
AND REMEMBER THEM IF THEY COMFORT YOU OR SOMETHING...
THANKS DAD...
NAH, THANK YOU STEVEN.
THE END

SLAM BUDDIES

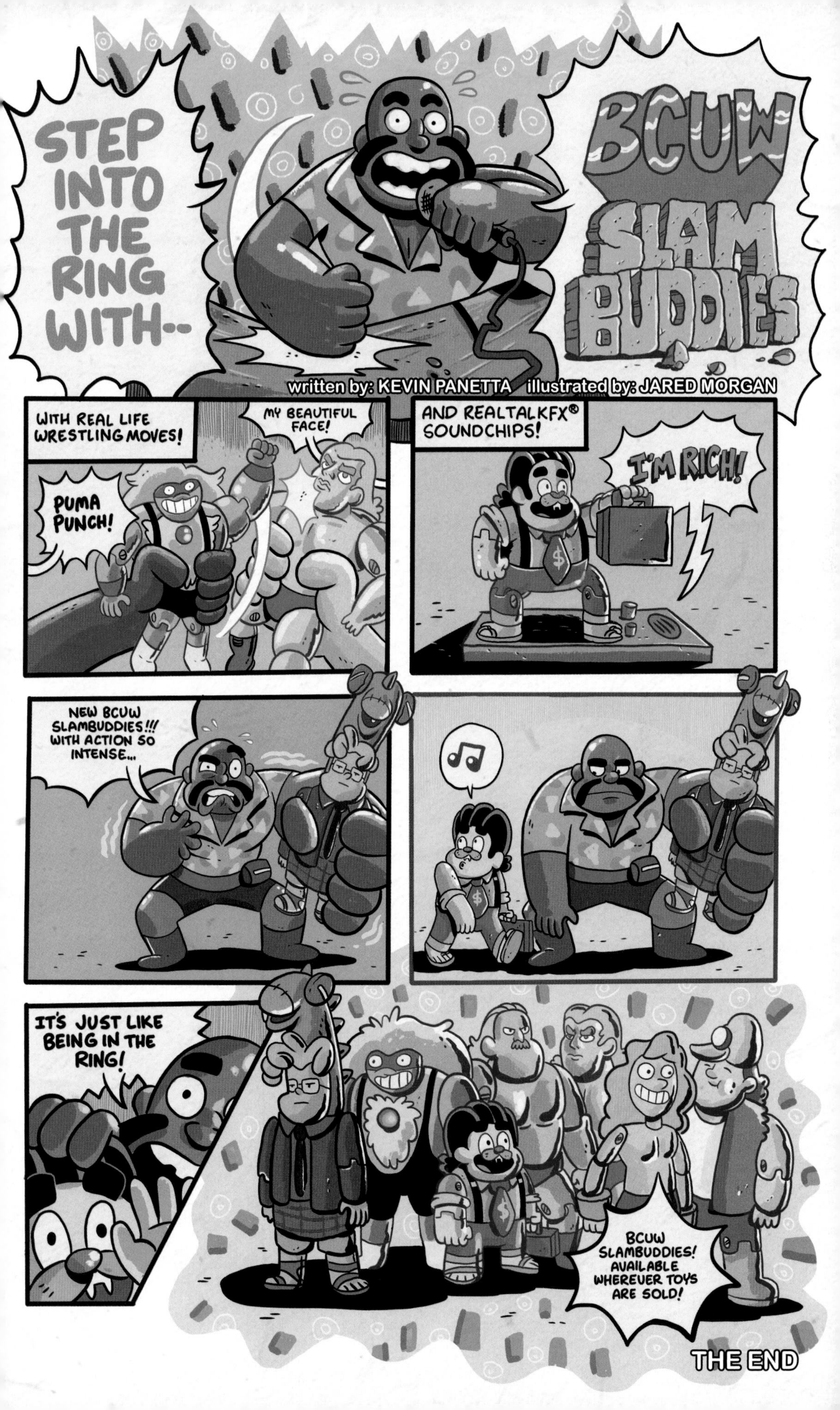
STEP INTO THE RING WITH--
BCUW SLAM BUDDIES
written by: KEVIN PANETTA illustrated by: JARED MORGAN
WITH REAL LIFE WRESTLING MOVES!
PUMA PUNCH!
MY BEAUTIFUL FACE!
AND REALTALKFX® SOUNDCHIPS!
I'M RICH!
NEW BCUW SLAMBUDDIES!!! WITH ACTION SO INTENSE...
IT'S JUST LIKE BEING IN THE RING!
BCUW SLAMBUDDIES! AVAILABLE WHEREVER TOYS ARE SOLD!
THE END

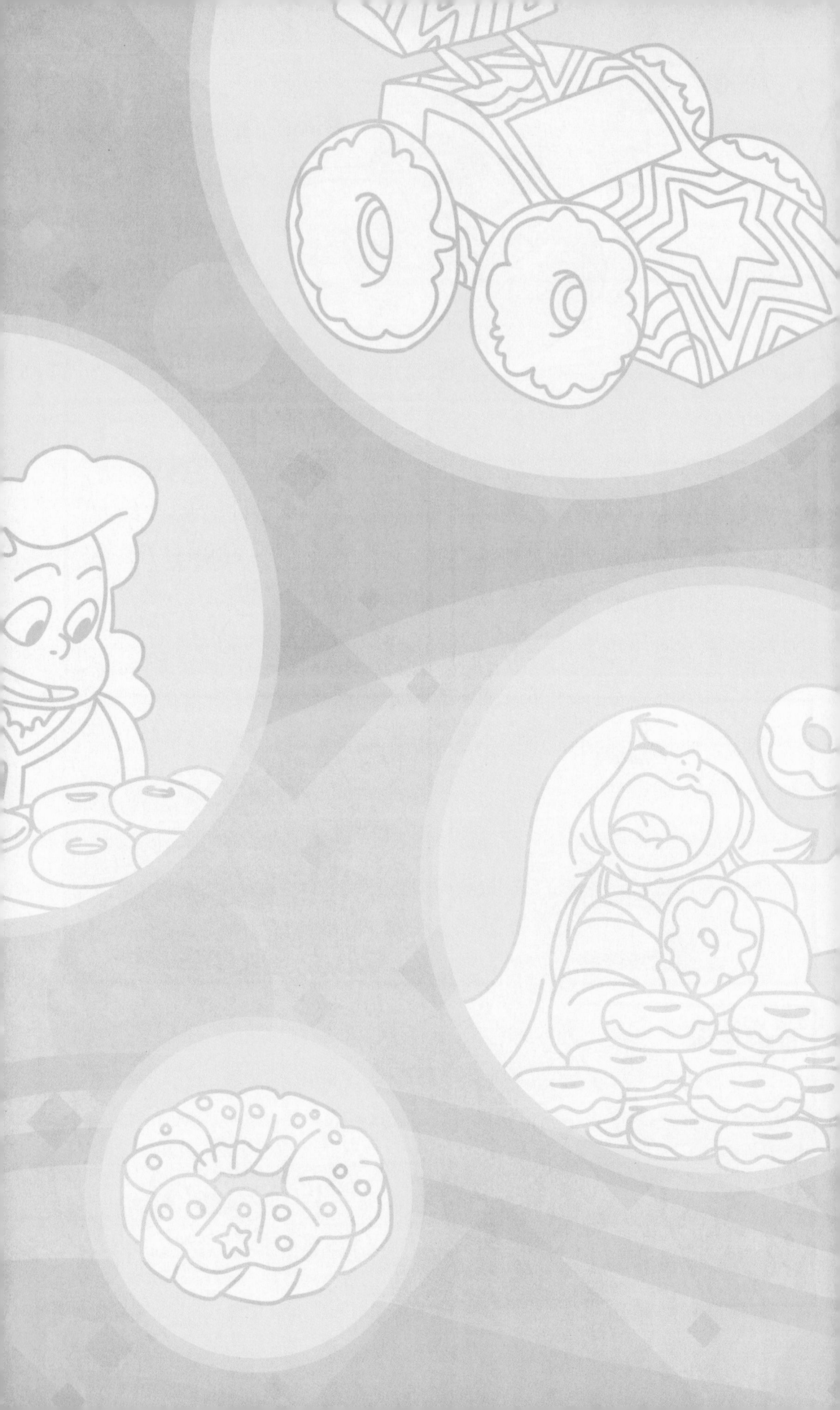

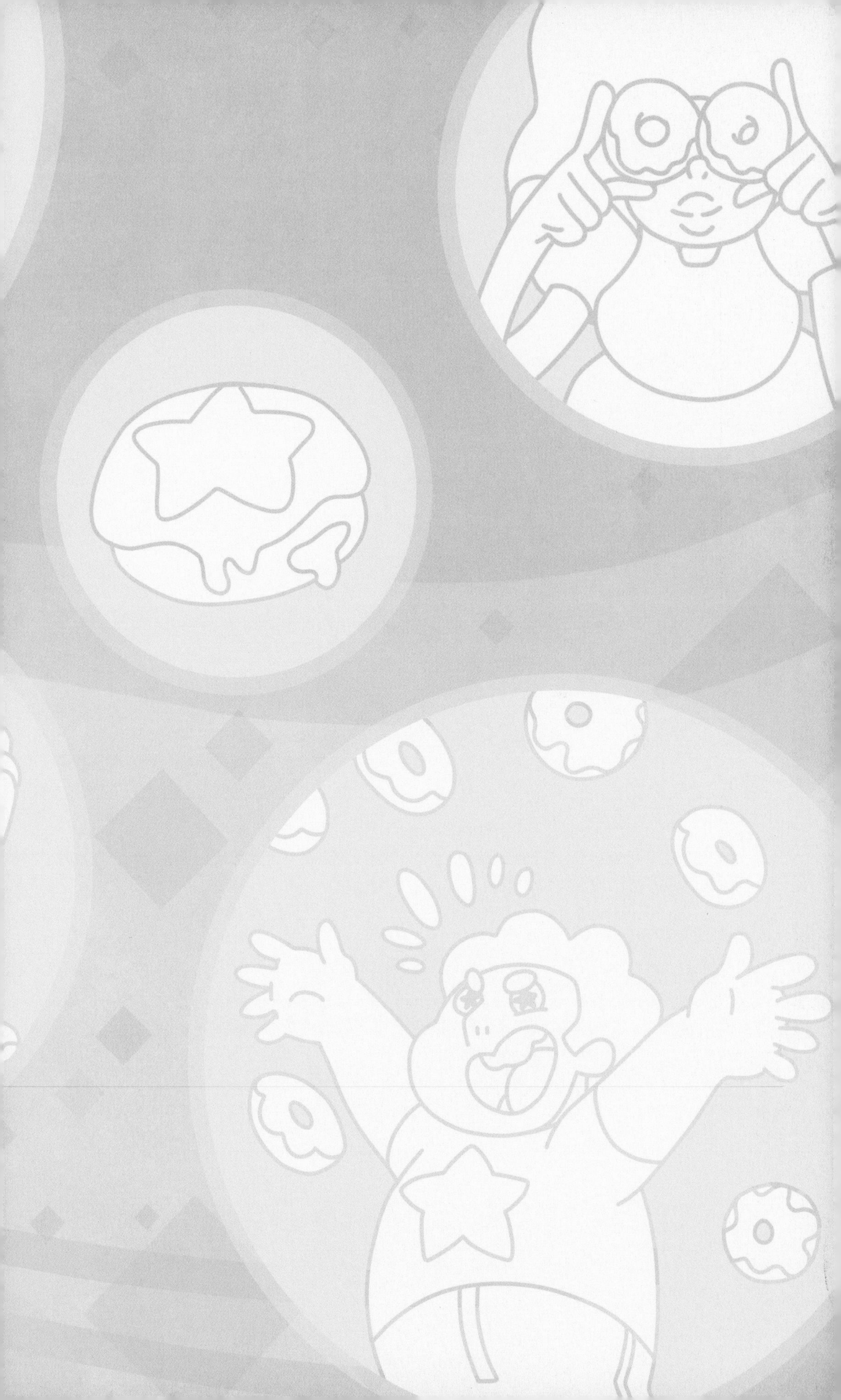

CLASH OF GLUTTONS

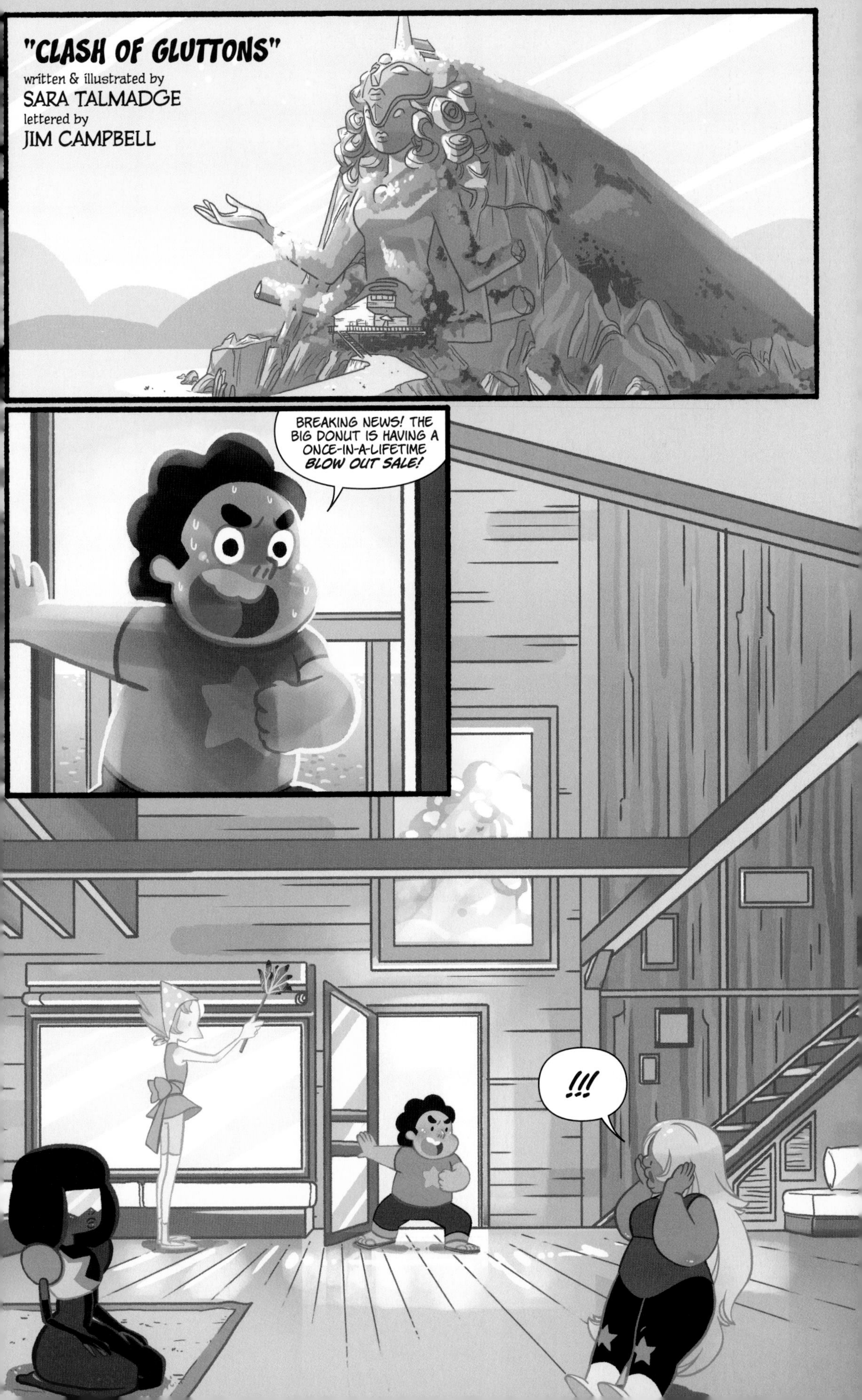
"CLASH OF GLUTTONS"
written & illustrated by
SARA TALMADGE
lettered by
JIM CAMPBELL
BREAKING NEWS! THE BIG DONUT IS HAVING A ONCE-IN-A-LIFETIME BLOW OUT SALE!
!!!

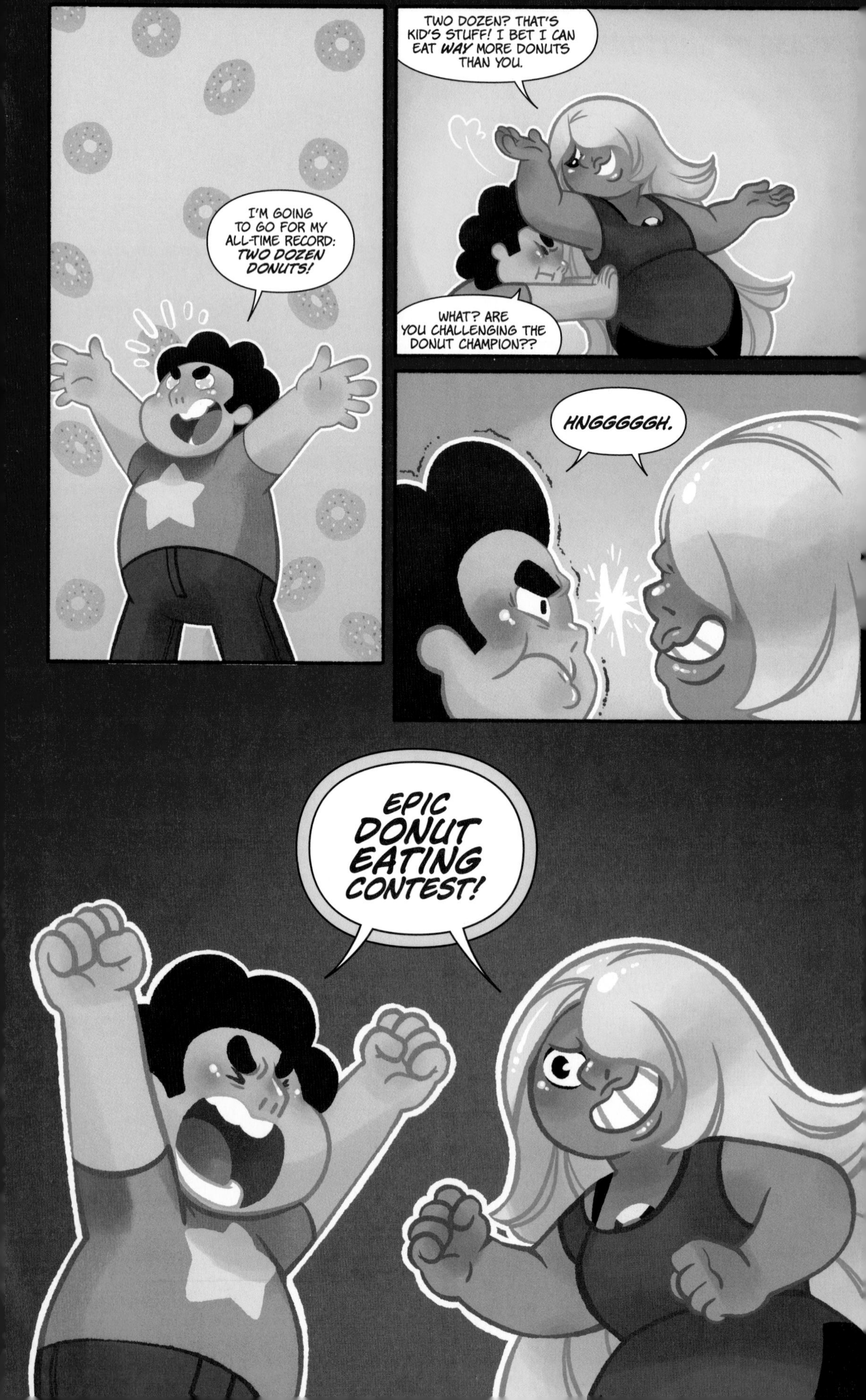
I'M GOING TO GO FOR MY ALL-TIME RECORD: TWO DOZEN DONUTS!
TWO DOZEN? THAT'S KID'S STUFF! I BET I CAN EAT WAY MORE DONUTS THAN YOU.
WHAT? ARE YOU CHALLENGING THE DONUT CHAMPION??
HNGGGGGH.
EPIC DONUT EATING CONTEST!

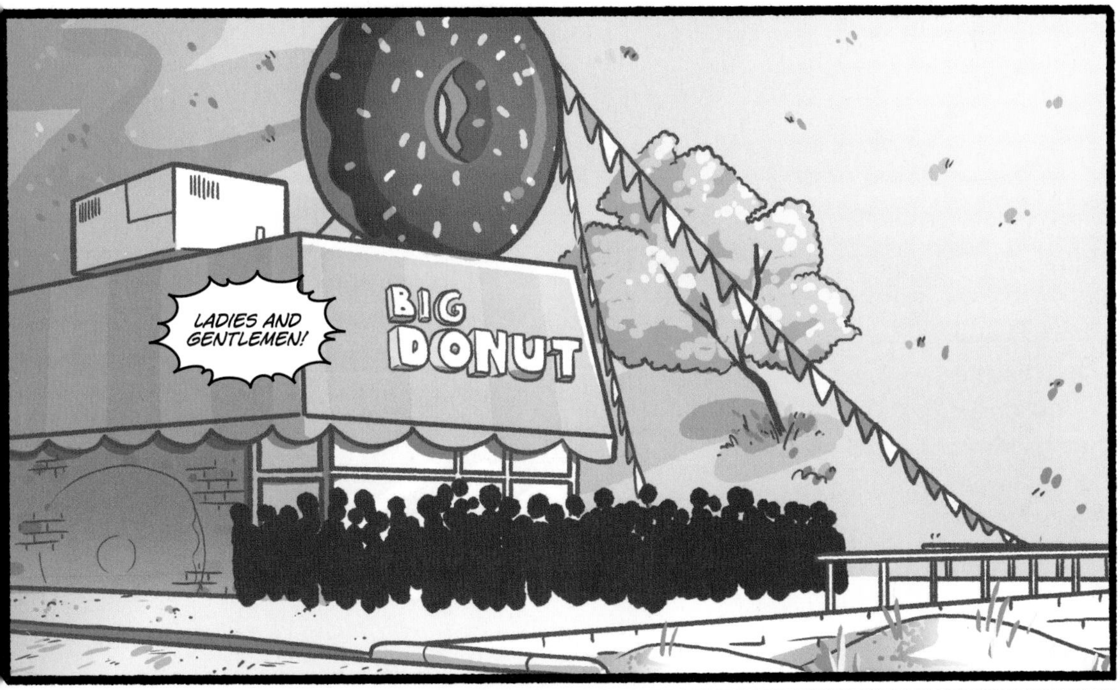
LADIES AND GENTLEMEN!
BIG DONUT

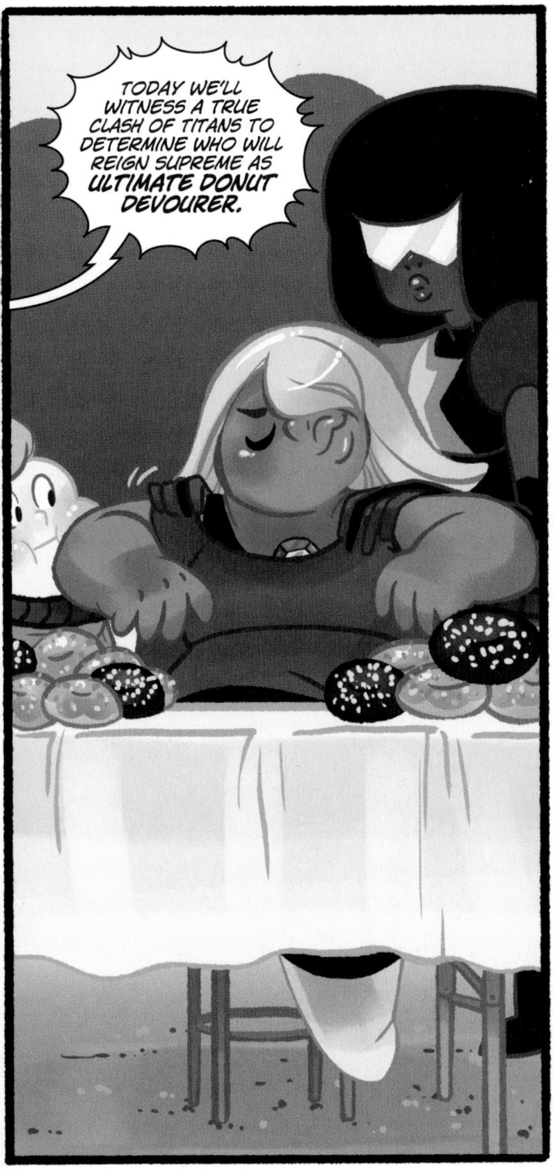
TODAY WE'LL WITNESS A TRUE CLASH OF TITANS TO DETERMINE WHO WILL REIGN SUPREME AS ULTIMATE DONUT DEVOURER.

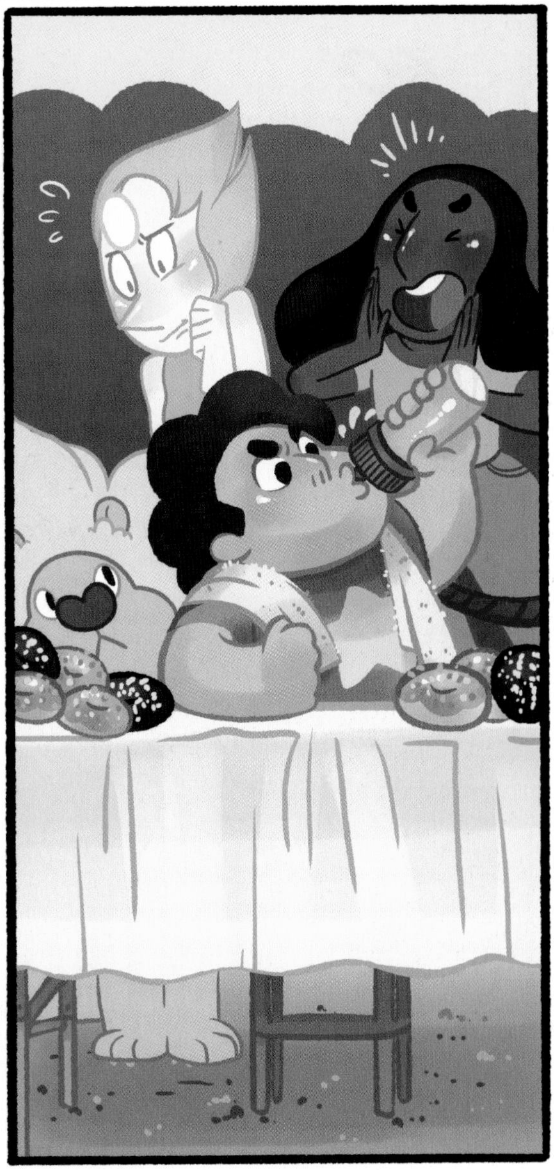

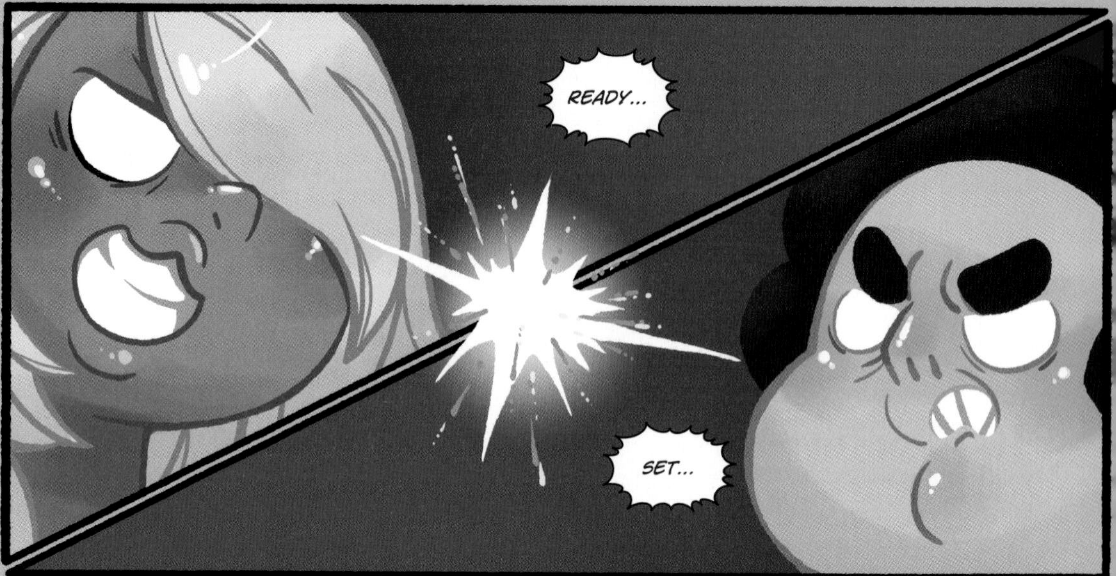
READY...
SET...
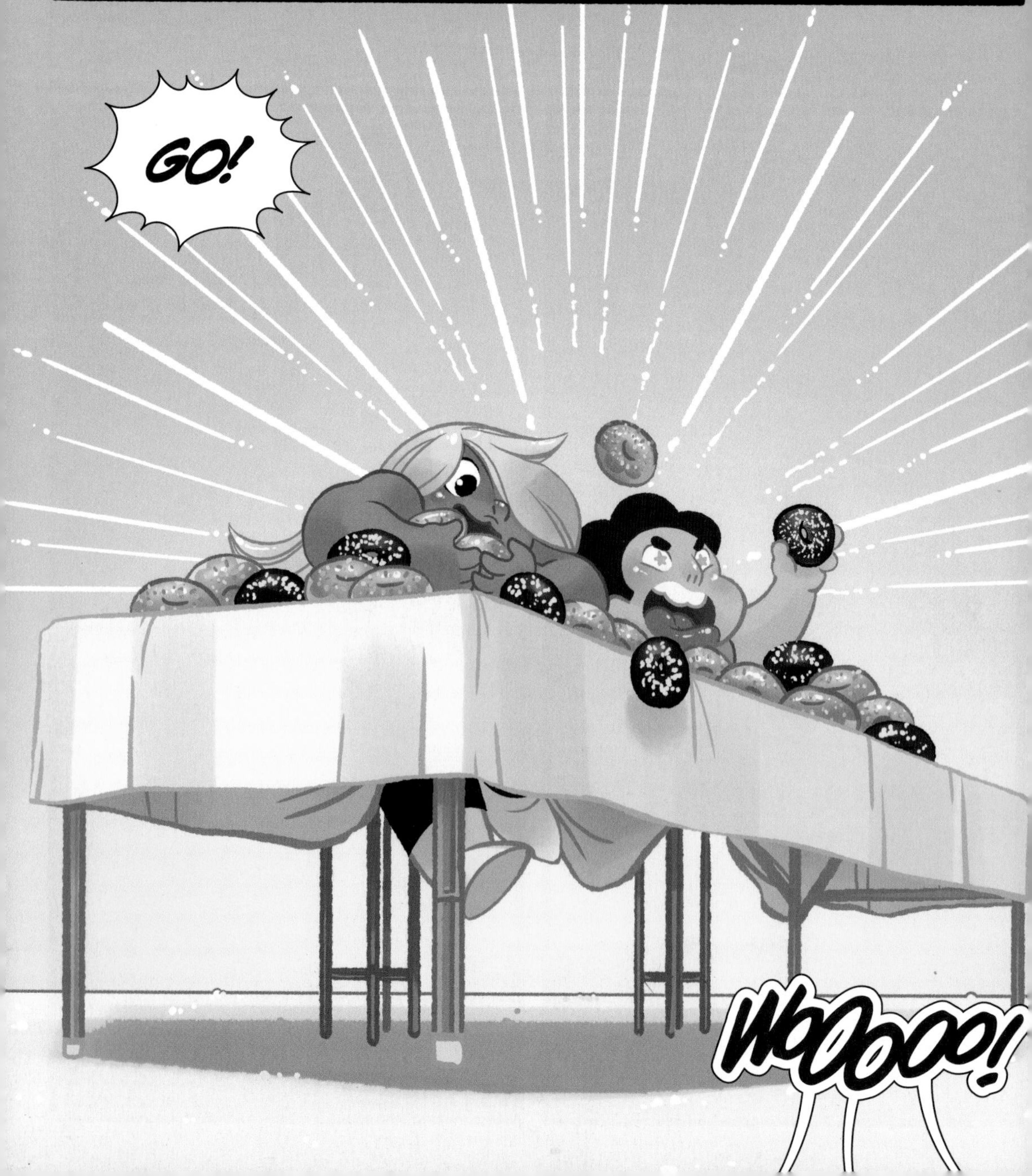
GO!
WOOOOOO!

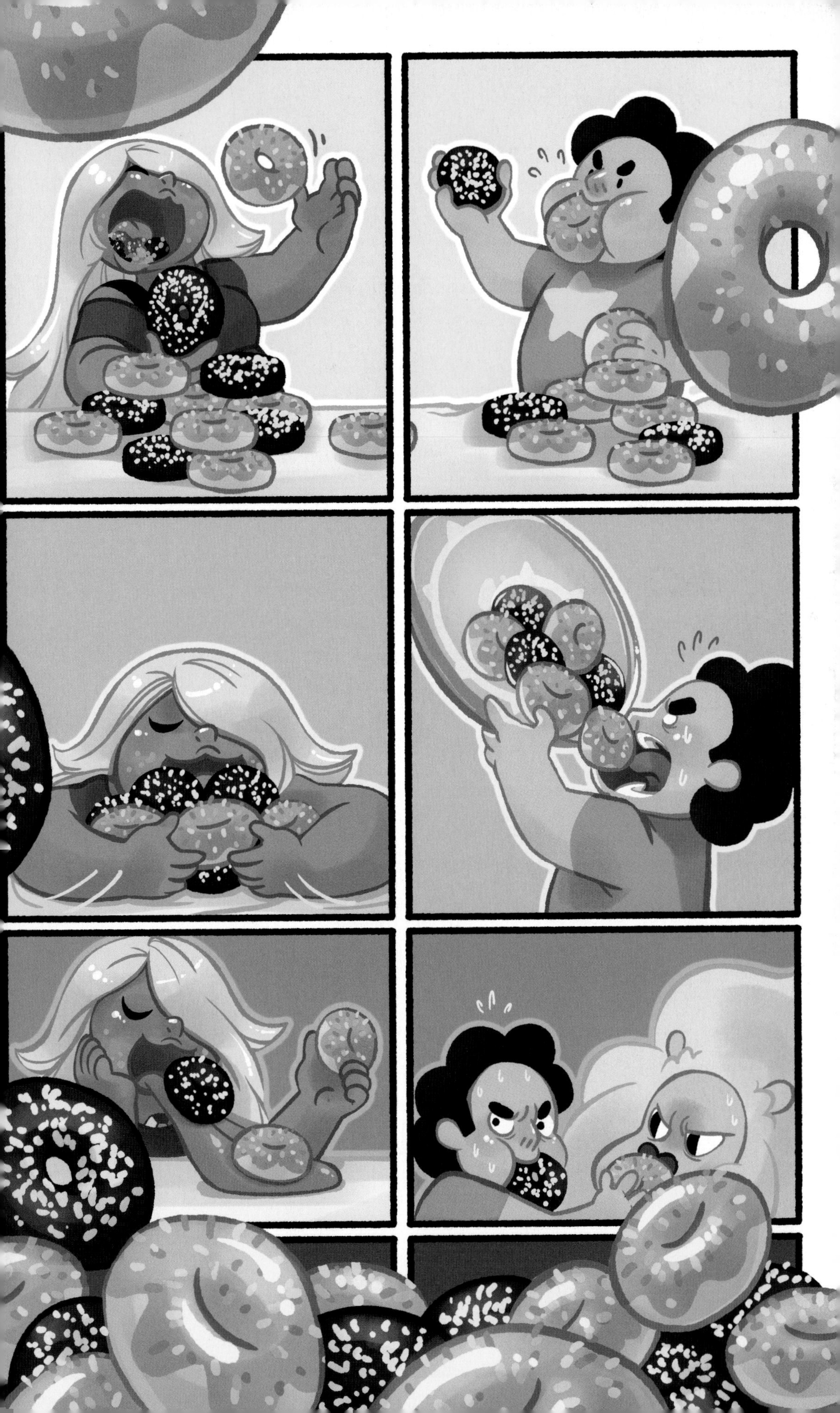

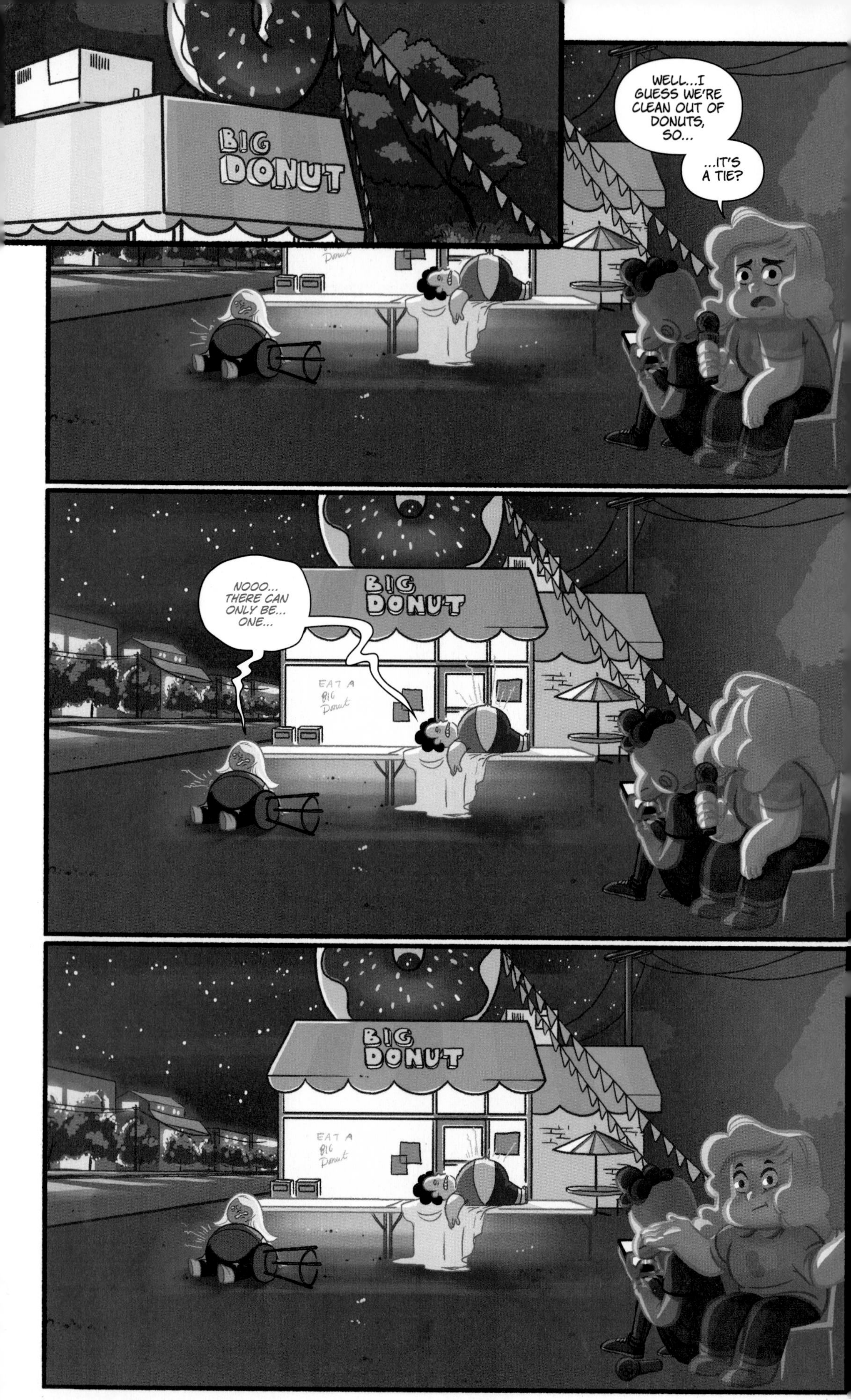
BIG DONUT
WELL...I GUESS WE'RE CLEAN OUT OF DONUTS, SO...
...IT'S A TIE?
BIG DONUT
EAT A BIG Donut
NOOO... THERE CAN ONLY BE... ONE...
BIG DONUT
EAT A BIG Donut

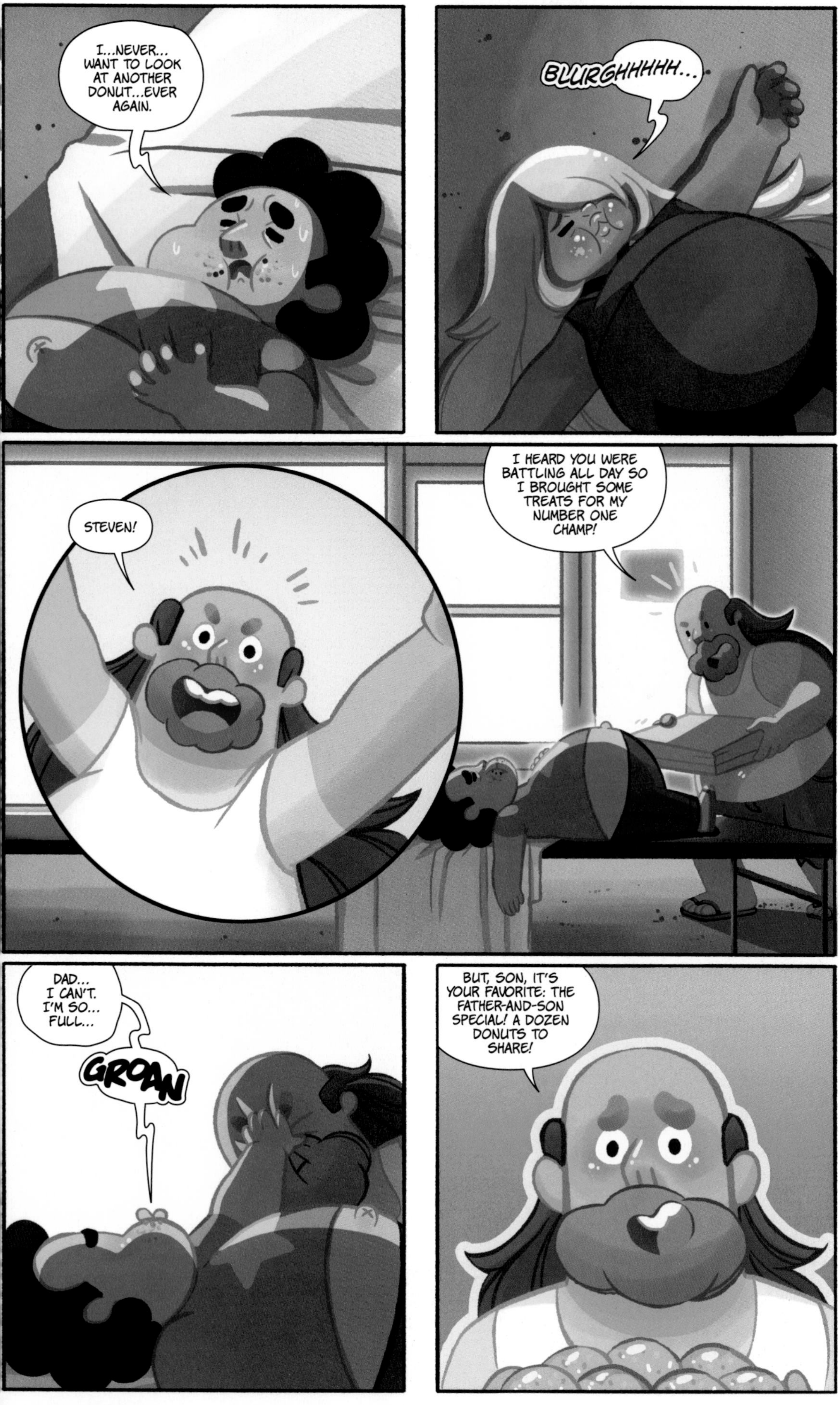
I...NEVER... WANT TO LOOK AT ANOTHER DONUT...EVER AGAIN.
BLURGHHHHH...
I HEARD YOU WERE BATTLING ALL DAY SO I BROUGHT SOME TREATS FOR MY NUMBER ONE CHAMP!
STEVEN!
DAD... I CAN'T. I'M SO... FULL...
GROAN
BUT, SON, IT'S YOUR FAVORITE: THE FATHER-AND-SON SPECIAL! A DOZEN DONUTS TO SHARE!

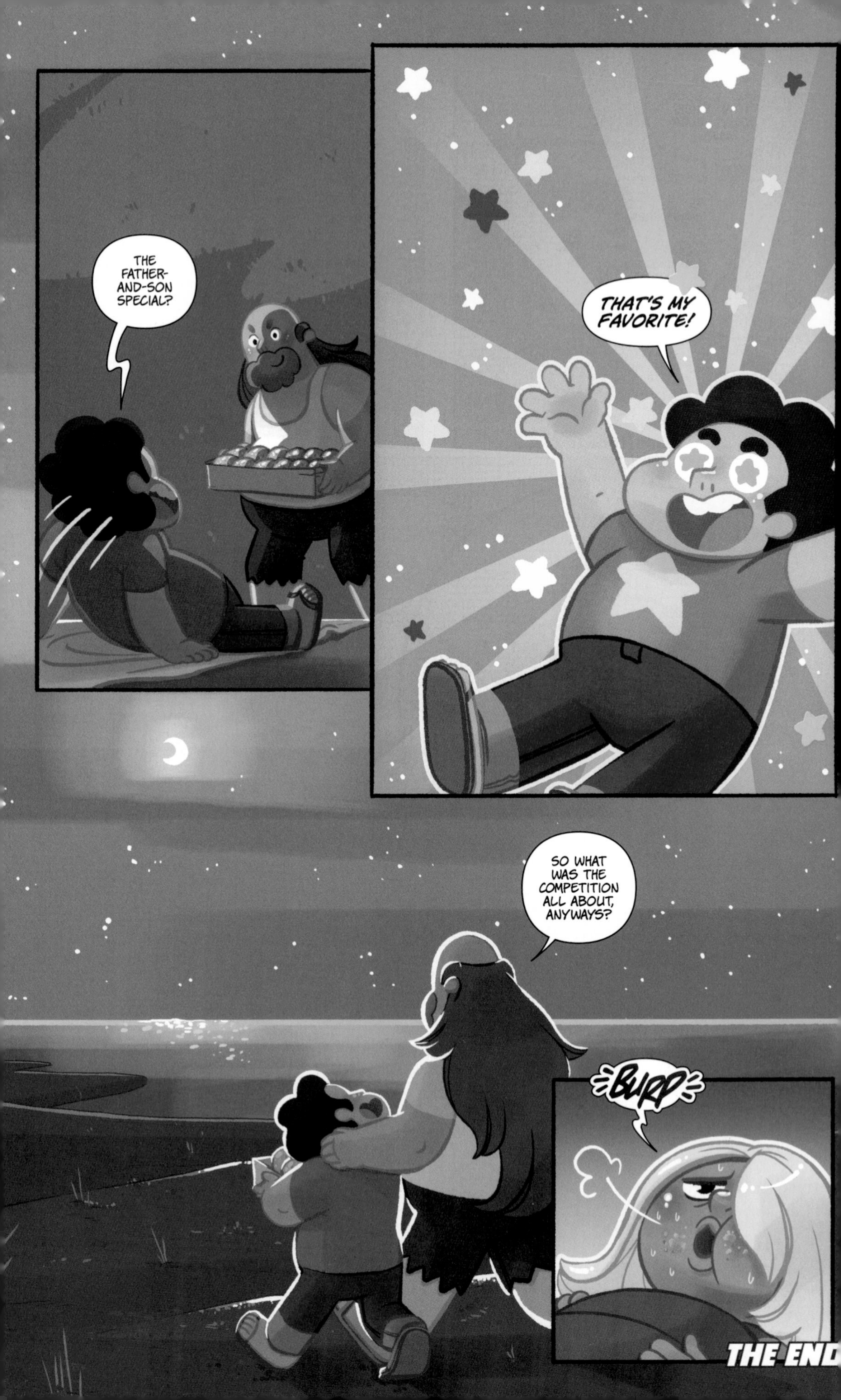
THE FATHER-AND-SON SPECIAL?
THAT'S MY FAVORITE!
SO WHAT WAS THE COMPETITION ALL ABOUT, ANYWAYS?
BURP
THE END

BIG DONUT CONTEST

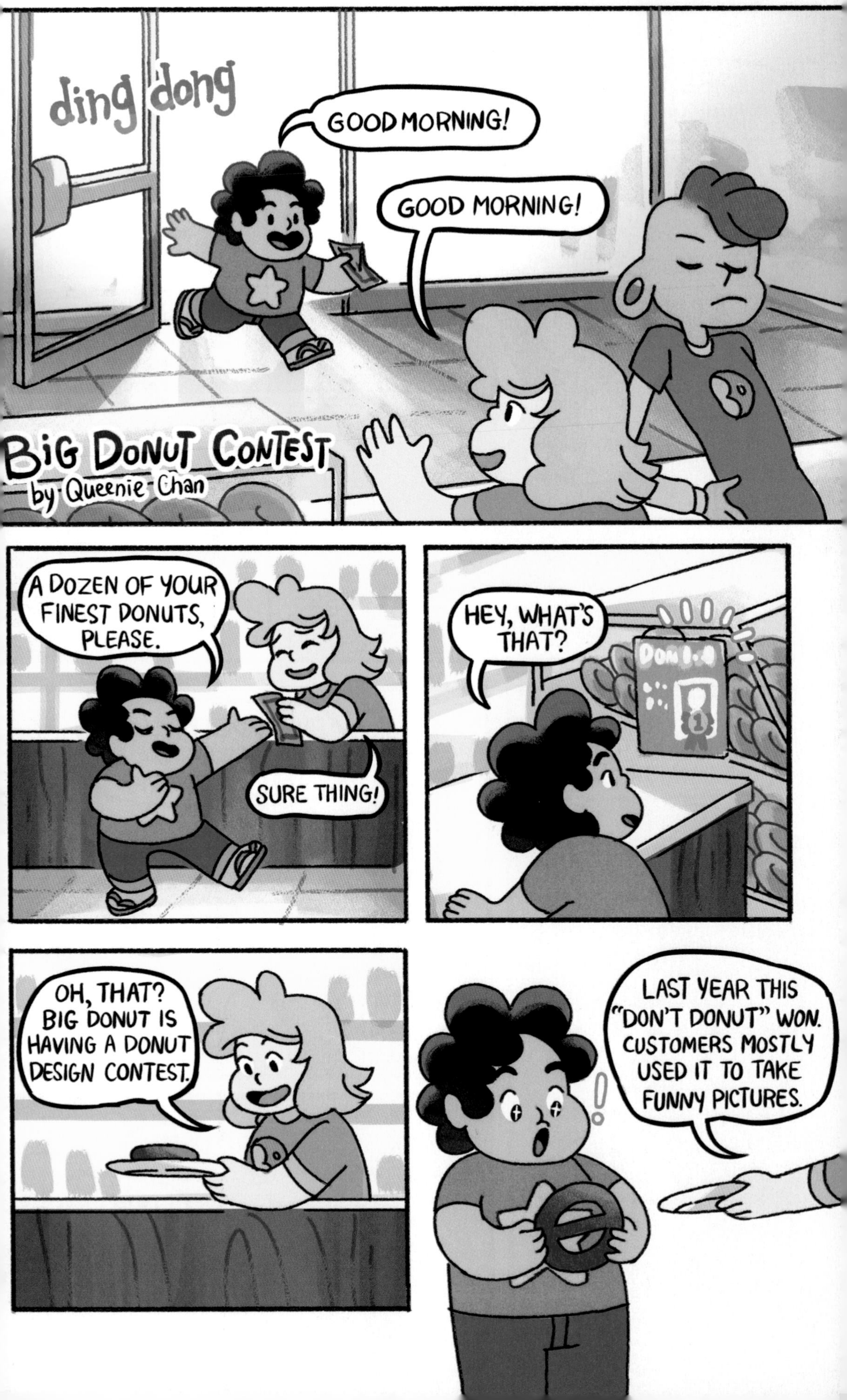
ding dong
GOOD MORNING!
GOOD MORNING!
BIG DONUT CONTEST
by Queenie Chan
A DOZEN OF YOUR FINEST DONUTS, PLEASE.
SURE THING!
HEY, WHAT'S THAT?
OH, THAT? BIG DONUT IS HAVING A DONUT DESIGN CONTEST.
LAST YEAR THIS "DON'T DONUT" WON. CUSTOMERS MOSTLY USED IT TO TAKE FUNNY PICTURES.

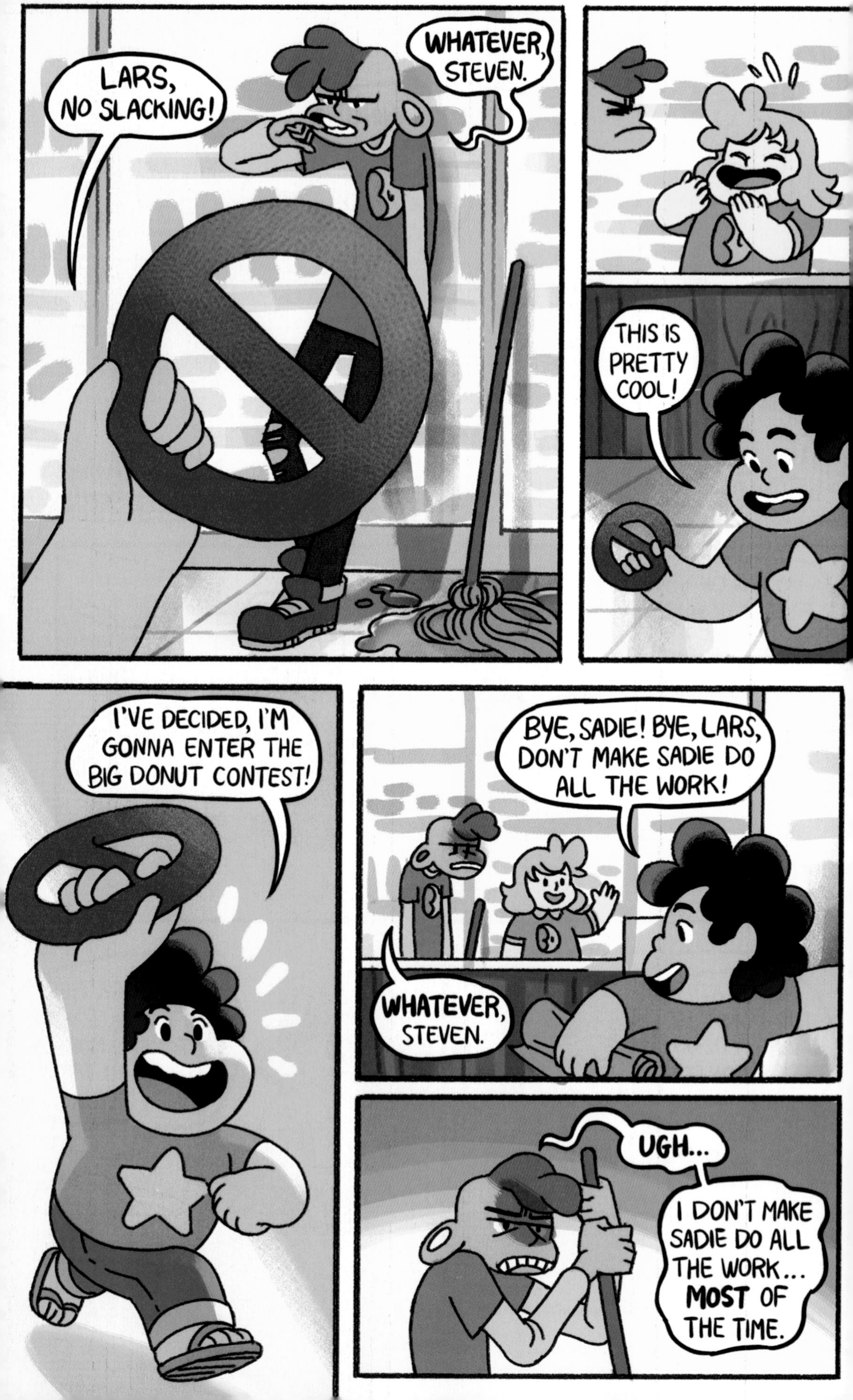
LARS, NO SLACKING!
WHATEVER, STEVEN.
THIS IS PRETTY COOL!
I'VE DECIDED, I'M GONNA ENTER THE BIG DONUT CONTEST!
BYE, SADIE! BYE, LARS, DON'T MAKE SADIE DO ALL THE WORK!
WHATEVER, STEVEN.
UGH...
I DON'T MAKE SADIE DO ALL THE WORK... **MOST** OF THE TIME.

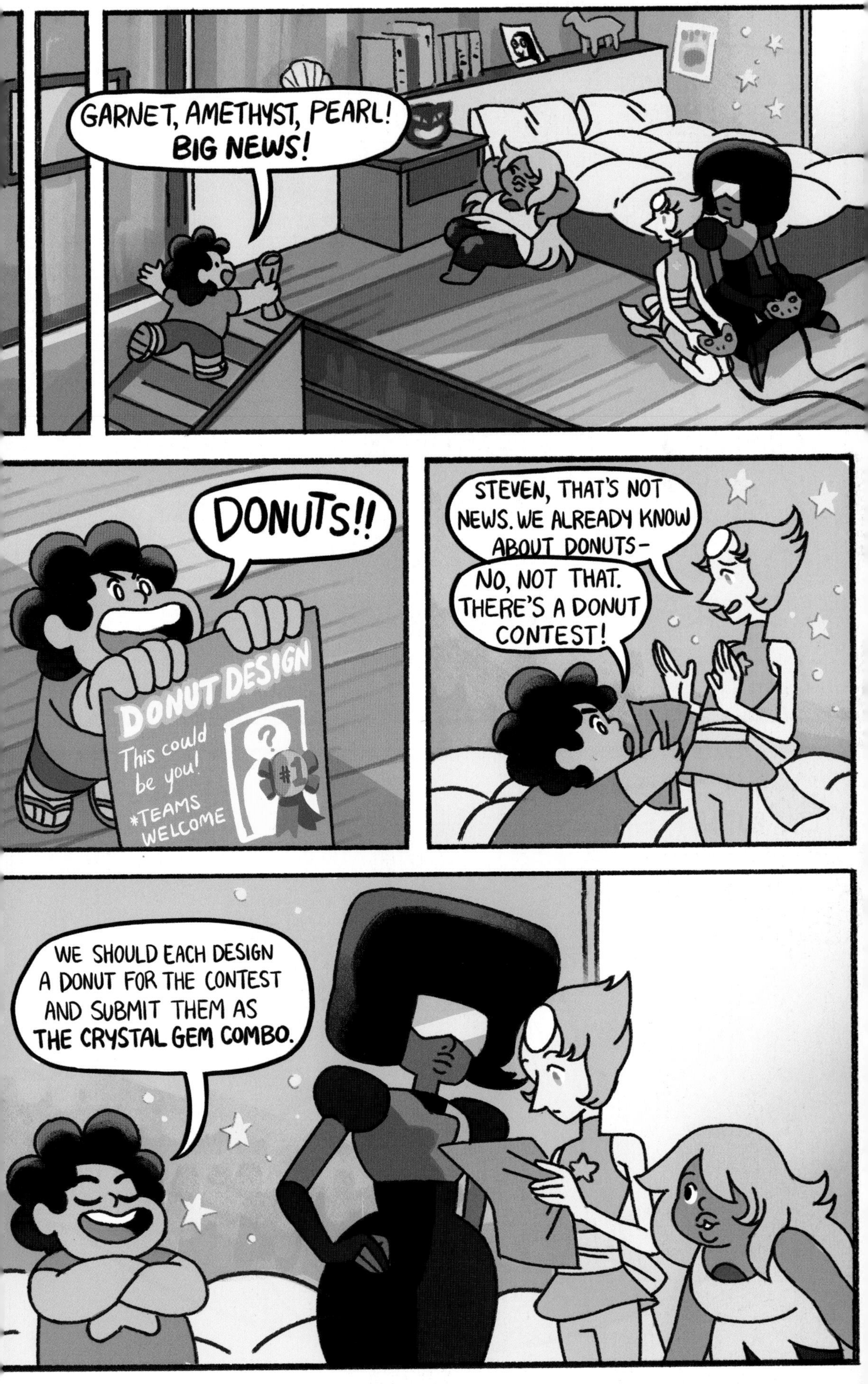
GARNET, AMETHYST, PEARL! BIG NEWS!
DONUTS!!
DONUT DESIGN
This could be you!
*TEAMS WELCOME
#1
STEVEN, THAT'S NOT NEWS. WE ALREADY KNOW ABOUT DONUTS—
NO, NOT THAT. THERE'S A DONUT CONTEST!
WE SHOULD EACH DESIGN A DONUT FOR THE CONTEST AND SUBMIT THEM AS THE CRYSTAL GEM COMBO.

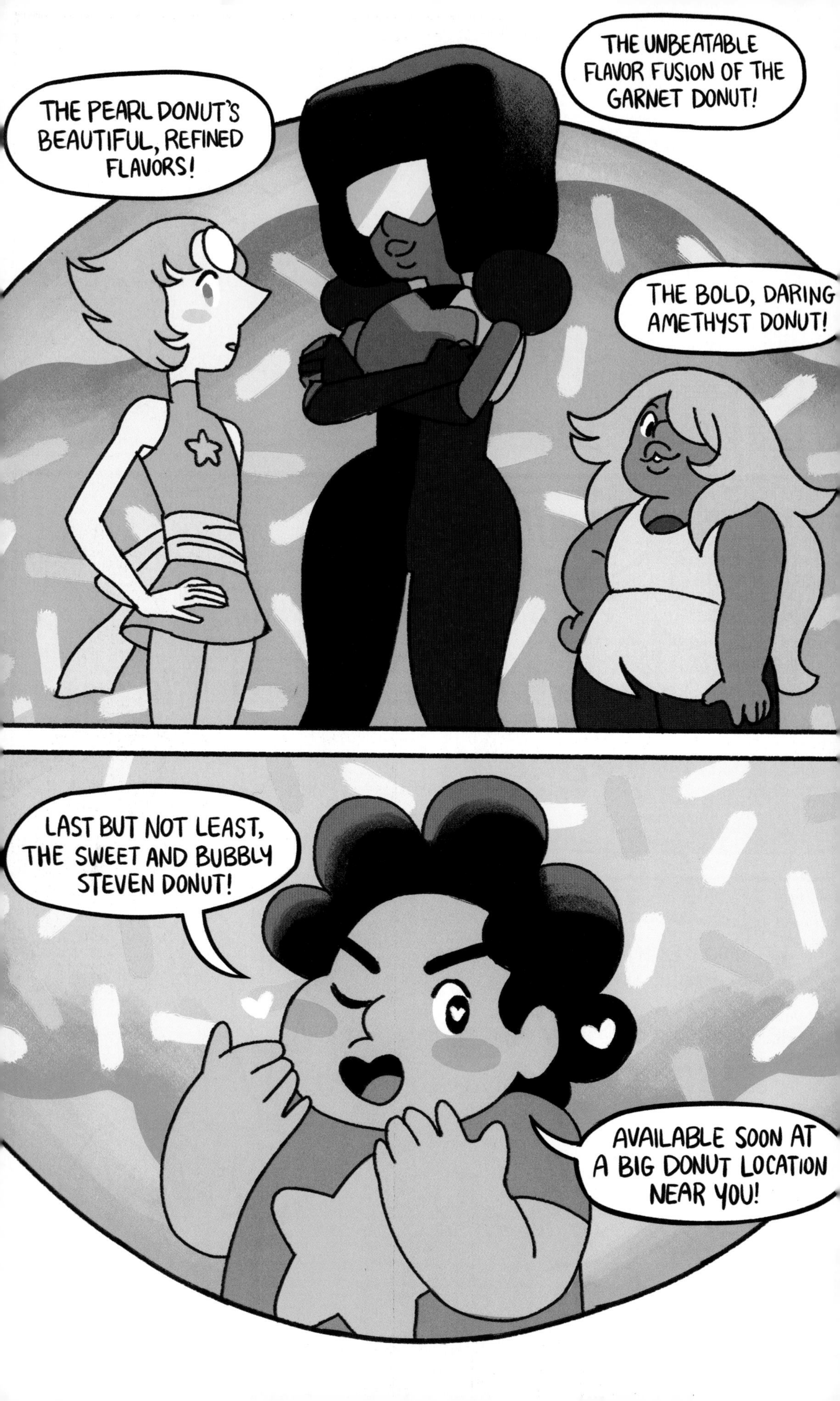
THE PEARL DONUT'S BEAUTIFUL, REFINED FLAVORS!
THE UNBEATABLE FLAVOR FUSION OF THE GARNET DONUT!
THE BOLD, DARING AMETHYST DONUT!
LAST BUT NOT LEAST, THE SWEET AND BUBBLY STEVEN DONUT!
AVAILABLE SOON AT A BIG DONUT LOCATION NEAR YOU!

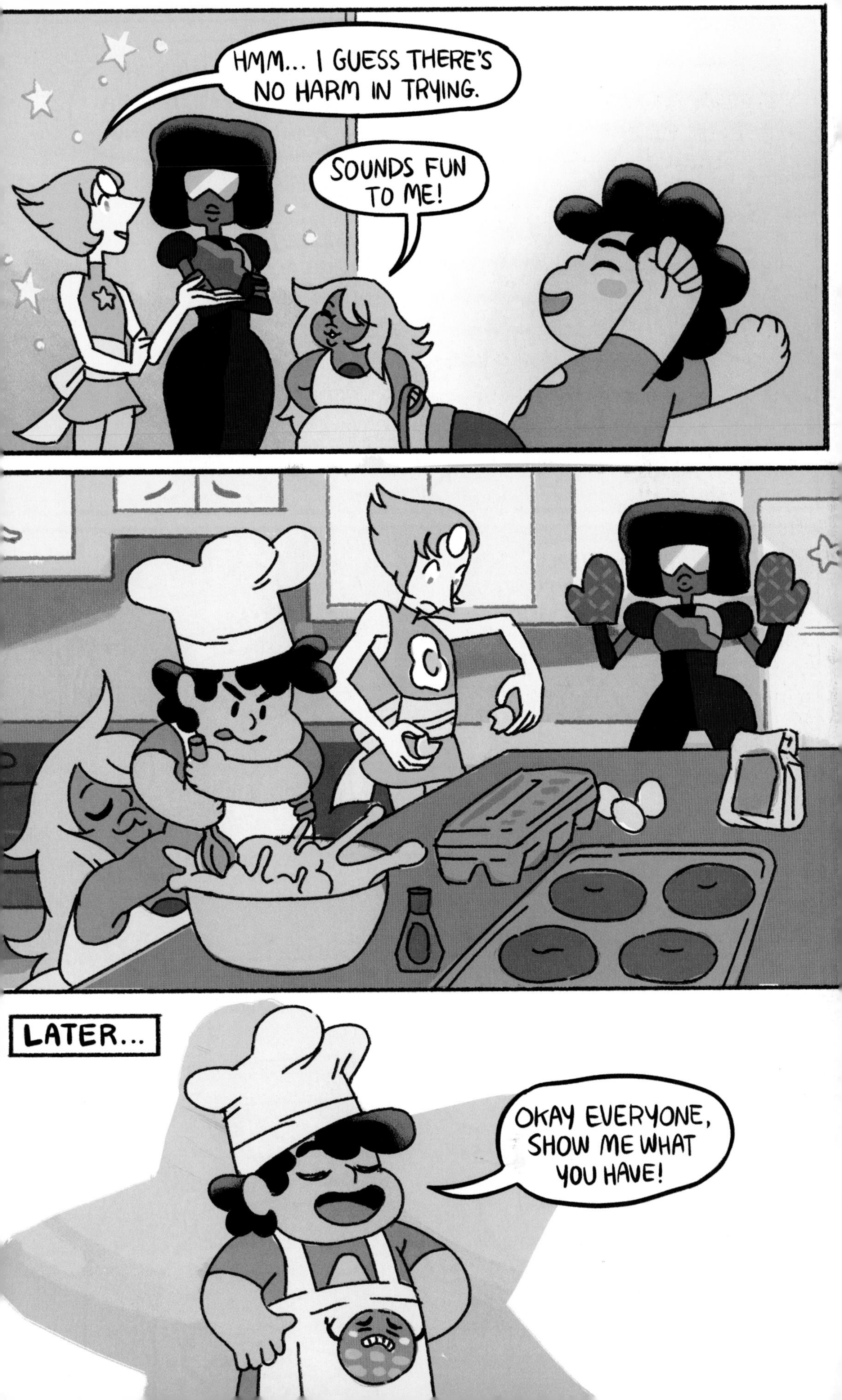
HMM... I GUESS THERE'S NO HARM IN TRYING.
SOUNDS FUN TO ME!
LATER...
OKAY EVERYONE, SHOW ME WHAT YOU HAVE!

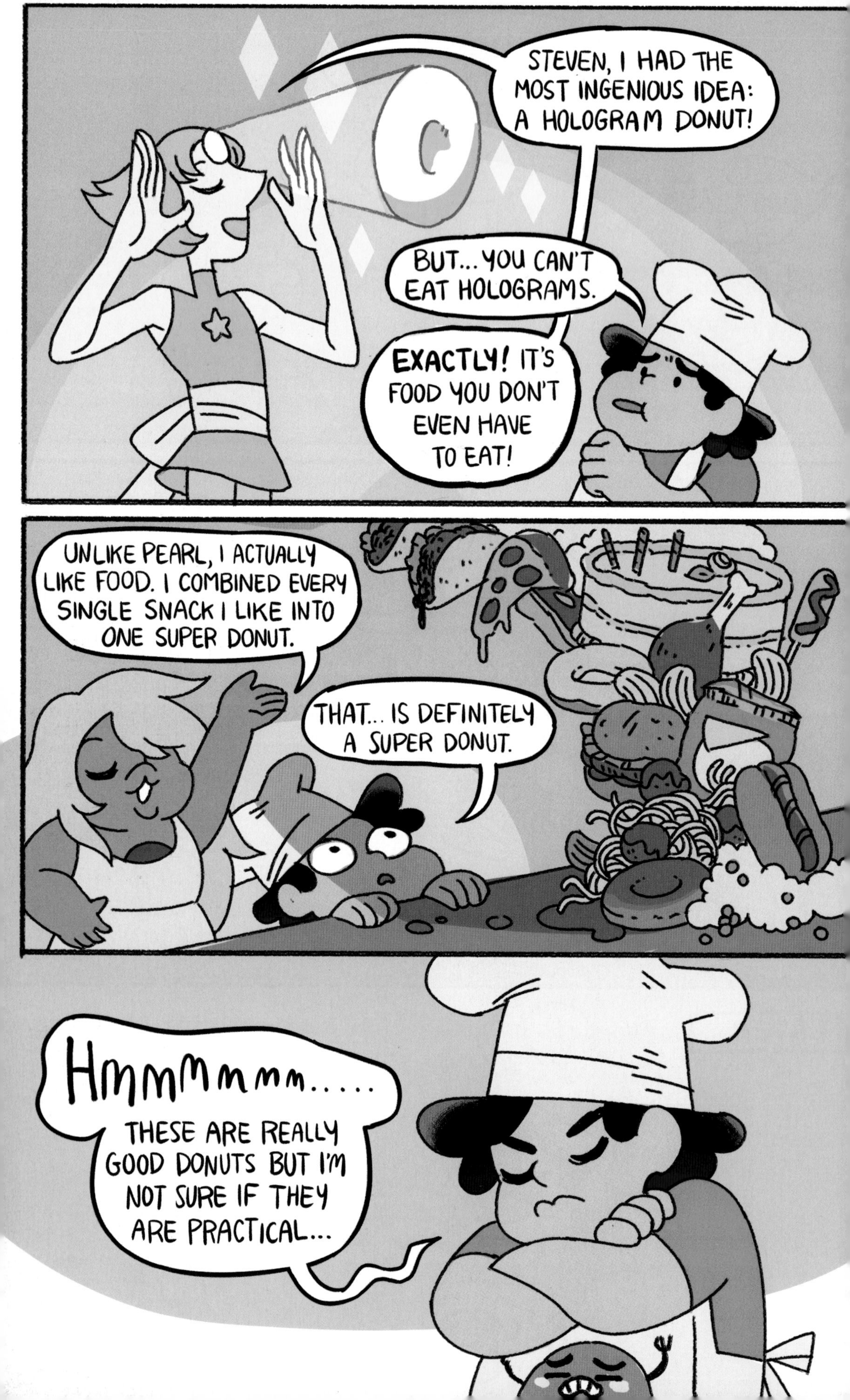
STEVEN, I HAD THE MOST INGENIOUS IDEA: A HOLOGRAM DONUT!
BUT... YOU CAN'T EAT HOLOGRAMS.
EXACTLY! IT'S FOOD YOU DON'T EVEN HAVE TO EAT!
UNLIKE PEARL, I ACTUALLY LIKE FOOD. I COMBINED EVERY SINGLE SNACK I LIKE INTO ONE SUPER DONUT.
THAT... IS DEFINITELY A SUPER DONUT.
Hmmmmmm......
THESE ARE REALLY GOOD DONUTS BUT I'M NOT SURE IF THEY ARE PRACTICAL...

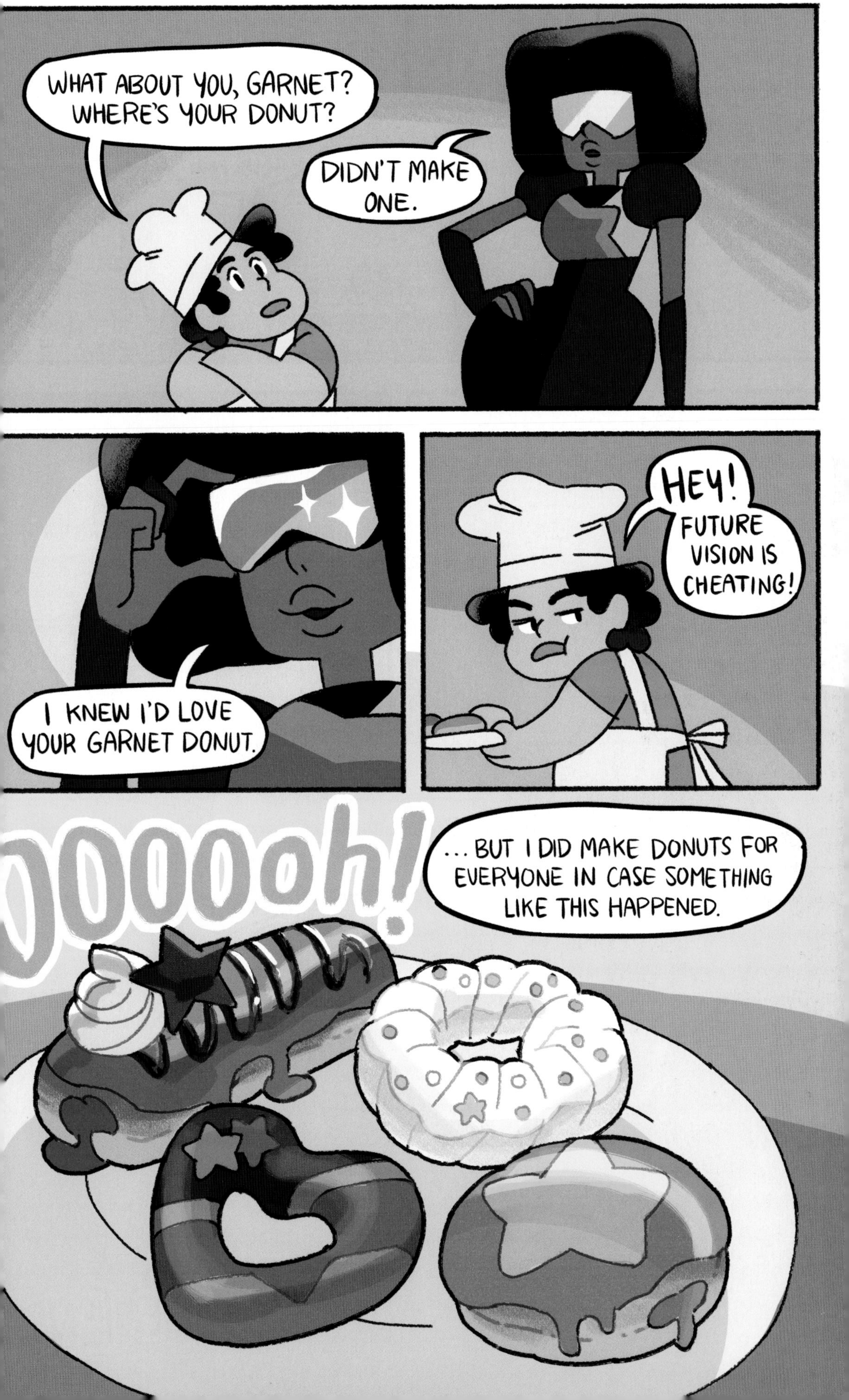
WHAT ABOUT YOU, GARNET? WHERE'S YOUR DONUT?
DIDN'T MAKE ONE.
I KNEW I'D LOVE YOUR GARNET DONUT.
HEY! FUTURE VISION IS CHEATING!
OOOOoh!
... BUT I DID MAKE DONUTS FOR EVERYONE IN CASE SOMETHING LIKE THIS HAPPENED.

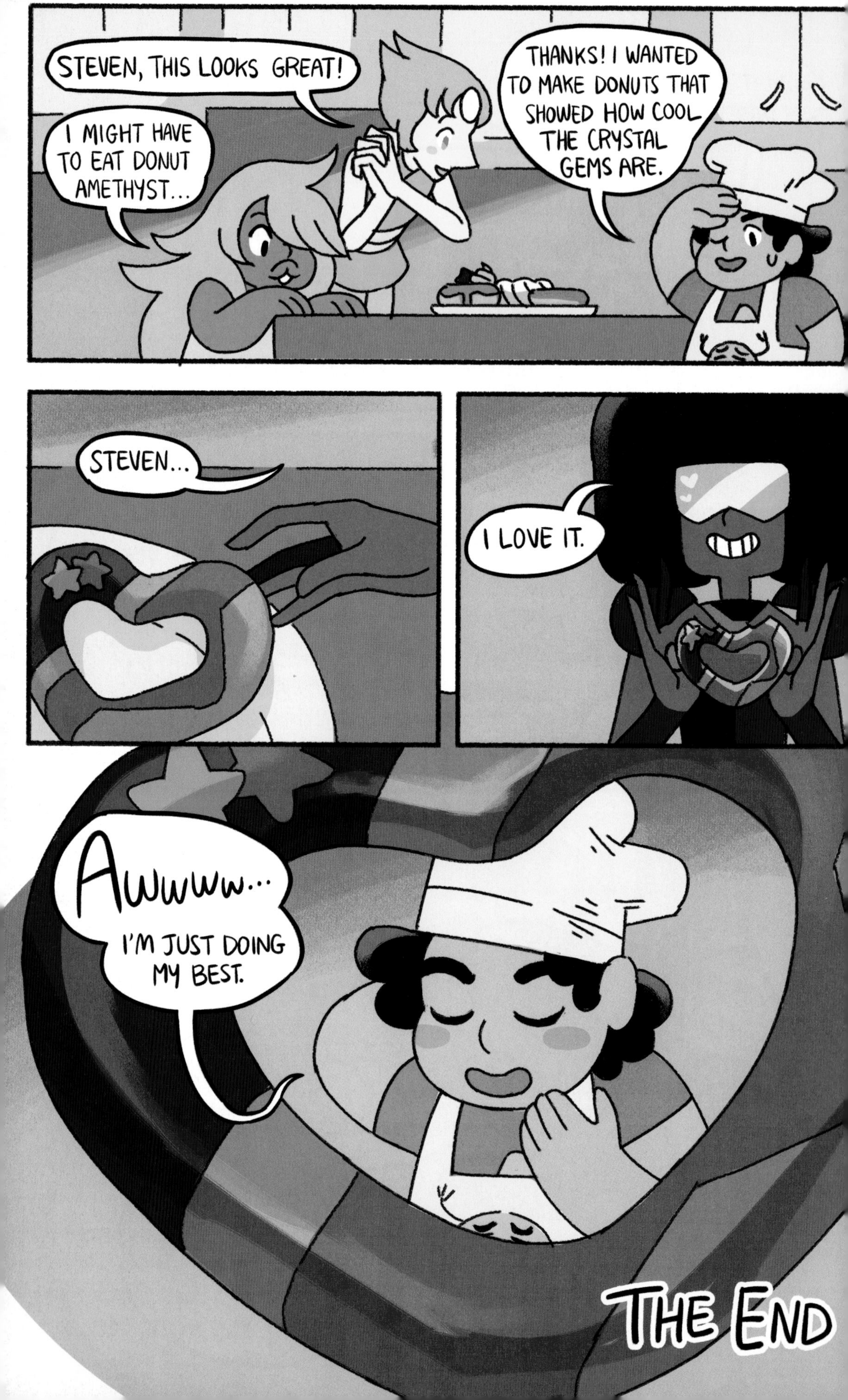
STEVEN, THIS LOOKS GREAT!
I MIGHT HAVE TO EAT DONUT AMETHYST...
THANKS! I WANTED TO MAKE DONUTS THAT SHOWED HOW COOL THE CRYSTAL GEMS ARE.
STEVEN...
I LOVE IT.
Awwww...
I'M JUST DOING MY BEST.
THE END

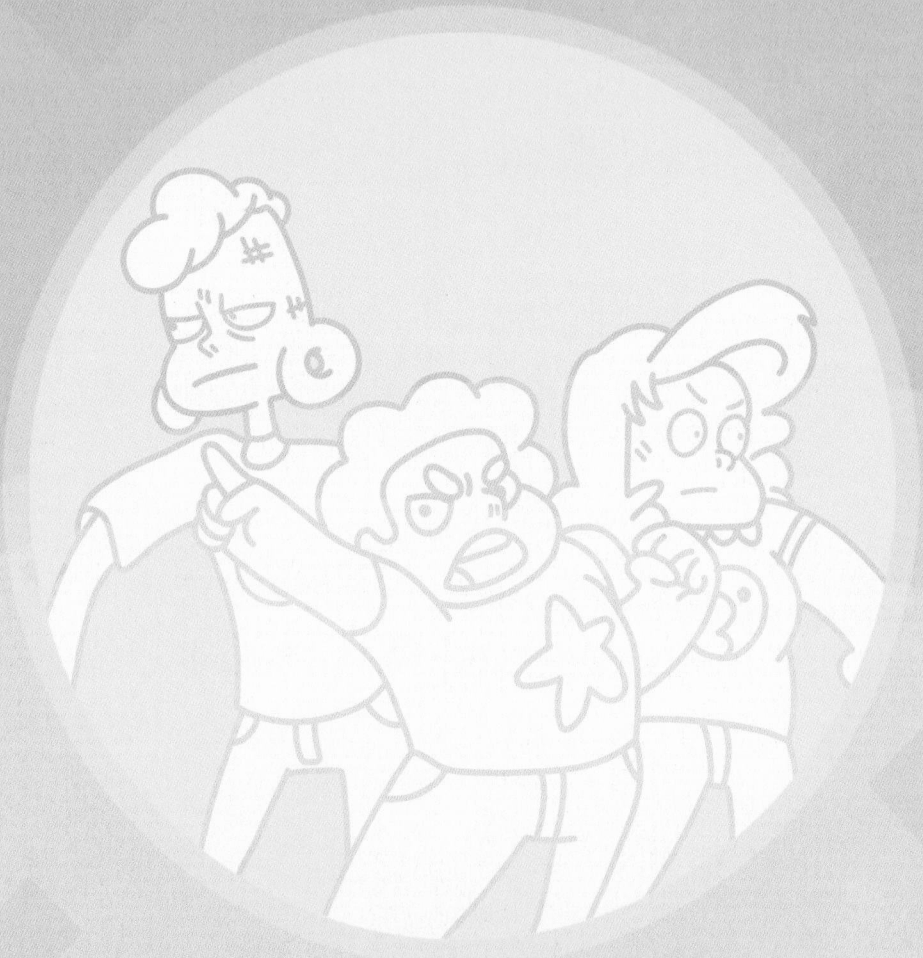

THE DONUT THIEF

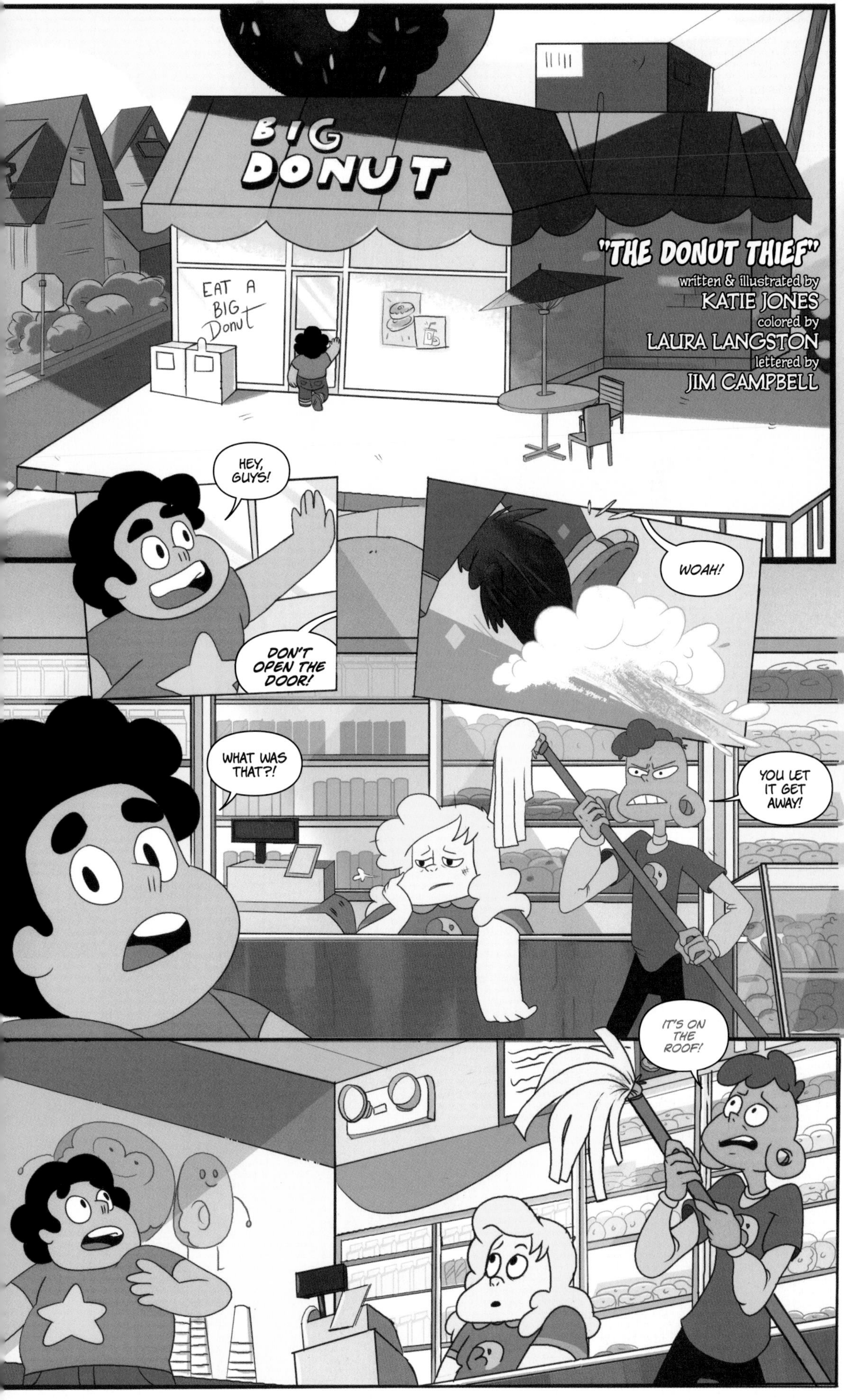
BIG
DONUT
EAT A BIG Donut
"THE DONUT THIEF"
written & illustrated by
KATIE JONES
colored by
LAURA LANGSTON
lettered by
JIM CAMPBELL
HEY, GUYS!
DON'T OPEN THE DOOR!
WOAH!
WHAT WAS THAT?!
YOU LET IT GET AWAY!
IT'S ON THE ROOF!

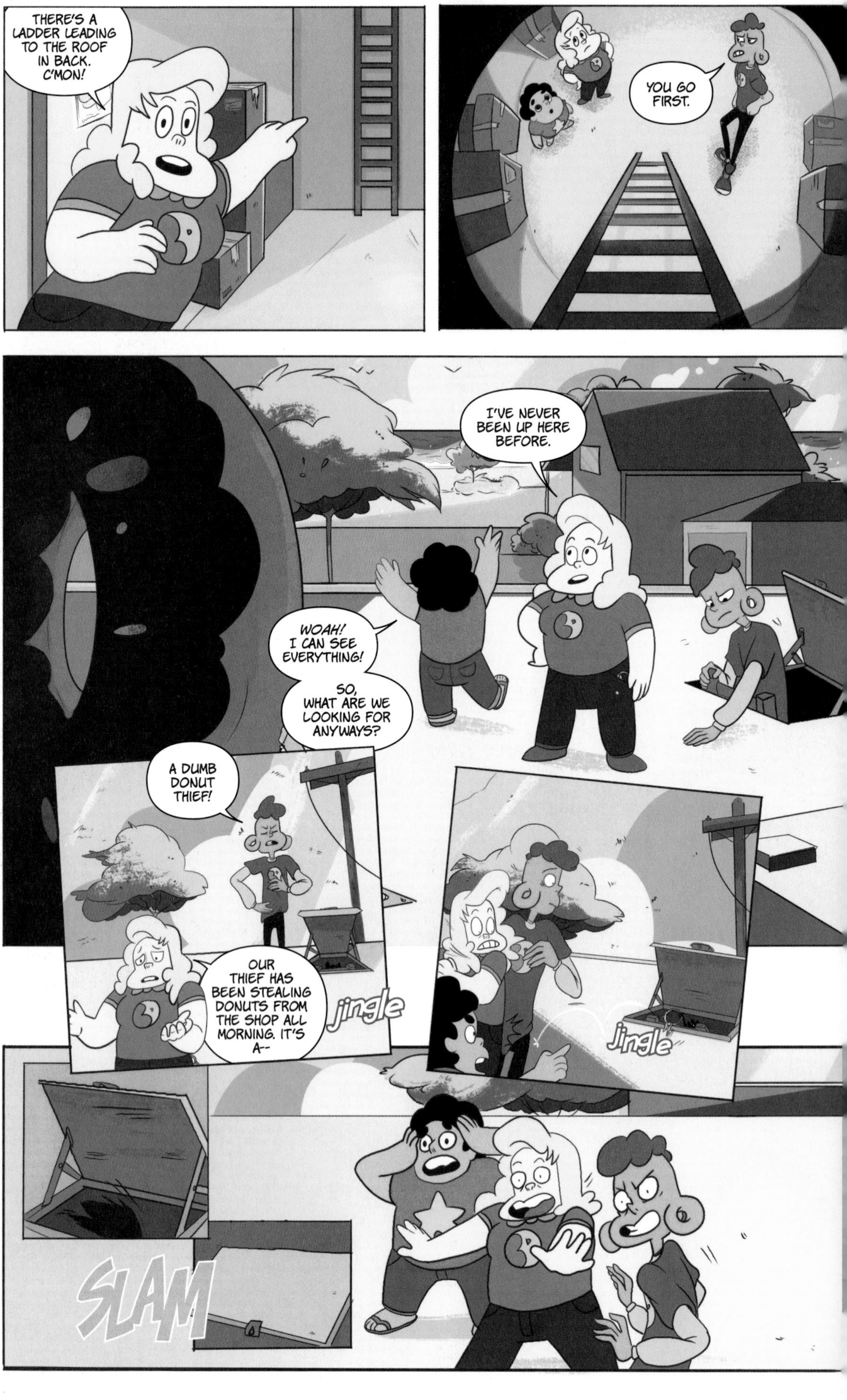
THERE'S A LADDER LEADING TO THE ROOF IN BACK. C'MON!
YOU GO FIRST.
I'VE NEVER BEEN UP HERE BEFORE.
WOAH! I CAN SEE EVERYTHING!
SO, WHAT ARE WE LOOKING FOR ANYWAYS?
A DUMB DONUT THIEF!
OUR THIEF HAS BEEN STEALING DONUTS FROM THE SHOP ALL MORNING. IT'S A--
jingle
jingle
SLAM

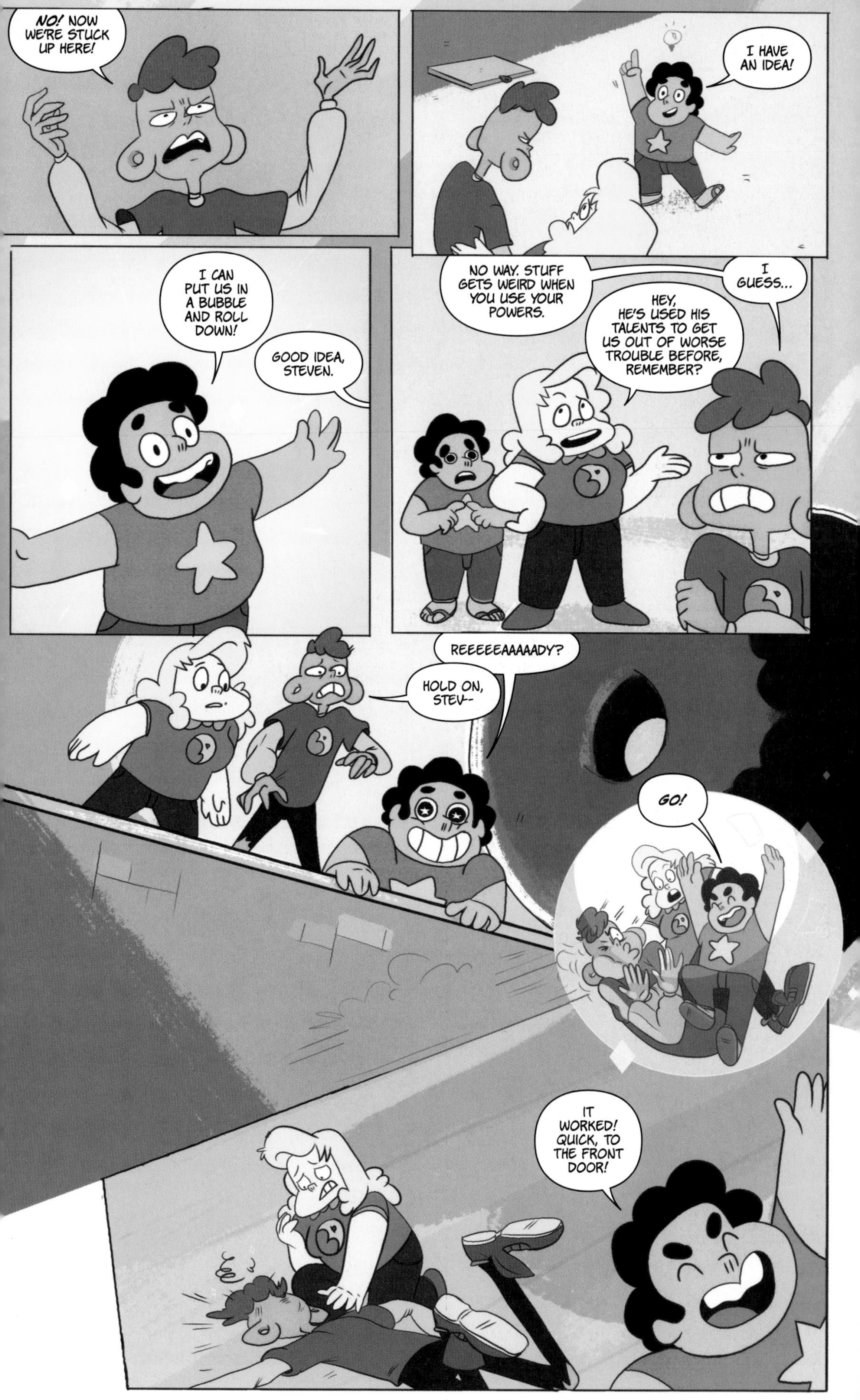
NO! NOW WE'RE STUCK UP HERE!
I HAVE AN IDEA!
I CAN PUT US IN A BUBBLE AND ROLL DOWN!
GOOD IDEA, STEVEN.
NO WAY. STUFF GETS WEIRD WHEN YOU USE YOUR POWERS.
HEY, HE'S USED HIS TALENTS TO GET US OUT OF WORSE TROUBLE BEFORE, REMEMBER?
I GUESS...
REEEEEAAAAADY?
HOLD ON, STEV-
GO!
IT WORKED! QUICK, TO THE FRONT DOOR!

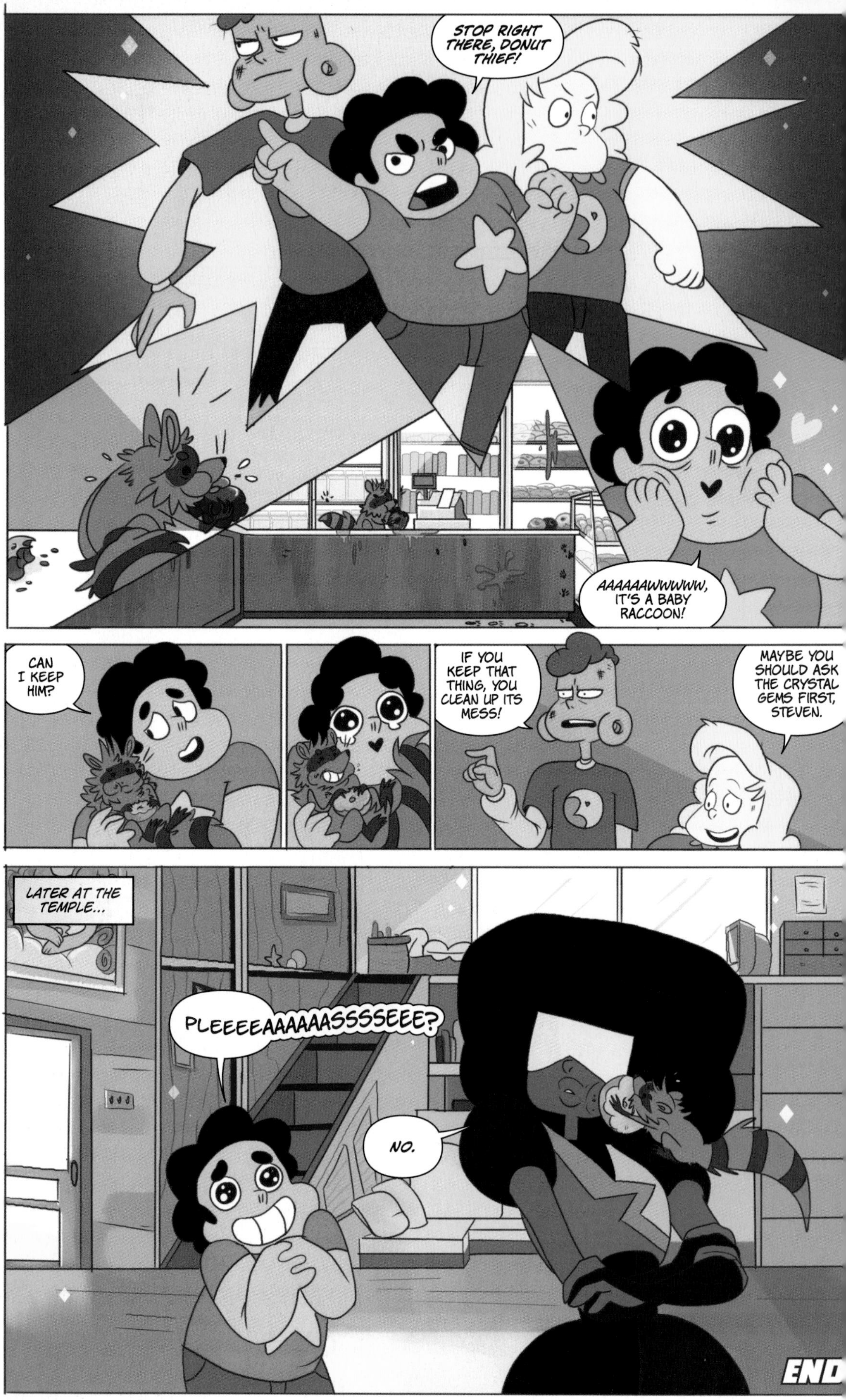
STOP RIGHT THERE, DONUT THIEF!
AAAAAAWWWWW, IT'S A BABY RACCOON!
CAN I KEEP HIM?
IF YOU KEEP THAT THING, YOU CLEAN UP ITS MESS!
MAYBE YOU SHOULD ASK THE CRYSTAL GEMS FIRST, STEVEN.
LATER AT THE TEMPLE...
PLEEEEAAAAAASSSSEEE?
NO.
END

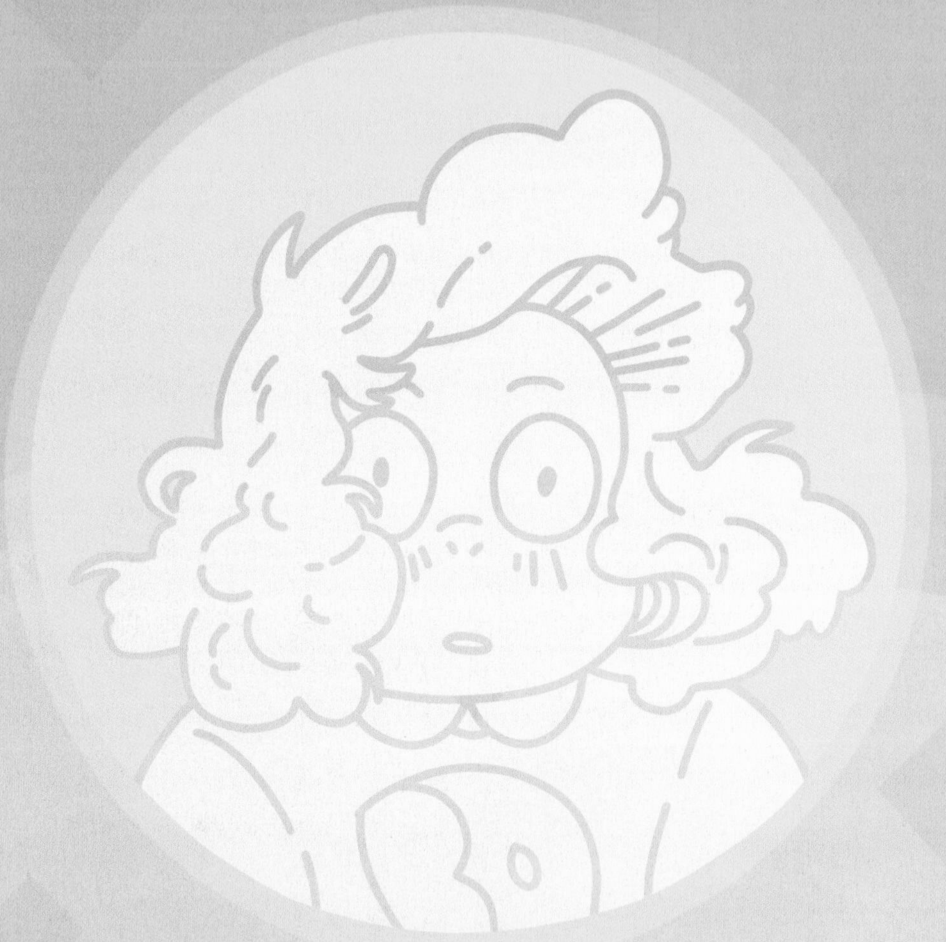

HEALTH INSPECTION

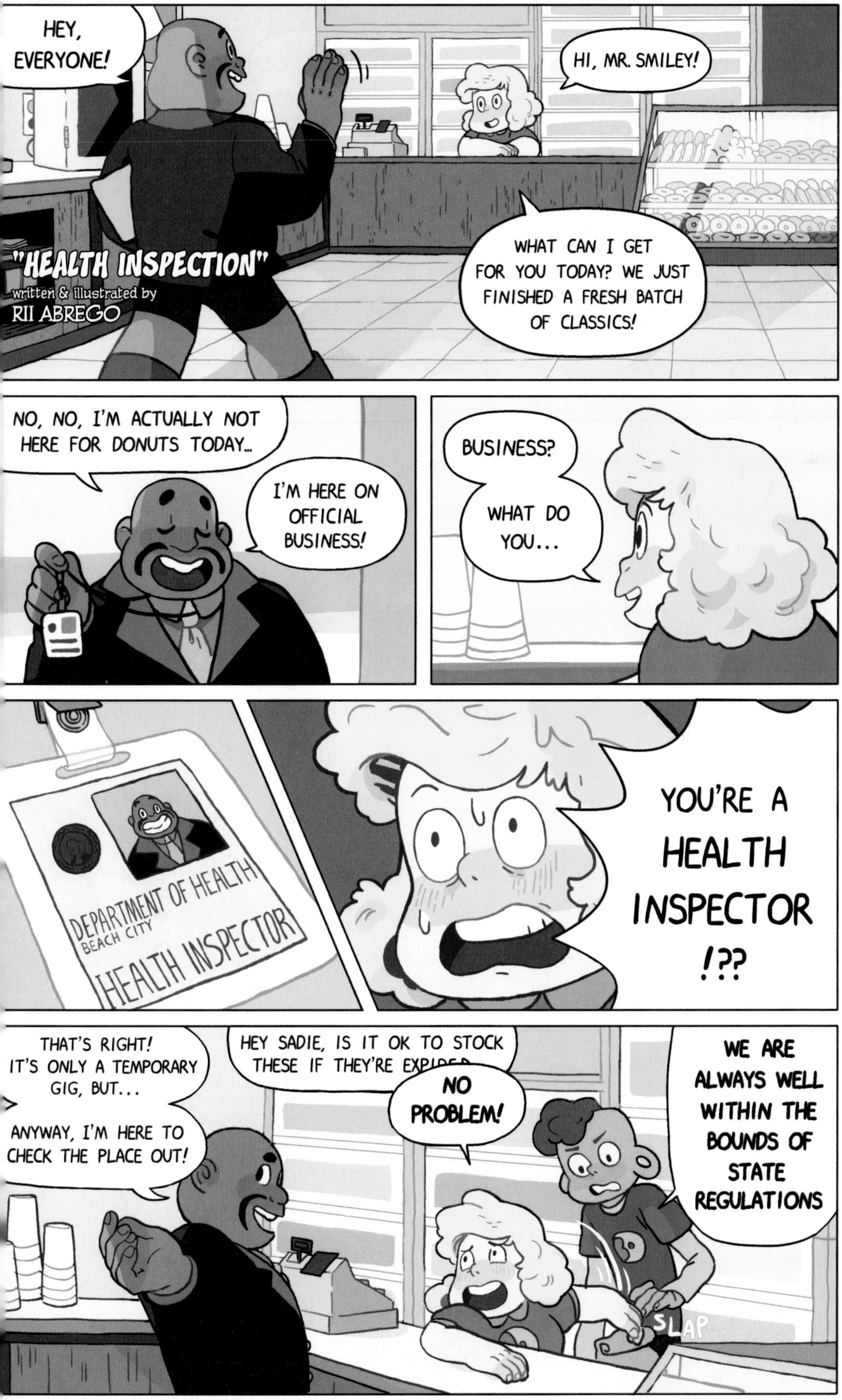
HEY, EVERYONE!
HI, MR. SMILEY!
"HEALTH INSPECTION"
written & illustrated by
RII ABREGO
WHAT CAN I GET FOR YOU TODAY? WE JUST FINISHED A FRESH BATCH OF CLASSICS!
NO, NO, I'M ACTUALLY NOT HERE FOR DONUTS TODAY...
I'M HERE ON OFFICIAL BUSINESS!
BUSINESS?
WHAT DO YOU...
DEPARTMENT OF HEALTH
BEACH CITY
HEALTH INSPECTOR
YOU'RE A HEALTH INSPECTOR !??
THAT'S RIGHT! IT'S ONLY A TEMPORARY GIG, BUT...
ANYWAY, I'M HERE TO CHECK THE PLACE OUT!
HEY SADIE, IS IT OK TO STOCK THESE IF THEY'RE EXP
NO PROBLEM!
WE ARE ALWAYS WELL WITHIN THE BOUNDS OF STATE REGULATIONS
SLAP

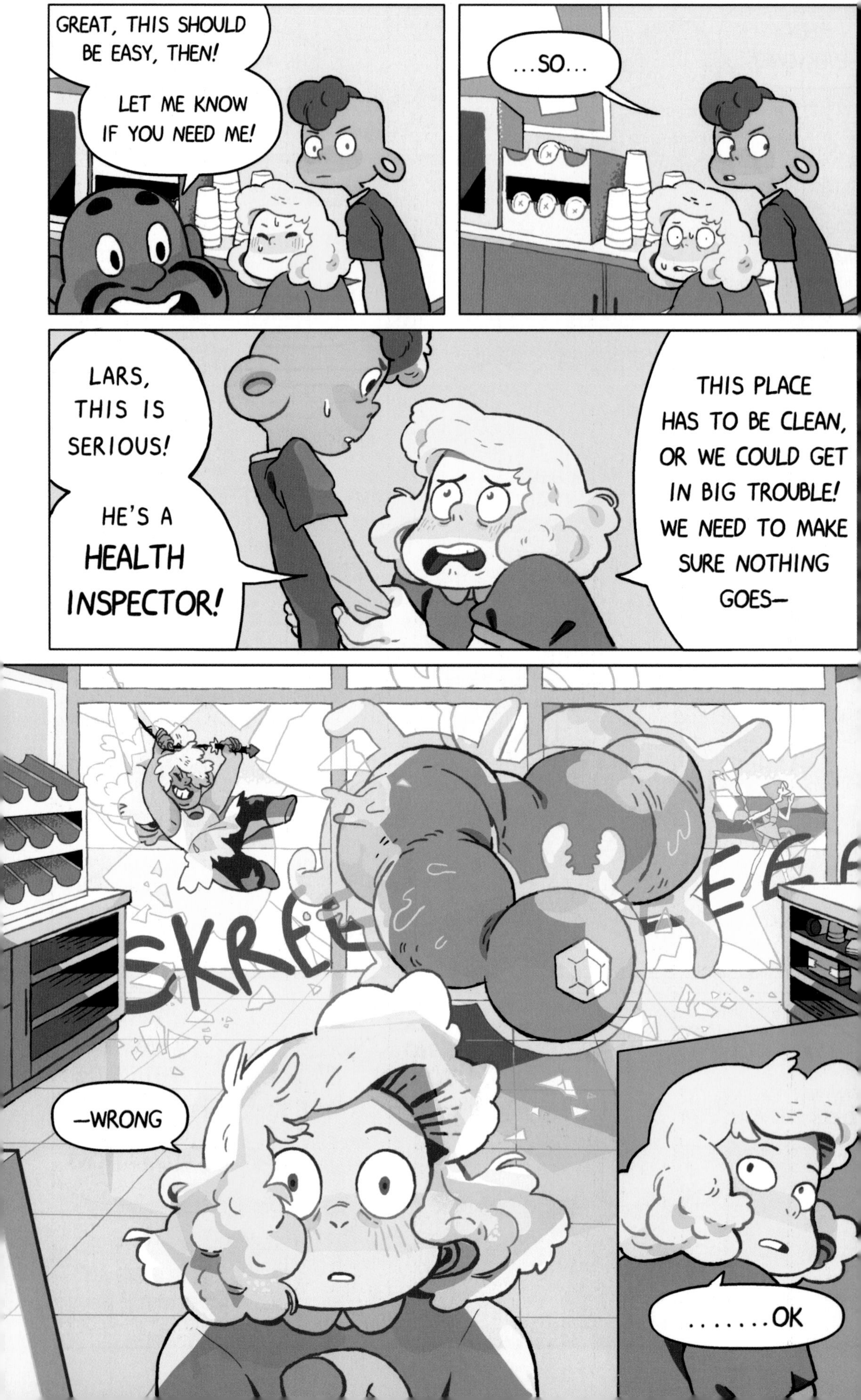
GREAT, THIS SHOULD BE EASY, THEN!
LET ME KNOW IF YOU NEED ME!
...SO...
LARS, THIS IS SERIOUS!
HE'S A HEALTH INSPECTOR!
THIS PLACE HAS TO BE CLEAN, OR WE COULD GET IN BIG TROUBLE! WE NEED TO MAKE SURE NOTHING GOES—
SKREEEEEE
—WRONG
........OK

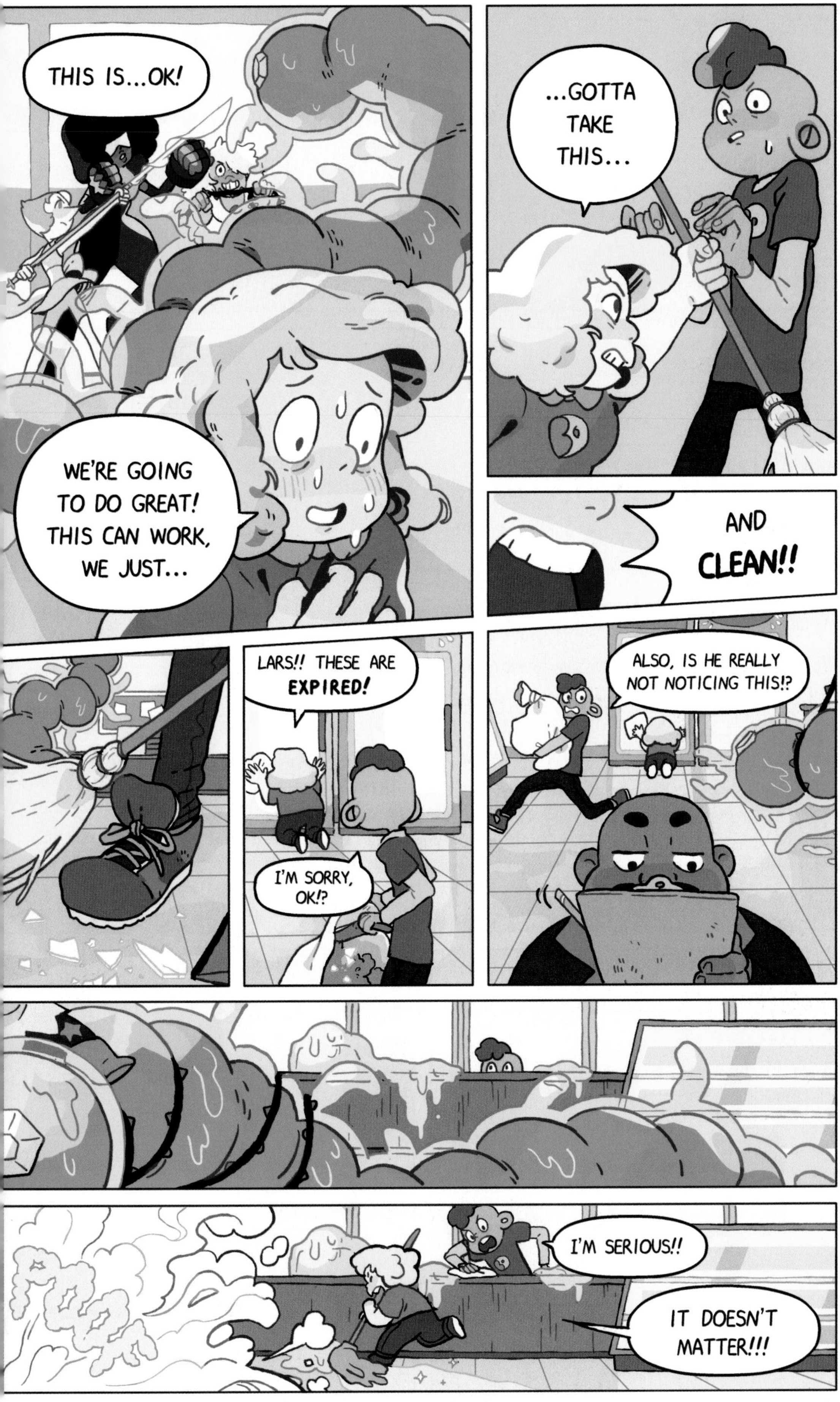

THIS IS...OK!
WE'RE GOING TO DO GREAT! THIS CAN WORK, WE JUST...
...GOTTA TAKE THIS...
AND CLEAN!!
LARS!! THESE ARE EXPIRED!
I'M SORRY, OK!?
ALSO, IS HE REALLY NOT NOTICING THIS!?
I'M SERIOUS!!
IT DOESN'T MATTER!!!

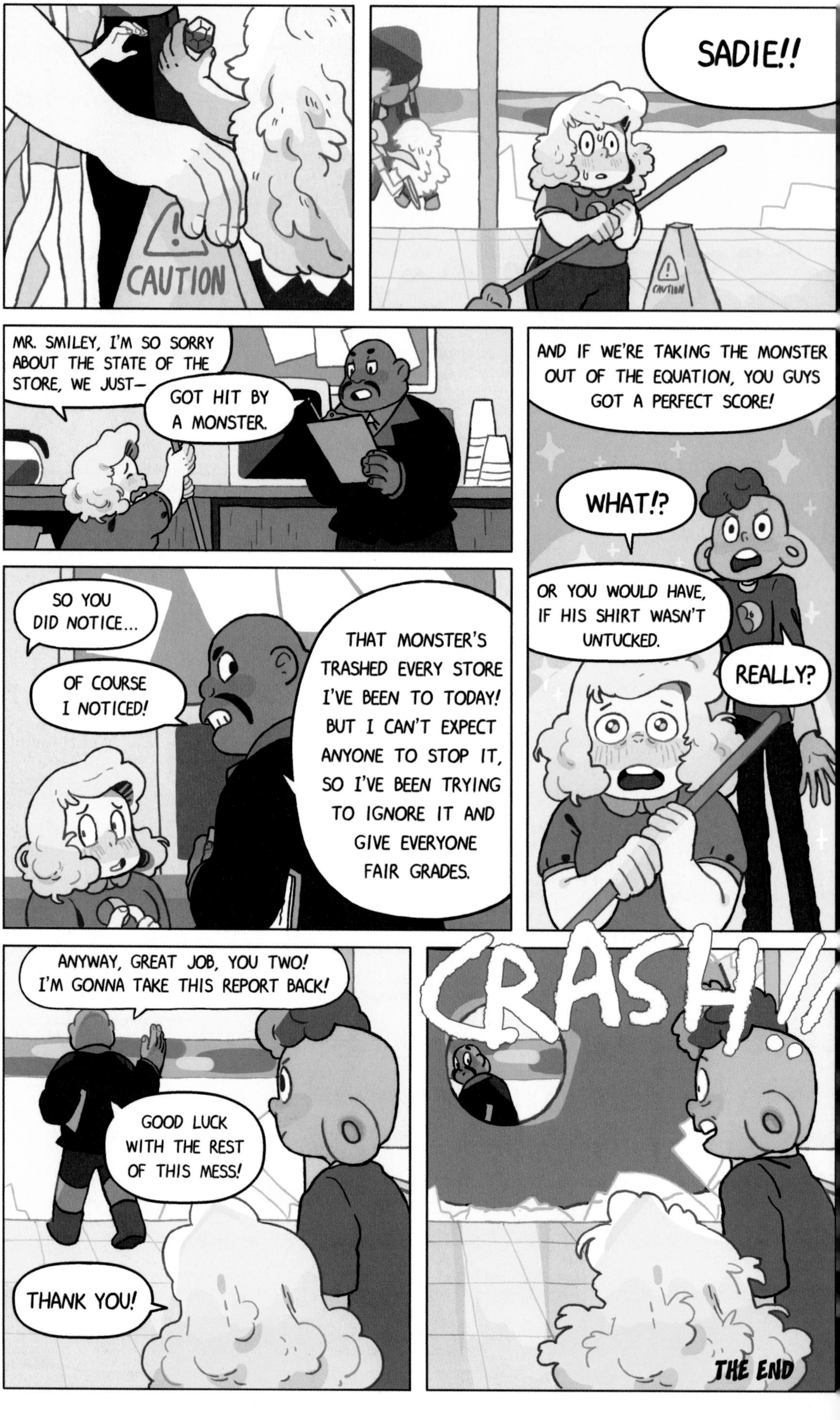
CAUTION
SADIE!!
CAUTION
MR. SMILEY, I'M SO SORRY ABOUT THE STATE OF THE STORE, WE JUST—
GOT HIT BY A MONSTER.
AND IF WE'RE TAKING THE MONSTER OUT OF THE EQUATION, YOU GUYS GOT A PERFECT SCORE!
WHAT!?
OR YOU WOULD HAVE, IF HIS SHIRT WASN'T UNTUCKED.
REALLY?
SO YOU DID NOTICE...
OF COURSE I NOTICED!
THAT MONSTER'S TRASHED EVERY STORE I'VE BEEN TO TODAY! BUT I CAN'T EXPECT ANYONE TO STOP IT, SO I'VE BEEN TRYING TO IGNORE IT AND GIVE EVERYONE FAIR GRADES.
ANYWAY, GREAT JOB, YOU TWO! I'M GONNA TAKE THIS REPORT BACK!
GOOD LUCK WITH THE REST OF THIS MESS!
THANK YOU!
CRASH!!
THE END

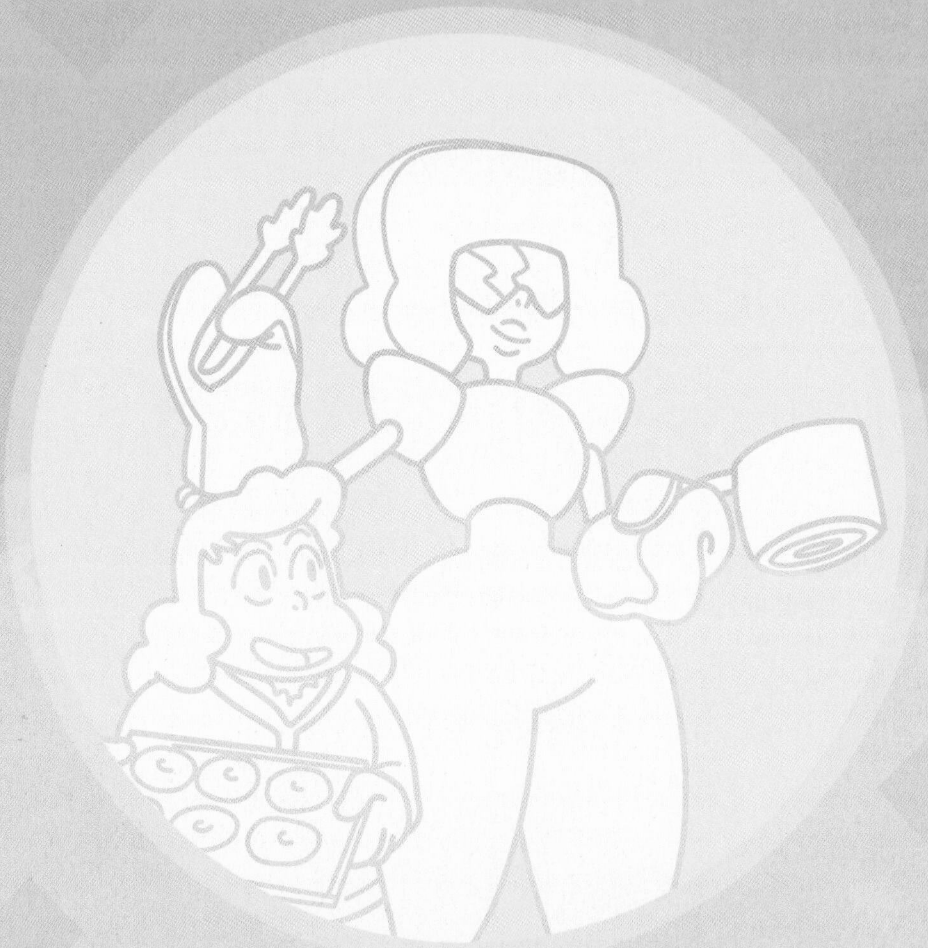

HOW TO DONUTS

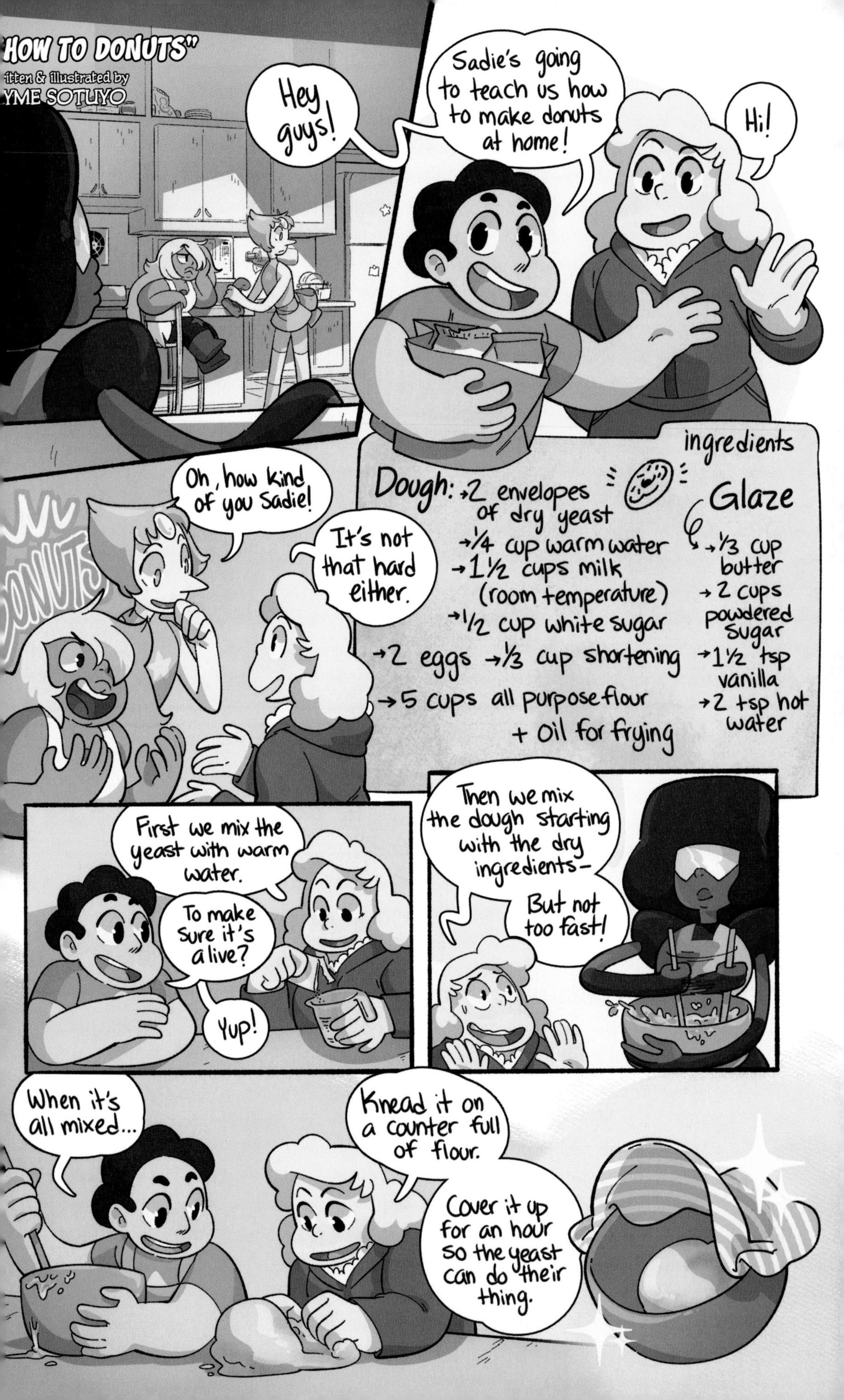
"HOW TO DONUTS"
itten & illustrated by
YME SOTUYO
Hey guys!
Sadie's going to teach us how to make donuts at home!
Hi!
DONUTS
Oh, how kind of you Sadie!
It's not that hard either.
ingredients
Dough: →2 envelopes of dry yeast
→1/4 cup warm water
→1 1/2 cups milk (room temperature)
→1/2 cup white sugar
→2 eggs →1/3 cup shortening
→5 cups all purpose flour
+ Oil for frying
Glaze
→1/3 cup butter
→2 cups powdered sugar
→1 1/2 tsp vanilla
→2 tsp hot water
First we mix the yeast with warm water.
To make sure it's a live?
Yup!
Then we mix the dough starting with the dry ingredients–
But not too fast!
When it's all mixed...
Knead it on a counter full of flour.
Cover it up for an hour so the yeast can do their thing.

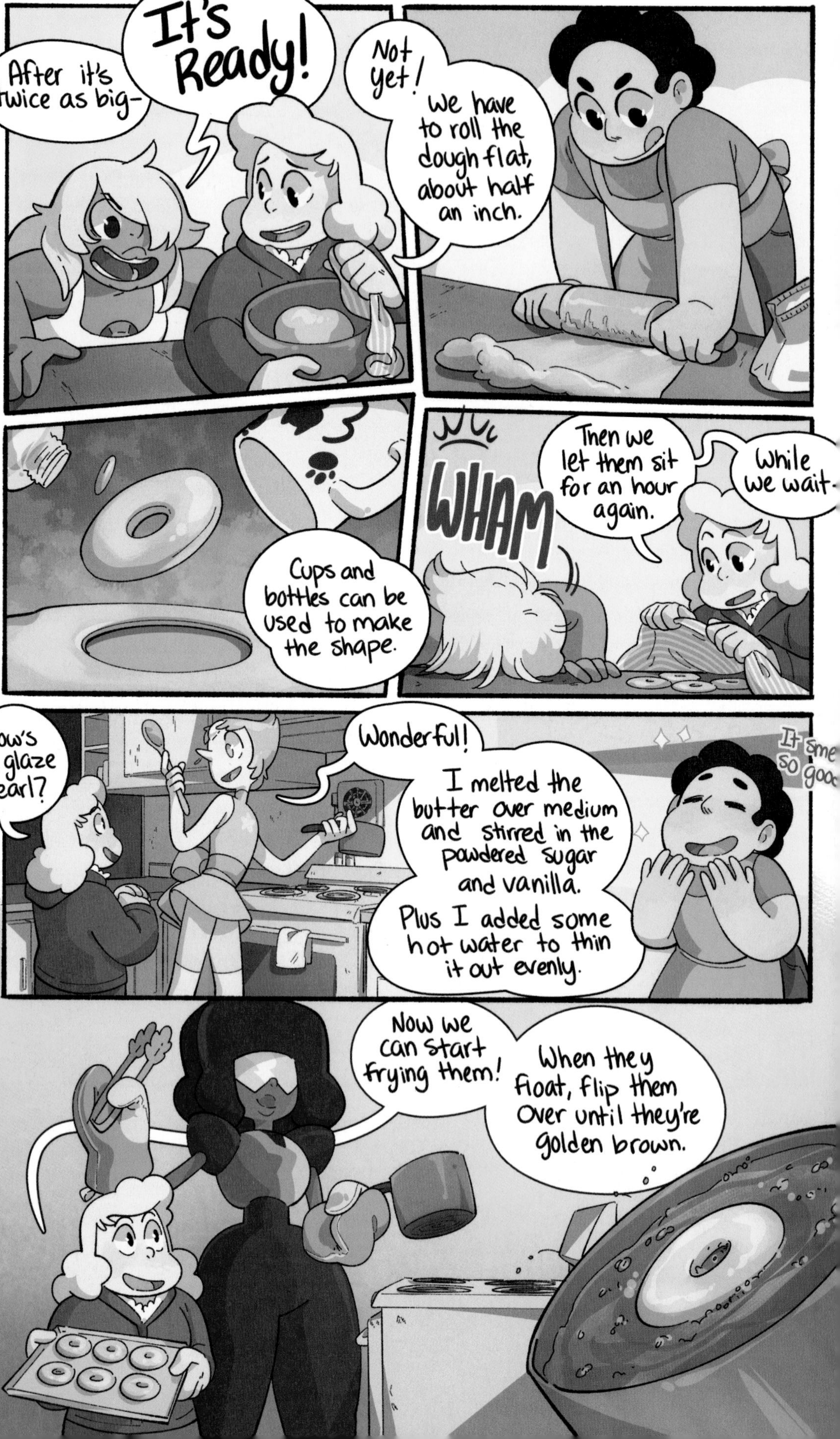
After it's twice as big-
It's Ready!
Not yet!
We have to roll the dough flat, about half an inch.
Cups and bottles can be used to make the shape.
WHAM
Then we let them sit for an hour again.
While we wait-
How's the glaze Pearl?
Wonderful!
I melted the butter over medium and stirred in the powdered sugar and vanilla.
Plus I added some hot water to thin it out evenly.
It sme
so goo
Now we can start frying them!
When they float, flip them over until they're golden brown.

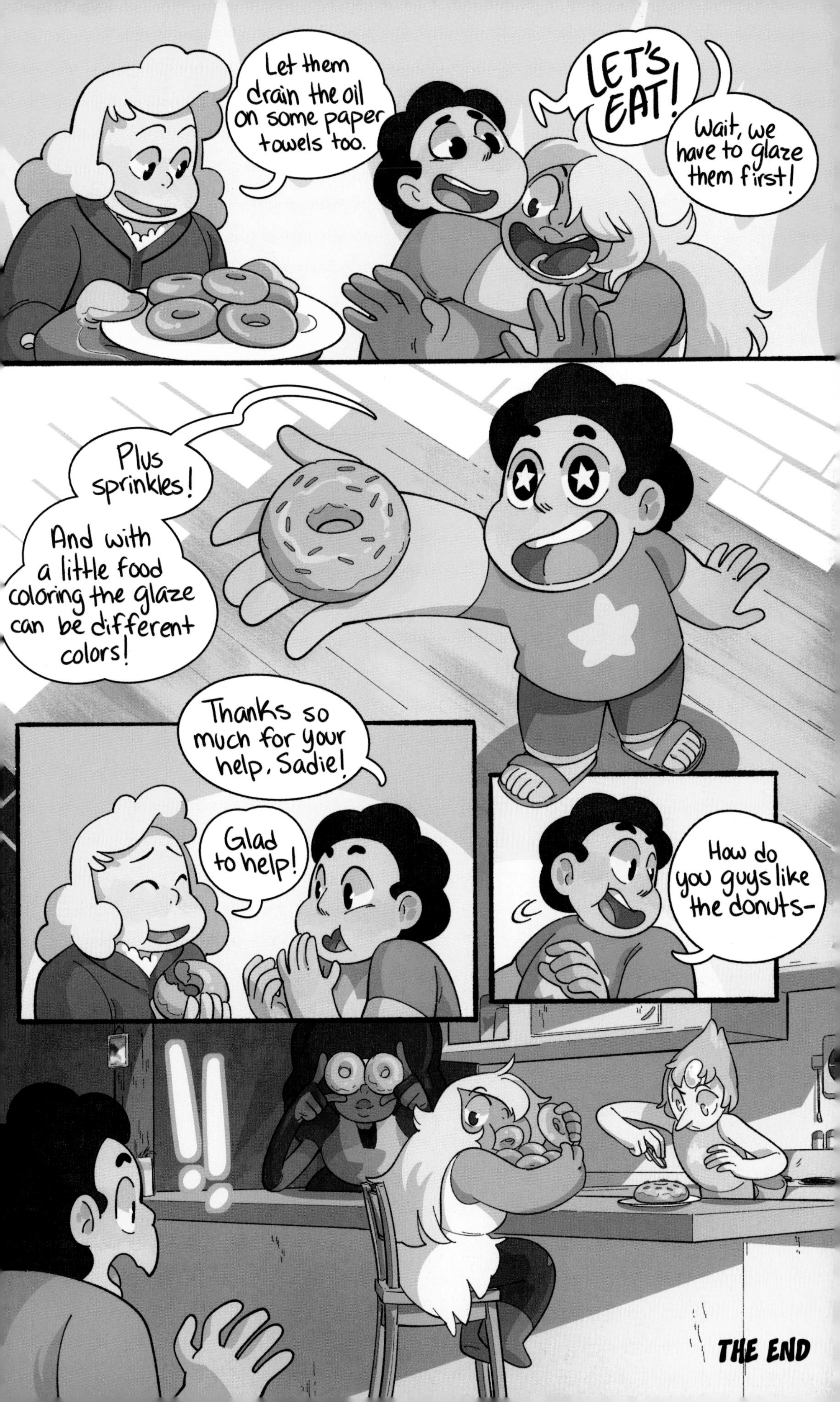

Let them drain the oil on some paper towels too.
LET'S EAT!
Wait, we have to glaze them first!
Plus sprinkles!
And with a little food coloring the glaze can be different colors!
Thanks so much for your help, Sadie!
Glad to help!
How do you guys like the donuts-
!!
THE END

FOOD FIGHT

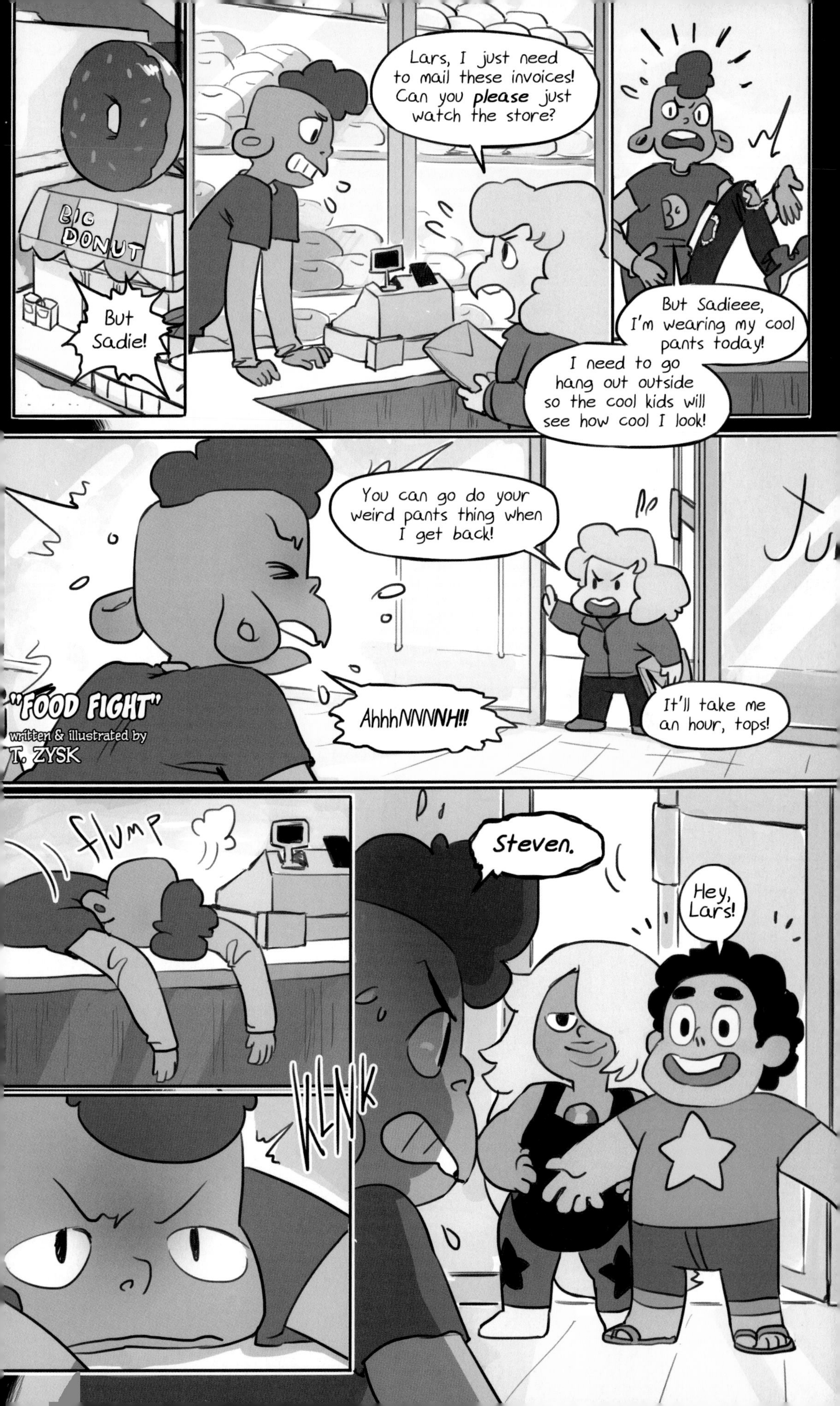
BIG DONUT
But Sadie!
Lars, I just need to mail these invoices! Can you *please* just watch the store?
But Sadieee, I'm wearing my cool pants today!
I need to go hang out outside so the cool kids will see how cool I look!
"FOOD FIGHT"
written & illustrated by
T. ZYSK
AhhhNNNNH!!
You can go do your weird pants thing when I get back!
It'll take me an hour, tops!
flump
KLNK
Steven.
Hey, Lars!

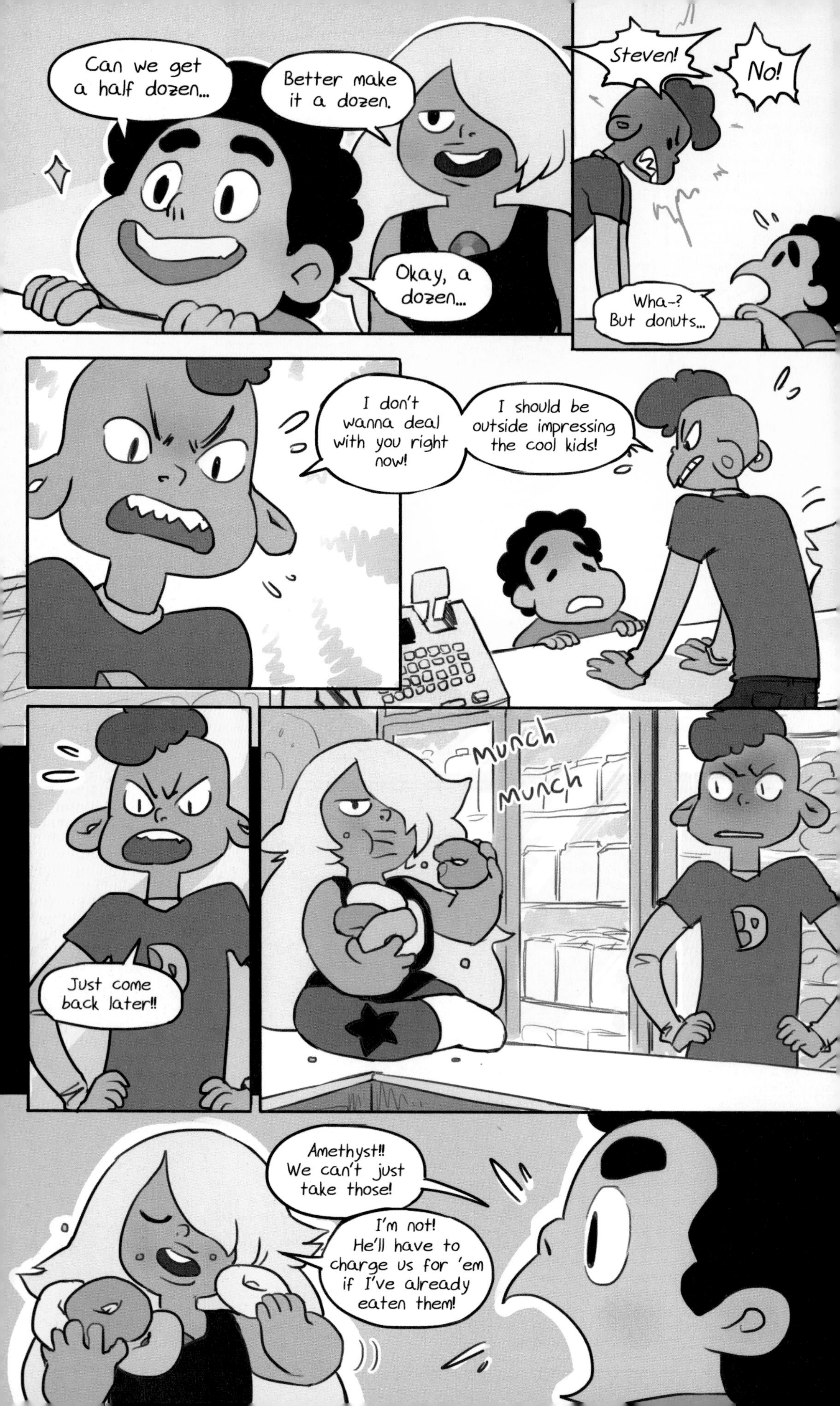
Can we get a half dozen...
Better make it a dozen.
Okay, a dozen...
Steven!
No!
Wha-? But donuts...
I don't wanna deal with you right now!
I should be outside impressing the cool kids!
Just come back later!!
Munch
Munch
Amethyst!! We can't just take those!
I'm not! He'll have to charge us for 'em if I've already eaten them!

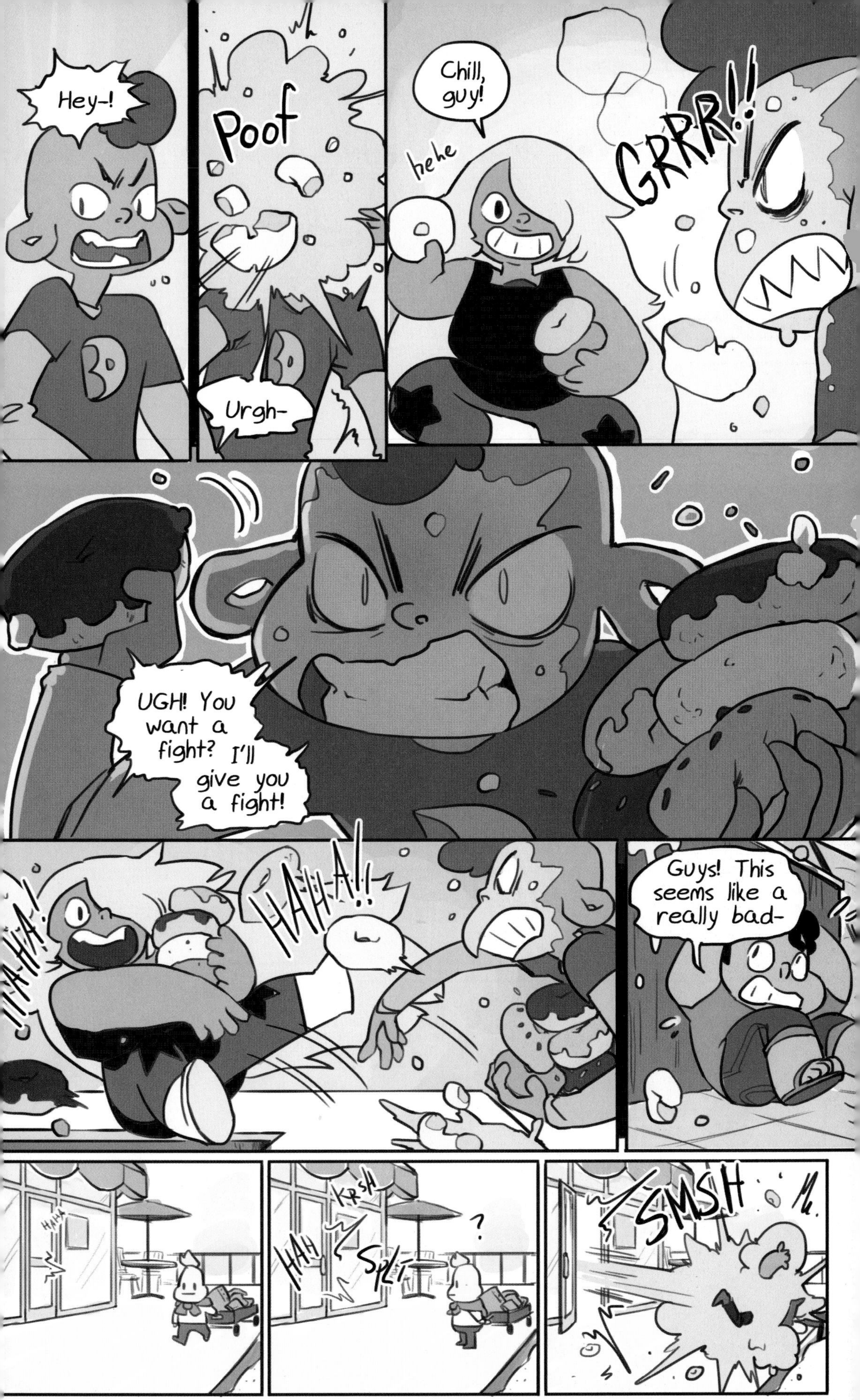

Hey-!
Poof
Urgh-
Chill, guy!
hehe
GRRR!!
UGH! You want a fight? I'll give you a fight!
HAHA!!
HAHA!
Guys! This seems like a really bad-
HAHA
KRSH
HAH
SPLT
?
SMSH

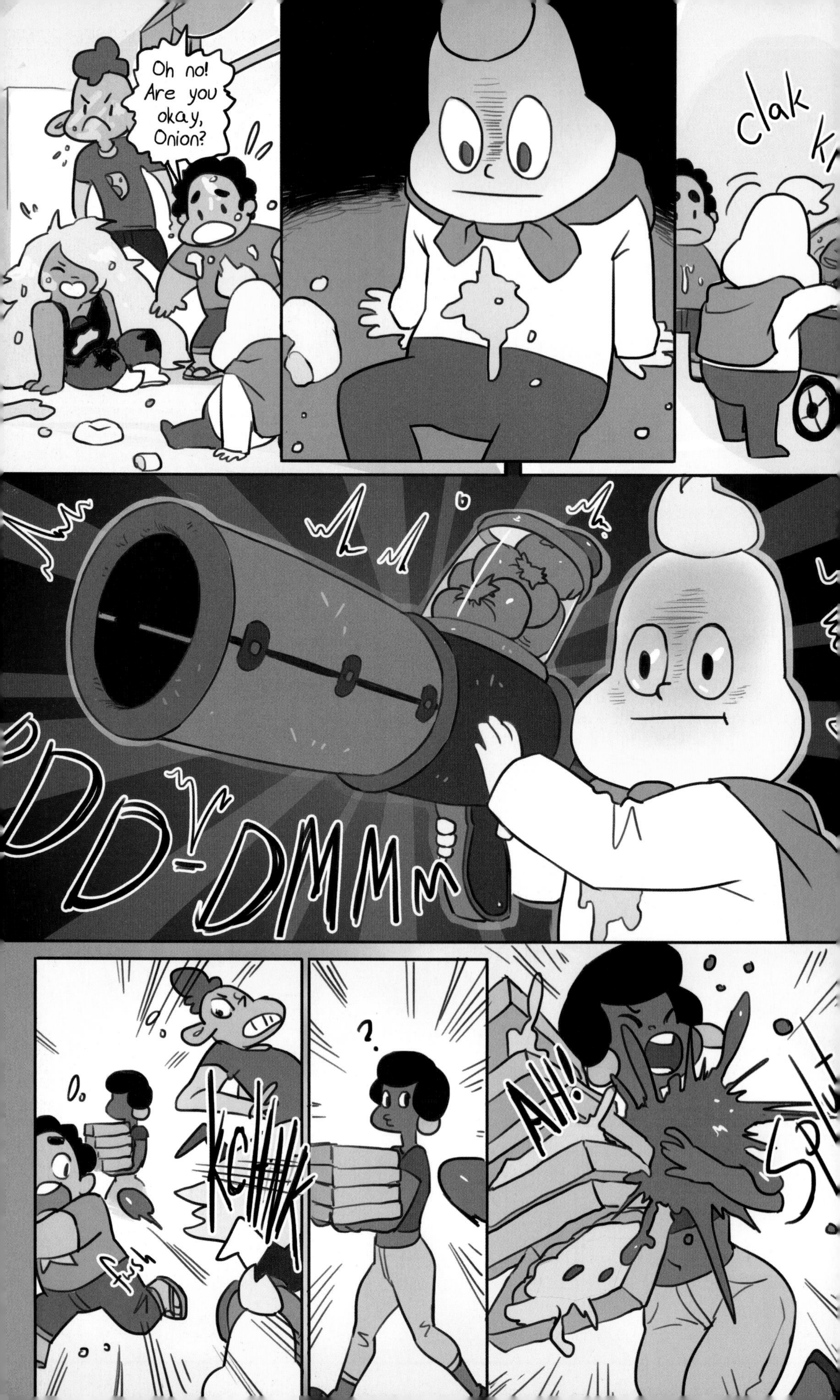

Oh no! Are you okay, Onion?
clak
DDD-DMMM
KCHK
fush
?
AH!
SPLUT

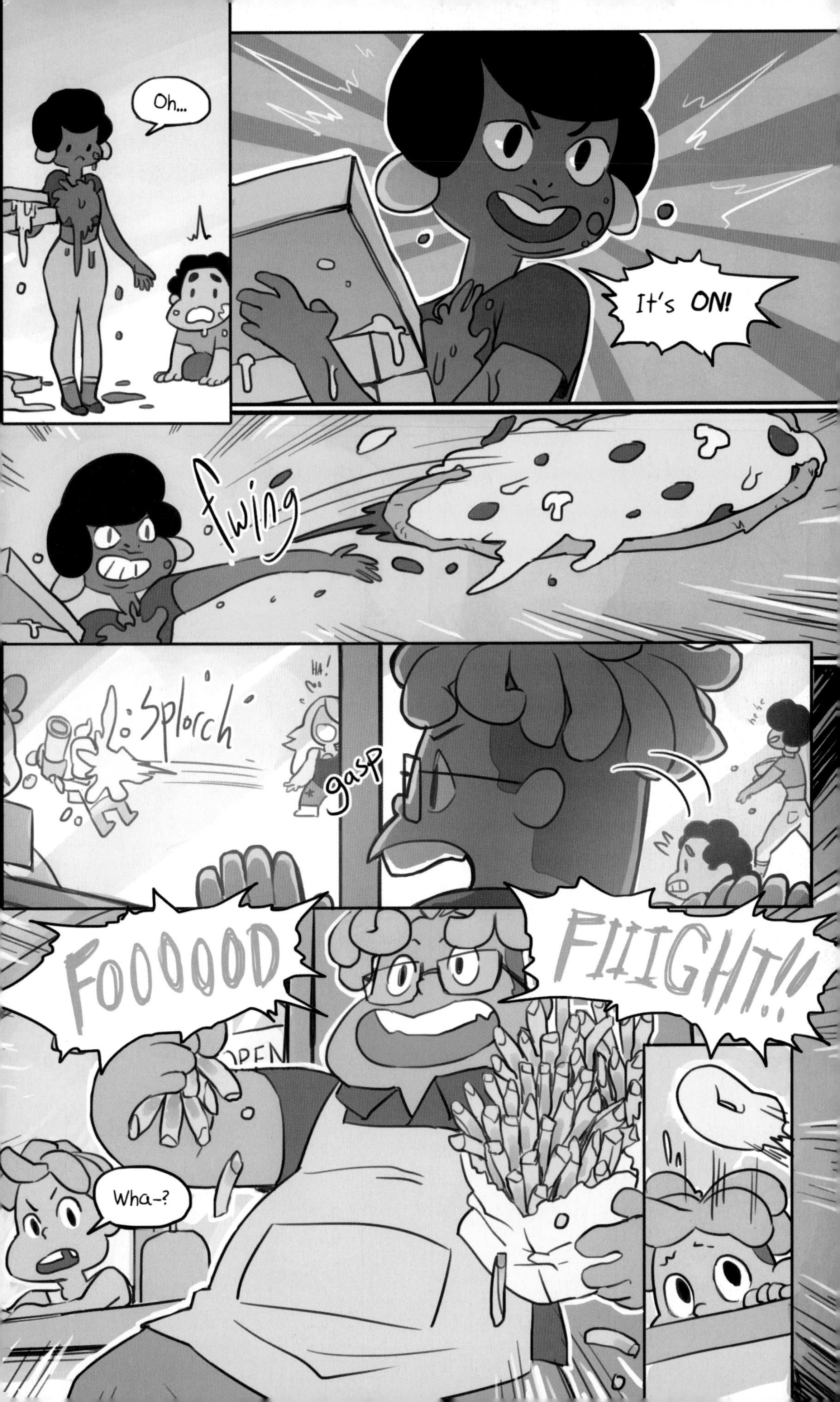
Oh...
It's ON!
fwing
Splorch
HA!
gasp
FOOOOOD
FIIIGHT!!
Wha-?

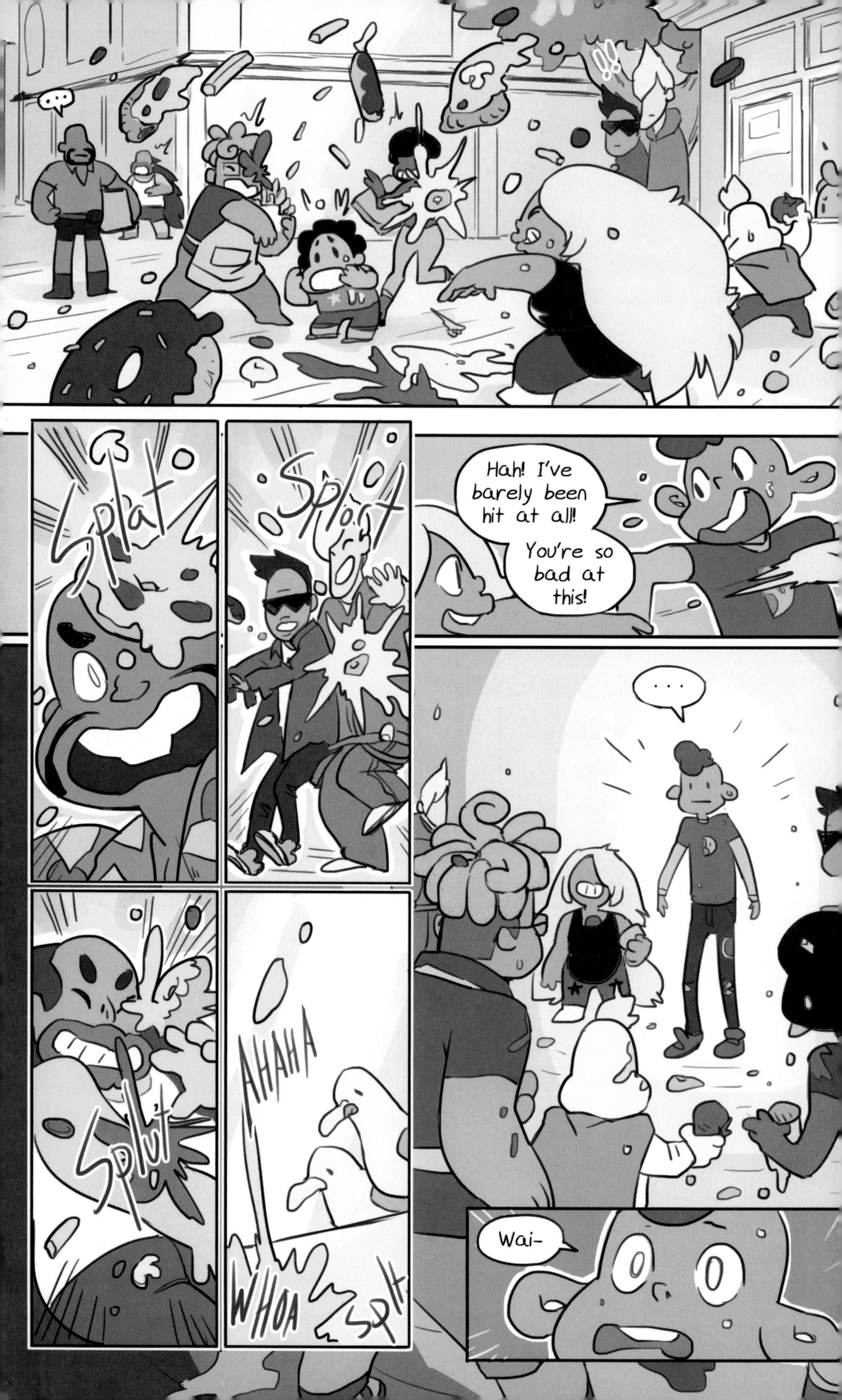

!!
Splat
Splort
Hah! I've barely been hit at all!
You're so bad at this!
...
Splut
AHAHA
WHOA
Splt
Wai-

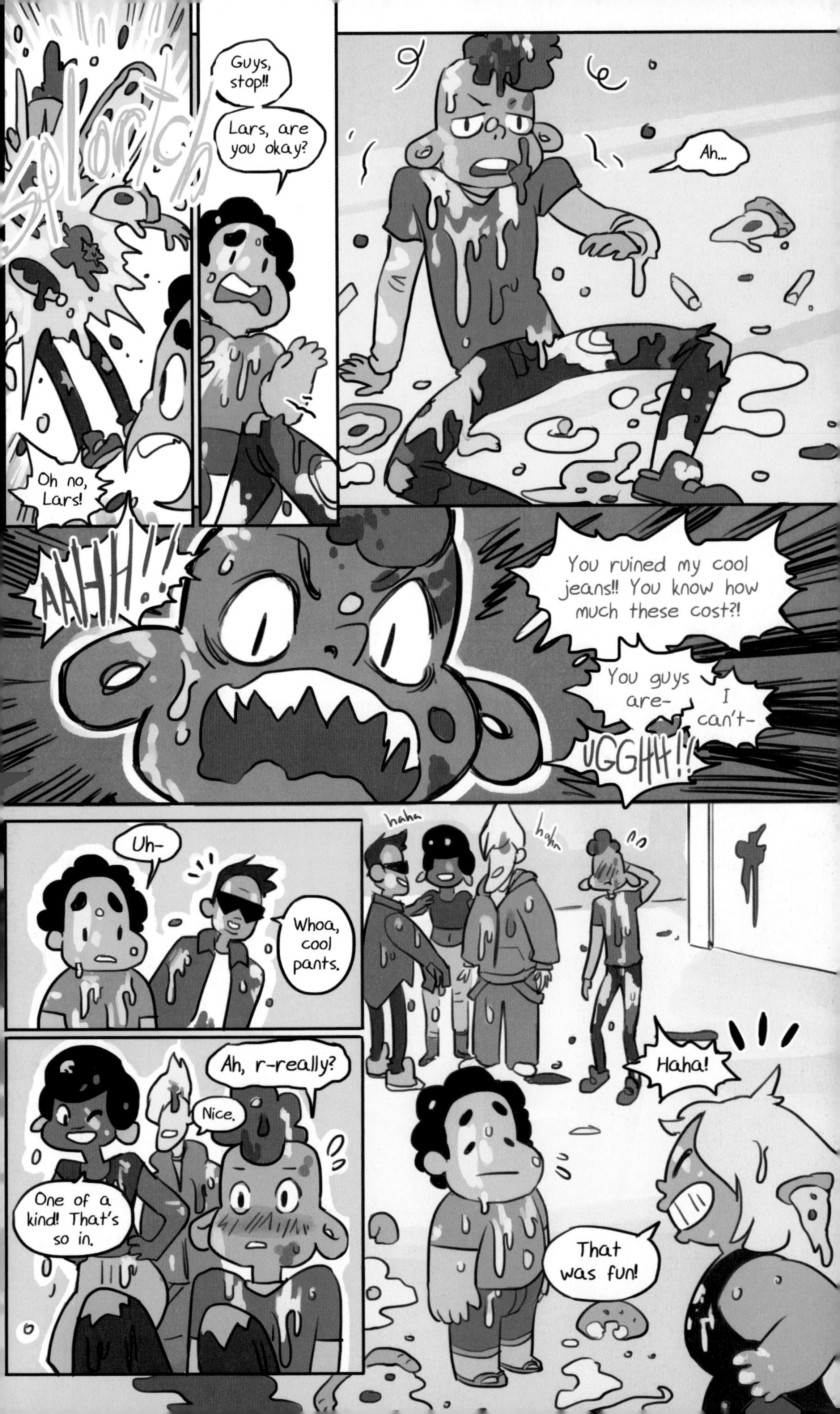
Splortch
Oh no, Lars!
Guys, stop!!
Lars, are you okay?
Ah...
AAHH!!
You ruined my cool jeans!! You know how much these cost?!
You guys are-
I can't-
UGGHH!!
Uh-
Whoa, cool pants.
haha
haha
Ah, r-really?
Nice.
One of a kind! That's so in.
Haha!
That was fun!

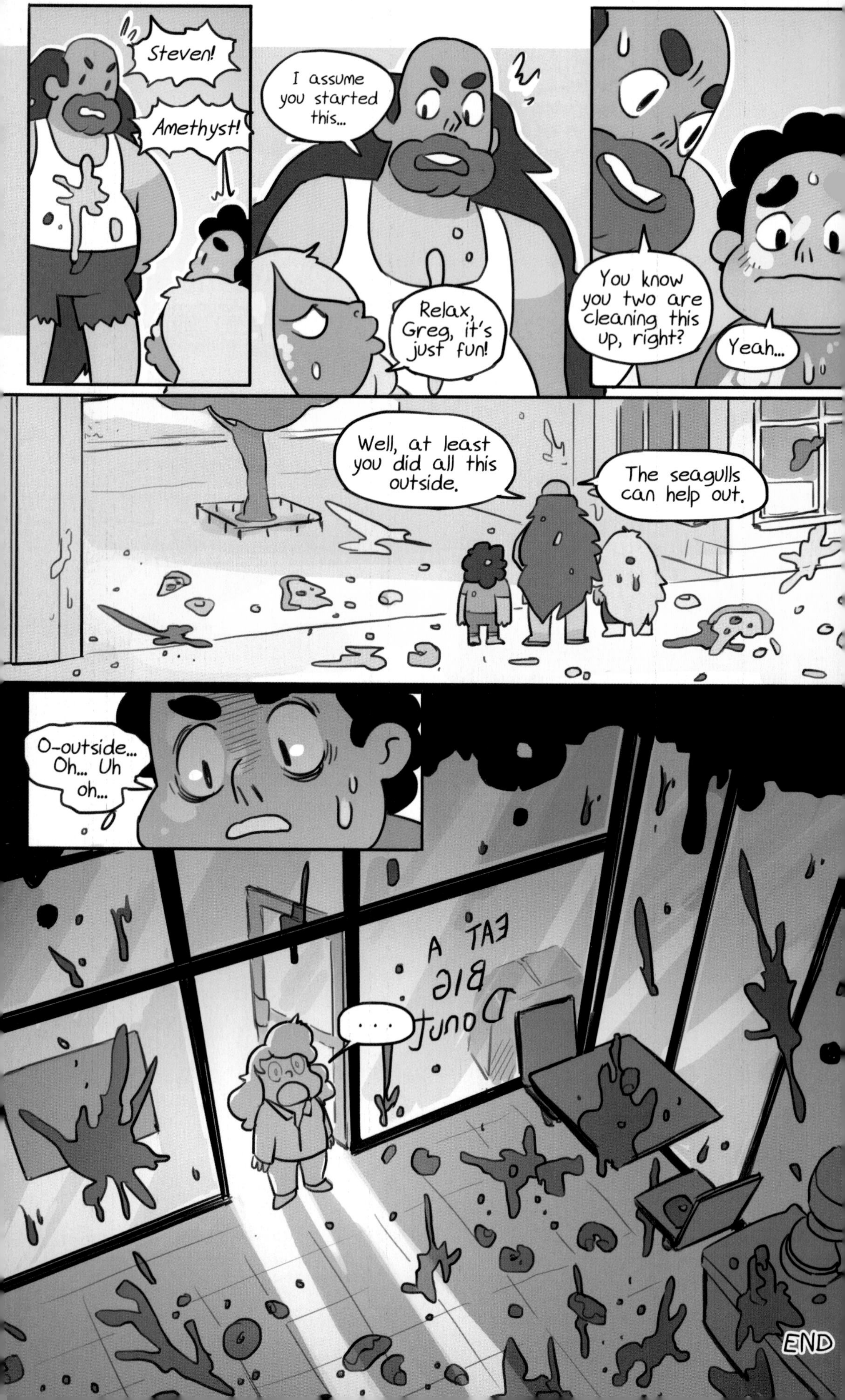

Steven!
Amethyst!
I assume you started this...
Relax, Greg, it's just fun!
You know you two are cleaning this up, right?
Yeah...
Well, at least you did all this outside.
The seagulls can help out.
O-outside... Oh... Uh oh...
EAT A BIG Donut
. . .
END

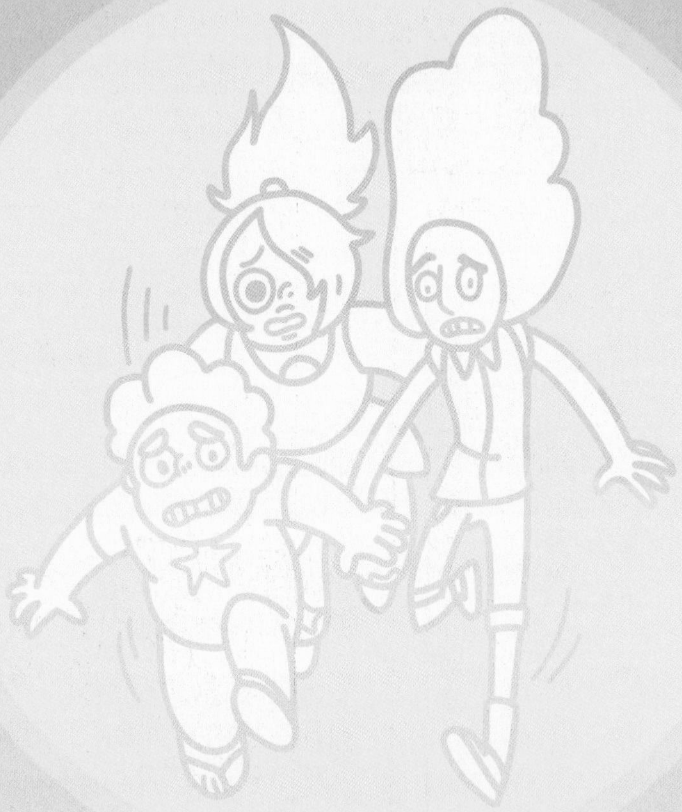

DONUT DERBY

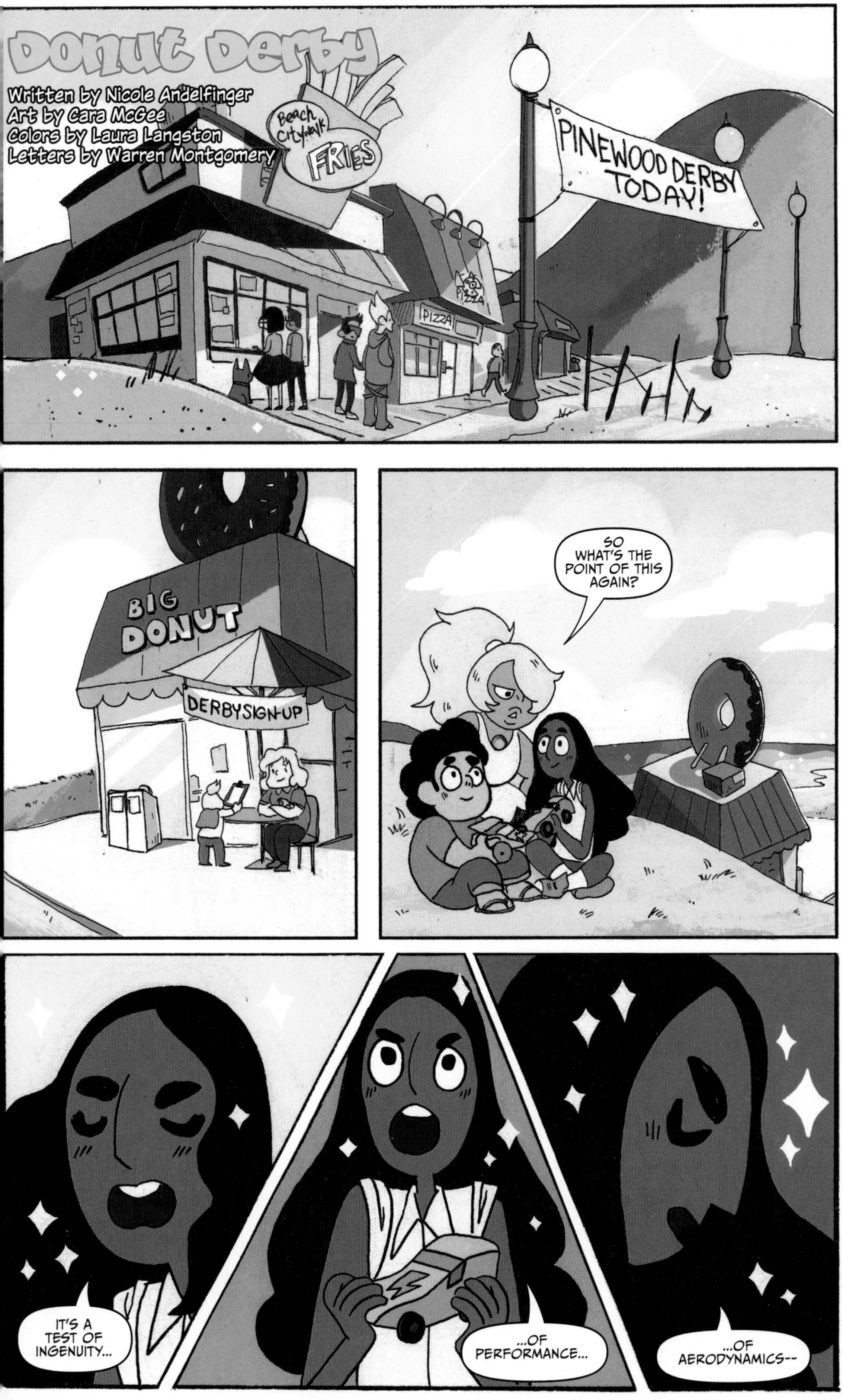
Donut Derby
Written by Nicole Andelfinger
Art by Cara McGee
Colors by Laura Langston
Letters by Warren Montgomery
Beach Citywalk FRIES
PINEWOOD DERBY TODAY!
PIZZA
BIG DONUT
DERBY SIGN-UP
SO WHAT'S THE POINT OF THIS AGAIN?
IT'S A TEST OF INGENUITY...
...OF PERFORMANCE...
...OF AERODYNAMICS--

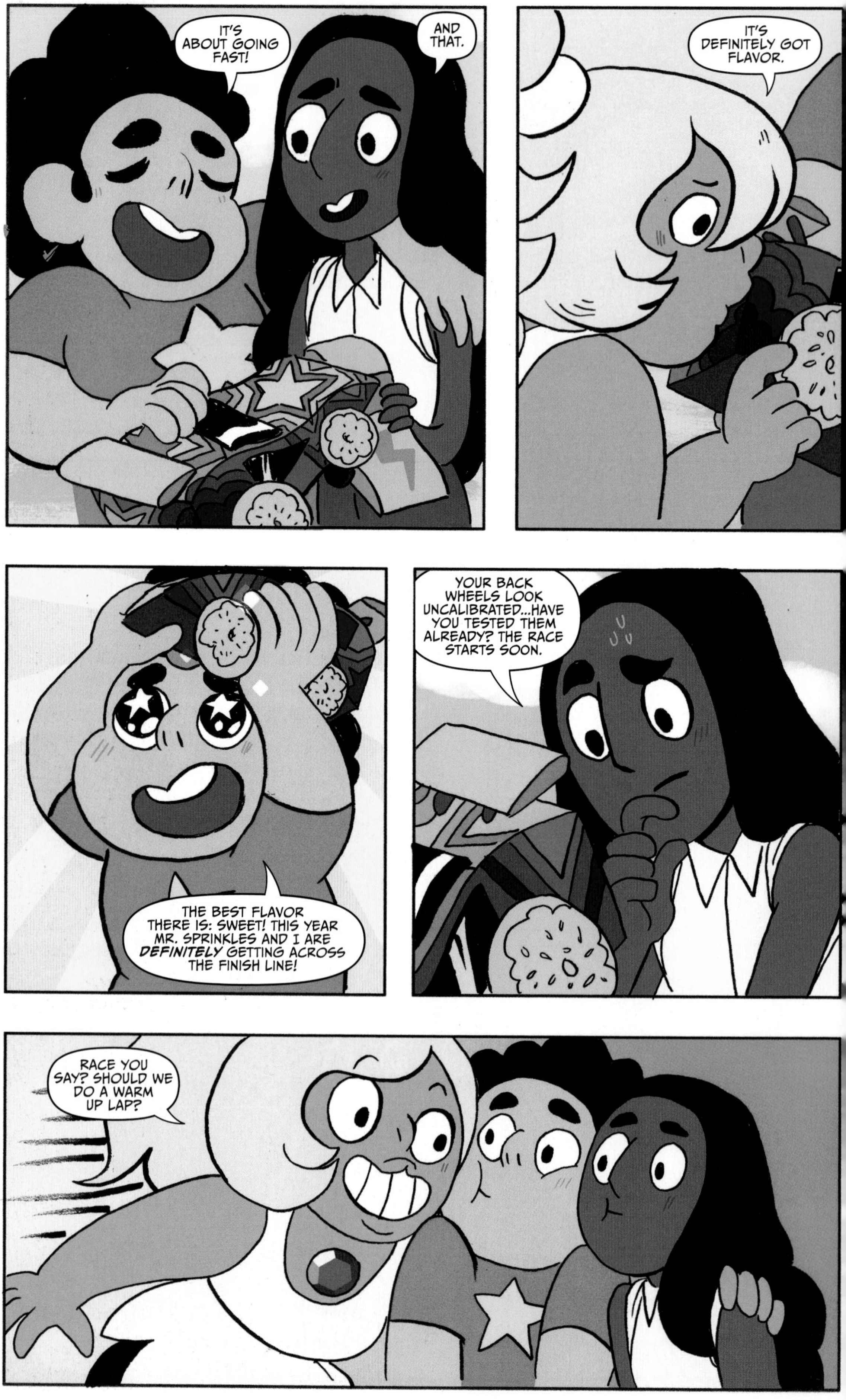

IT'S ABOUT GOING FAST!
AND THAT.
IT'S DEFINITELY GOT FLAVOR.
THE BEST FLAVOR THERE IS: SWEET! THIS YEAR MR. SPRINKLES AND I ARE *DEFINITELY* GETTING ACROSS THE FINISH LINE!
YOUR BACK WHEELS LOOK UNCALIBRATED...HAVE YOU TESTED THEM ALREADY? THE RACE STARTS SOON.
RACE YOU SAY? SHOULD WE DO A WARM UP LAP?

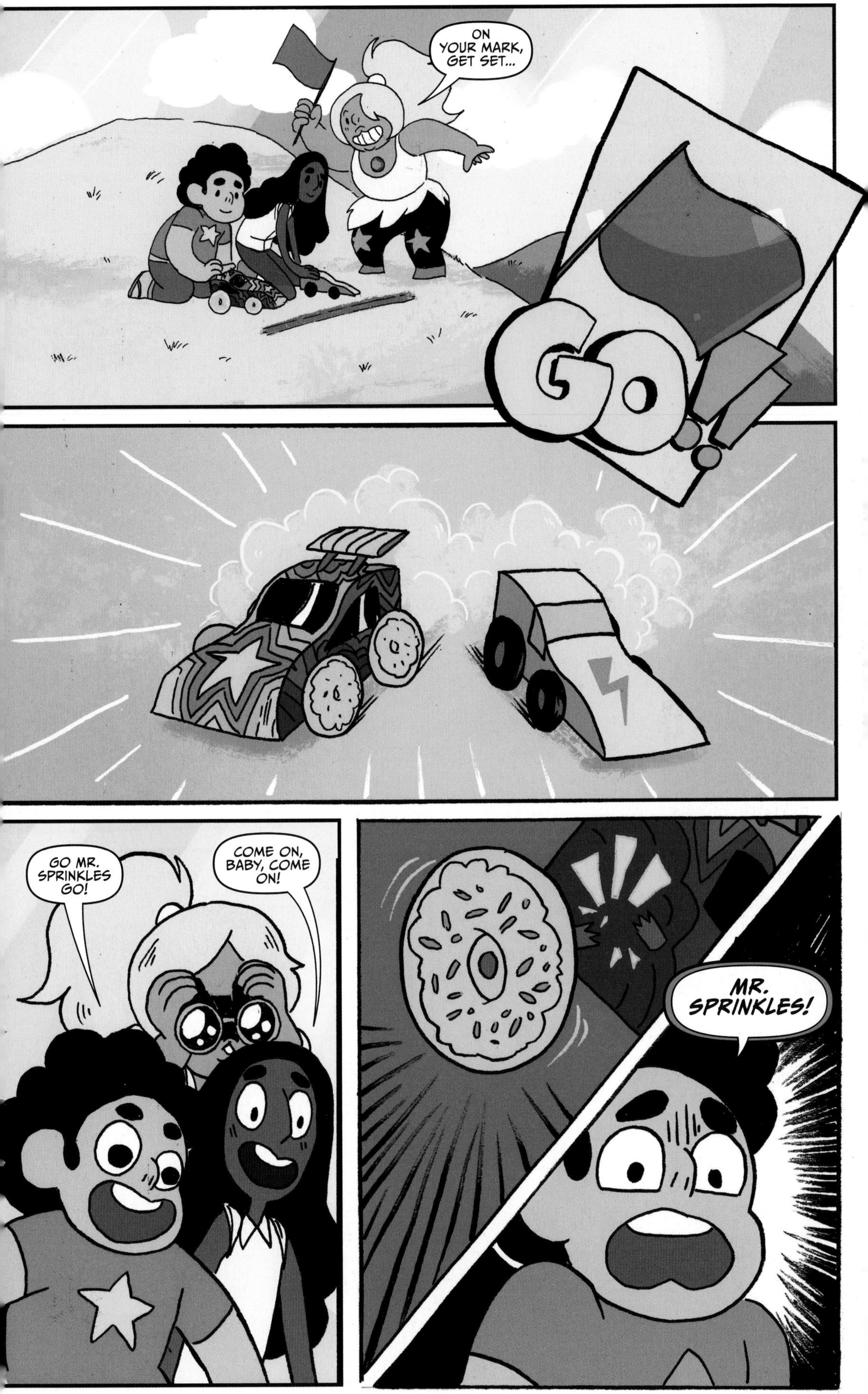

ON YOUR MARK, GET SET...
GO!!
GO MR. SPRINKLES GO!
COME ON, BABY, COME ON!
MR. SPRINKLES!

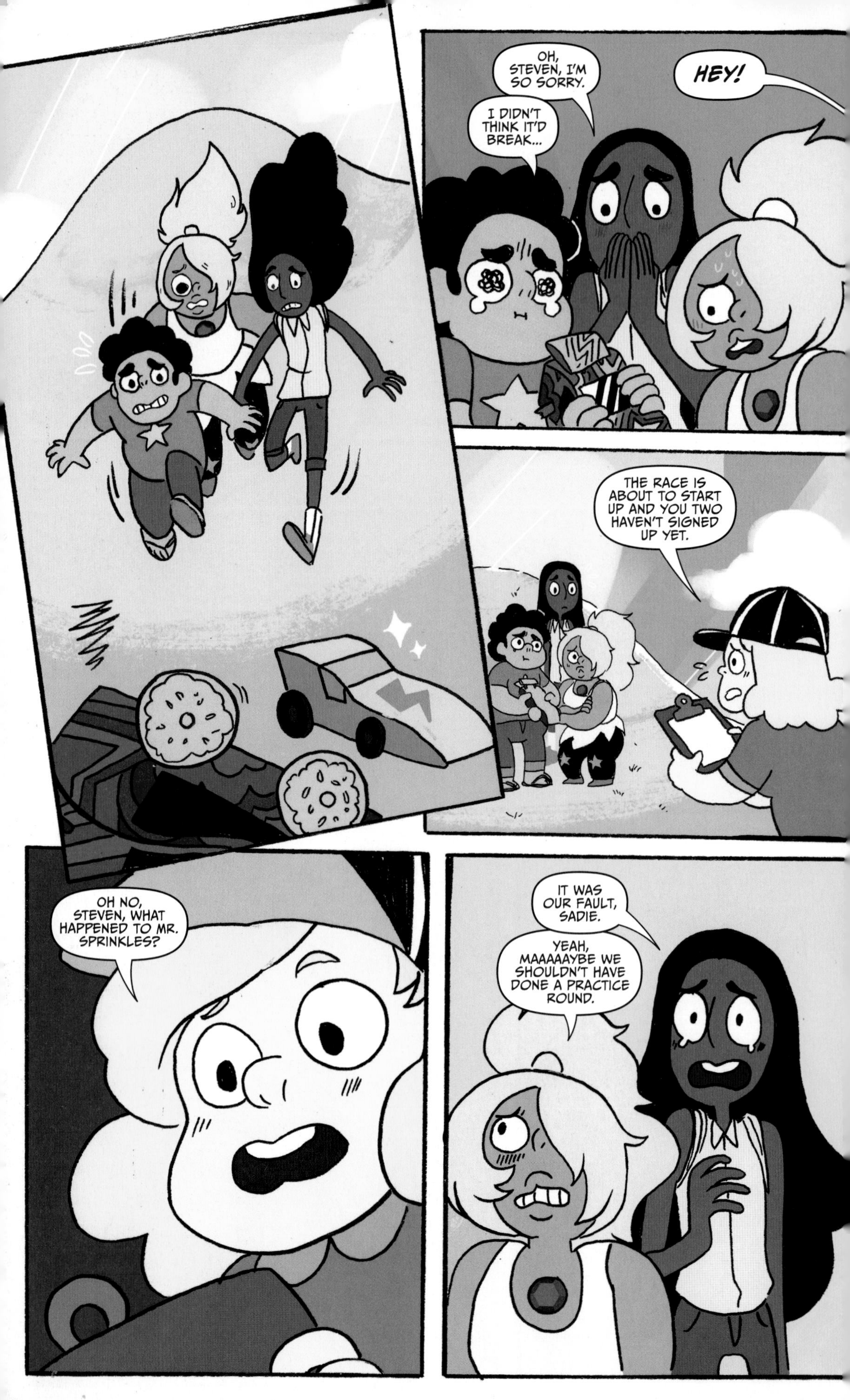
OH, STEVEN, I'M SO SORRY.
I DIDN'T THINK IT'D BREAK...
HEY!
THE RACE IS ABOUT TO START UP AND YOU TWO HAVEN'T SIGNED UP YET.
OH NO, STEVEN, WHAT HAPPENED TO MR. SPRINKLES?
IT WAS OUR FAULT, SADIE.
YEAH, MAAAAAYBE WE SHOULDN'T HAVE DONE A PRACTICE ROUND.

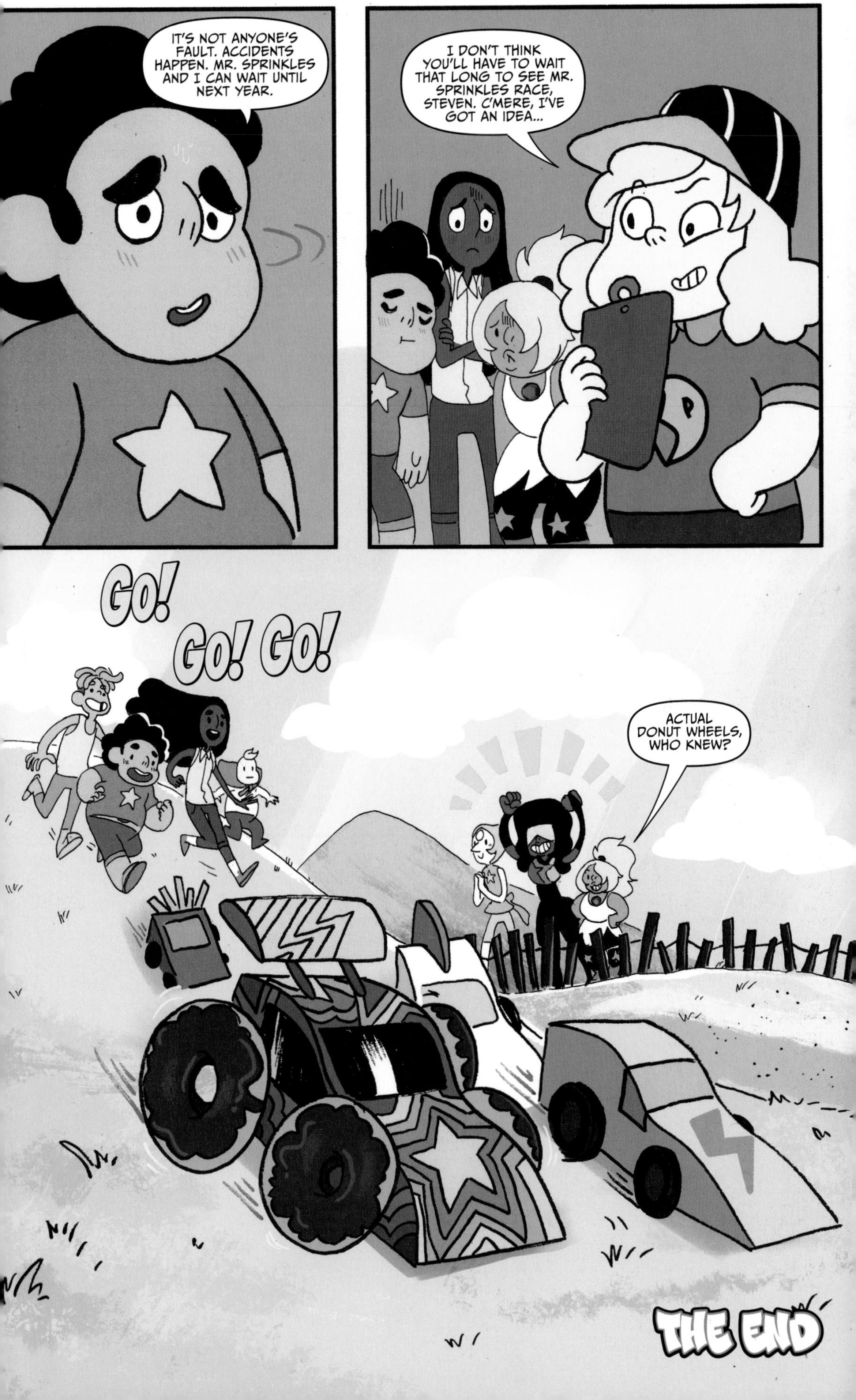
IT'S NOT ANYONE'S FAULT. ACCIDENTS HAPPEN. MR. SPRINKLES AND I CAN WAIT UNTIL NEXT YEAR.
I DON'T THINK YOU'LL HAVE TO WAIT THAT LONG TO SEE MR. SPRINKLES RACE, STEVEN. C'MERE, I'VE GOT AN IDEA...
GO!
GO! GO!
ACTUAL DONUT WHEELS, WHO KNEW?
THE END

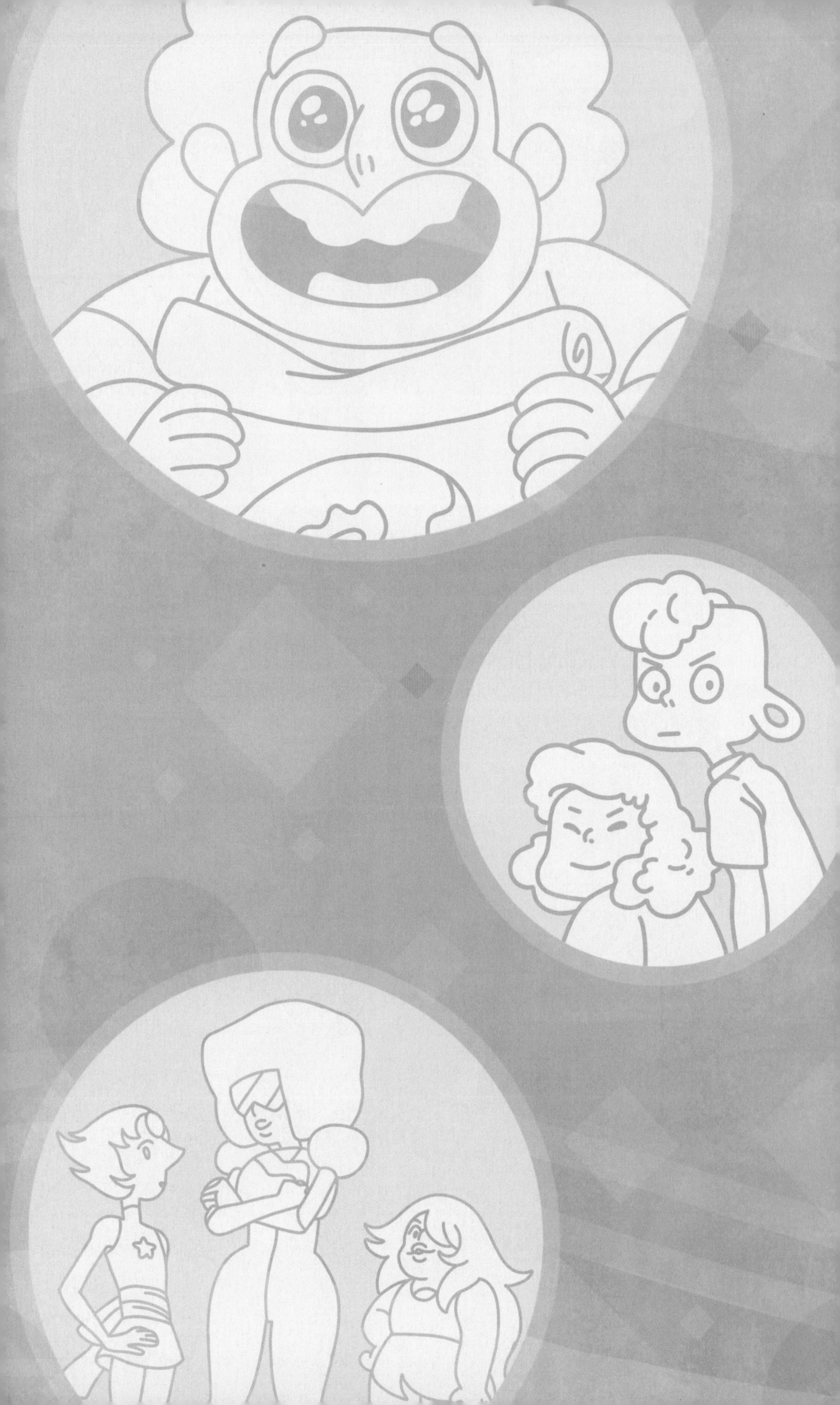

COVER GALLERY

Steven Universe: Greg Universe #1 Main Cover by
RU XU

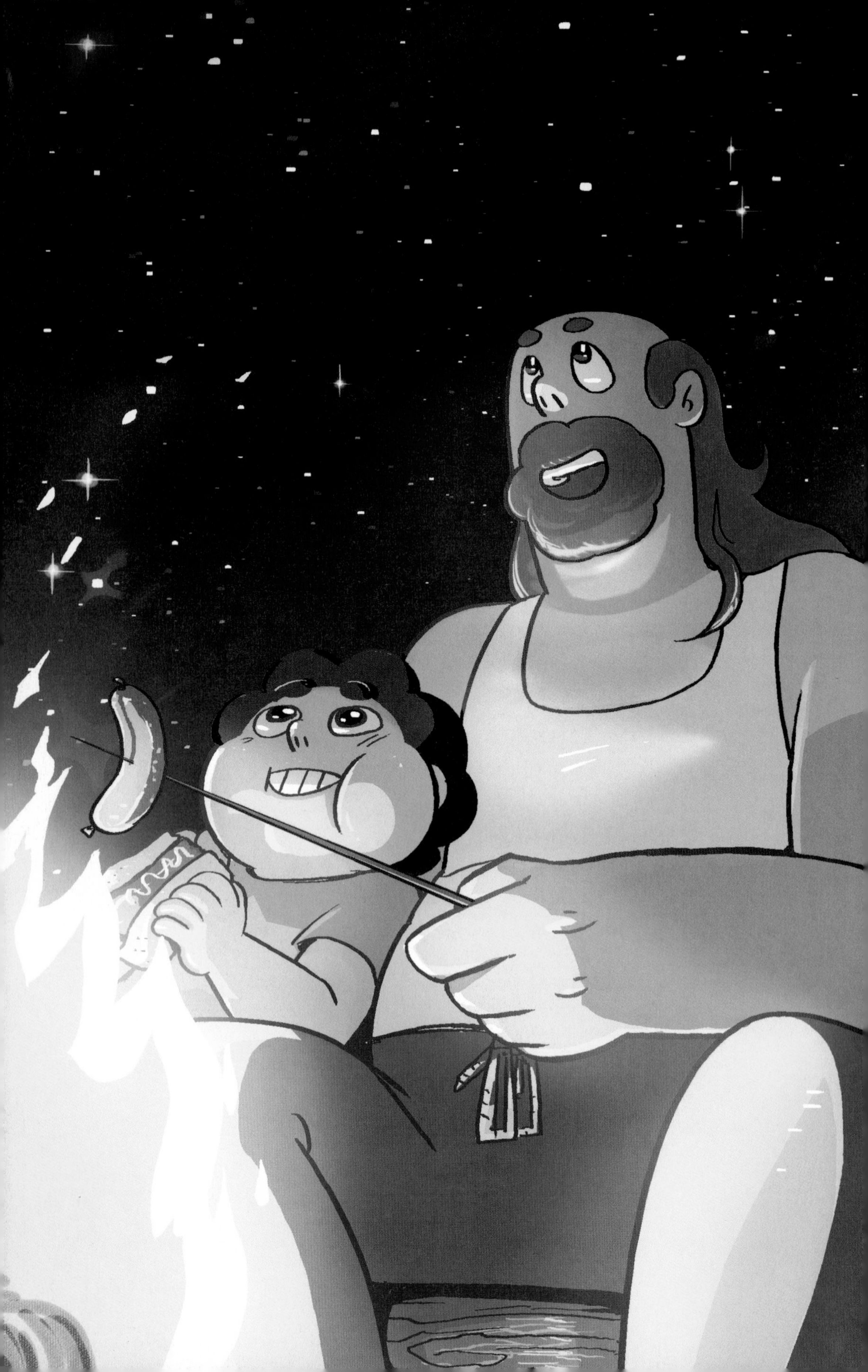

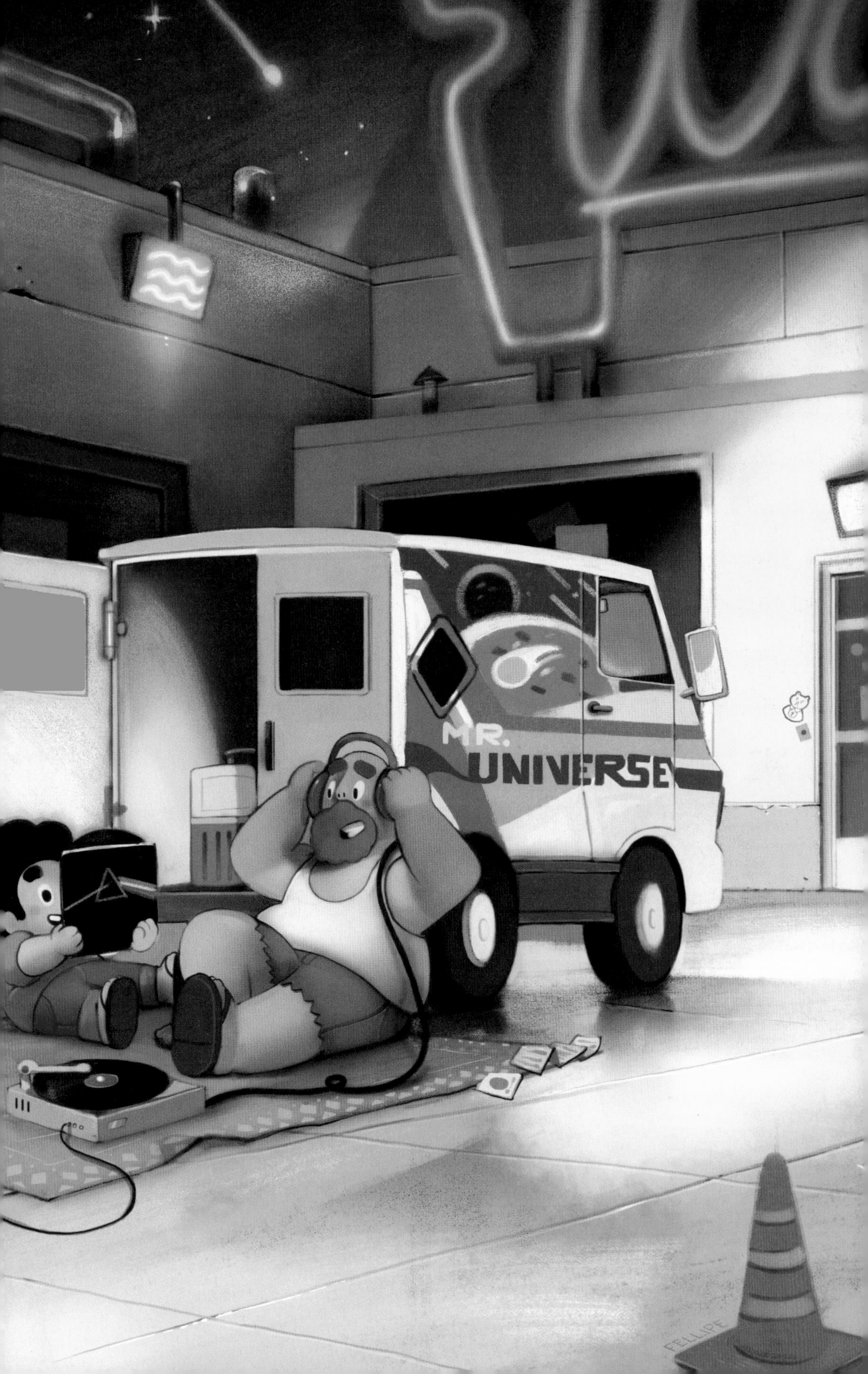
MR.
UNIVERSE
FELLIPE

Steven Universe: Greg Universe #1 Variant Cover by
FELLIPE MARTINS

Steven Universe 2016 Special #1 Variant Cover by
KATIE JONES

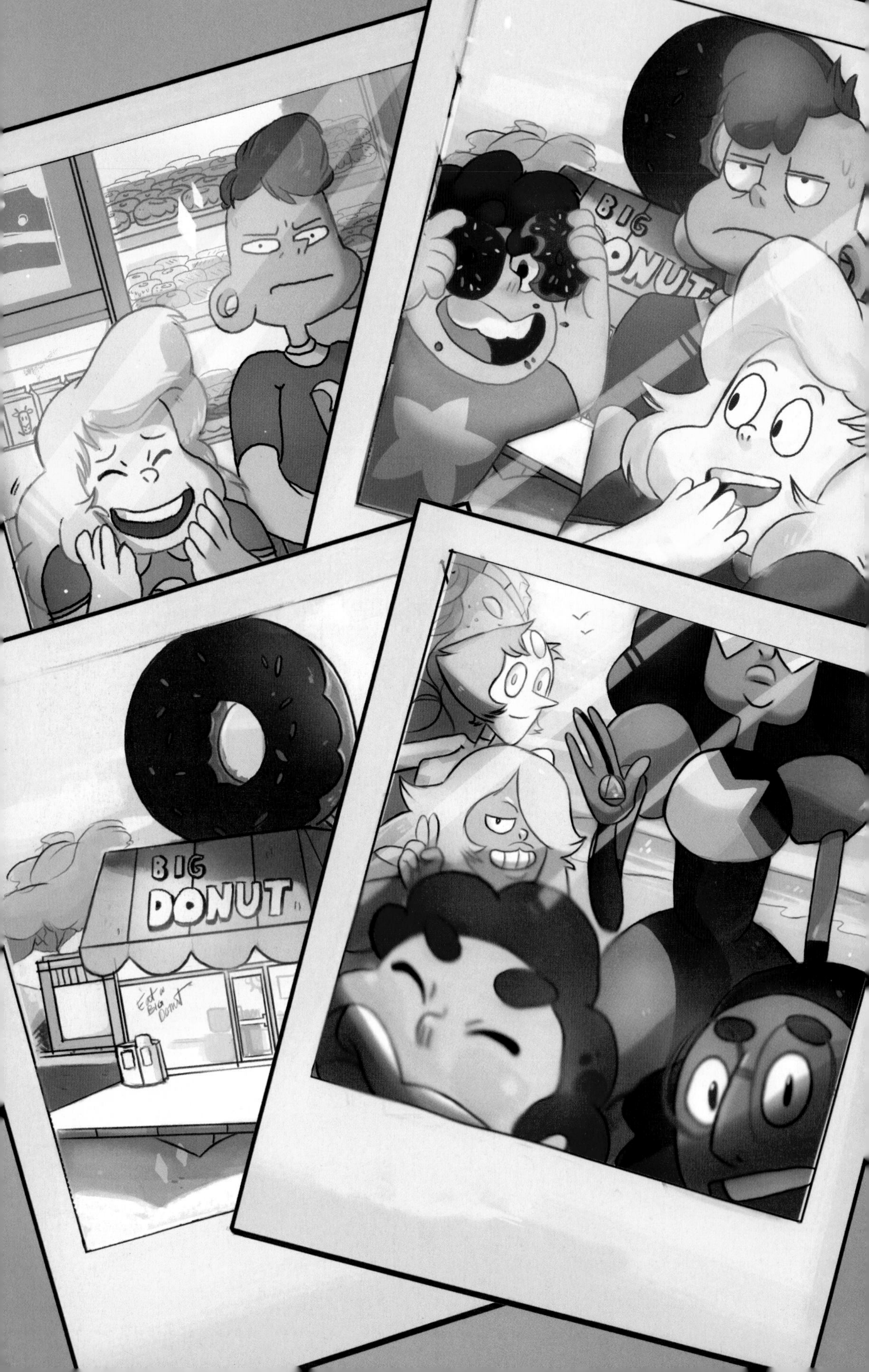
BIG
DONUT

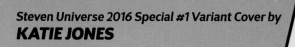

Steven Universe 2016 Special #1 Fried Pie Exclusive Cover by
MISSY PEÑA

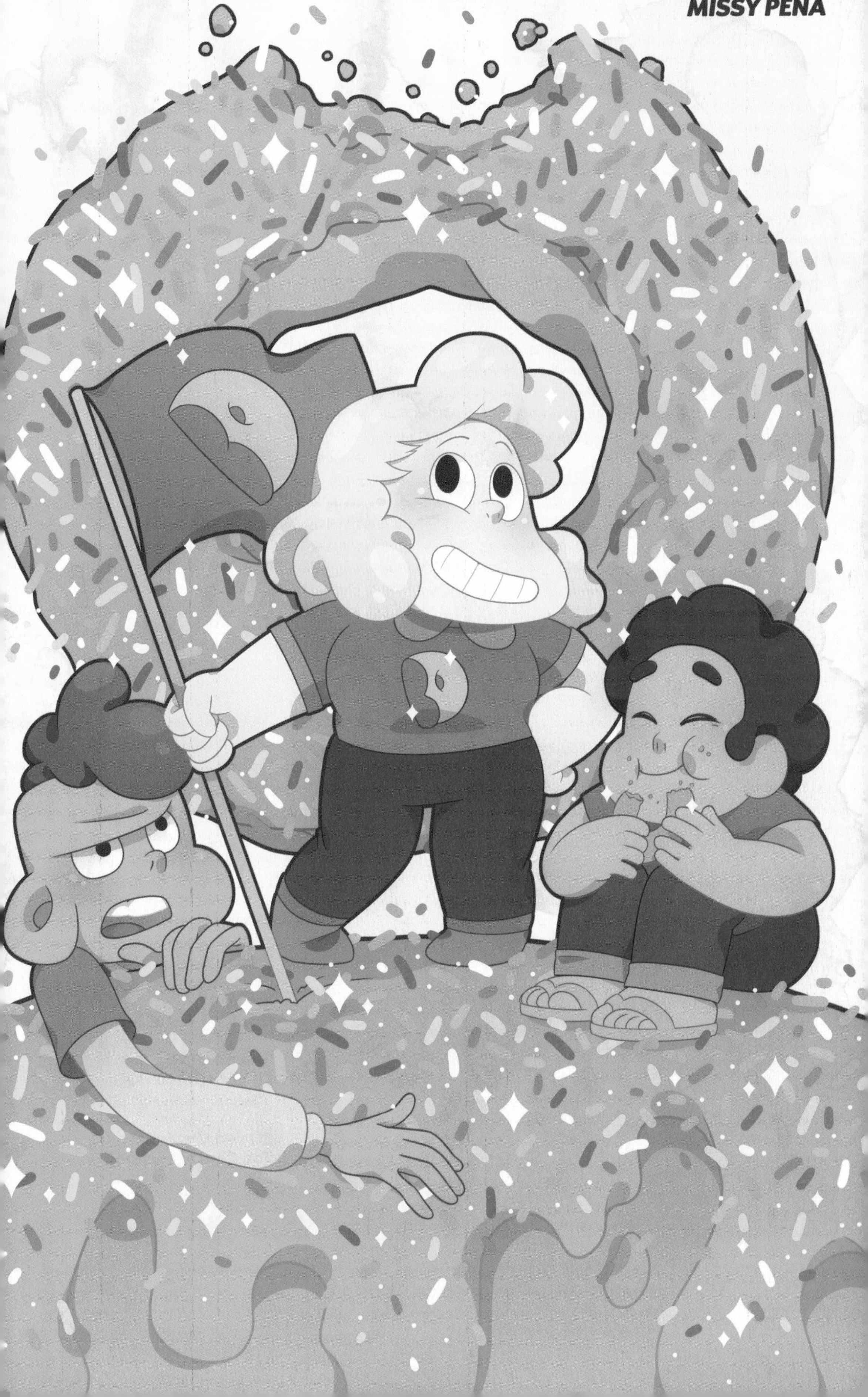